DO IT FOR DAISY

DO IT FOR DAISY

William Ade

LeVel
BEST BOOKS

First published by Level Best Books 2021

Copyright © 2021 by William Ade

This novel is entirely a work of fiction. The names, characters and incidents portrayed in it are the work of the author's imagination. Any resemblance to actual persons, living or dead, events or localities is entirely coincidental.

William Ade asserts the moral right to be identified as the author of this work.

AUTHOR PHOTO CREDIT: William Ade

First edition

ISBN: 978-1-953789-56-3

Cover art by Level Best Designs

*This book was professionally typeset on Reedsy.
Find out more at reedsy.com*

Ellen Brinkman, Beta Reader and Baby Sister

Praise for DO IT FOR DAISY

"William Ade's *Do it for Daisy* is that rare treat—an exquisitely crafted novel that lives comfortably in a range of genres, and sets the highest possible bar in any of them. Funny, sad, suspenseful, thrilling, reflective, maddening, and ultimately triumphant, with this impressive debut Ade proves himself a master storyteller and a powerful new voice in crime fiction." — Kerry K. Cox, author of the Nick Tanner Crime Thriller Series.

Chapter One

Daisy and Eric's verbal ju-jitsu had gotten so nasty that it forced me to walk out of my dining room.

"I'll check on the eggplant," I said, doubting whether my sister and her husband heard me as they unloaded on each other. Even with the kitchen door shut, the sizzle of their fighting came through the walls.

My big sister, Daisy, did the screaming.

"I know you're cheating with some floozy."

You didn't find too many women in New Jersey named Daisy, but our mother loved the old television program, The Dukes of Hazard. I guess she hoped Sis would grow up to be a beauty with long legs and big boobs. That didn't happen. My sister stood about five feet four and a little on the chubby side.

That didn't stop her from being tougher than any woman I knew, real or on TV. She had to be, growing up like we did.

"I'm sick and tired of your craziness. You spoiled brat."

My brother-in-law, Eric Pressman, provided the low-key yet brutal assessments. He liked to accuse Daisy of being mentally deranged and self-centered. I hated him. Why she ever married the idiot in the first place, I never understood. Sure, Eric had the good looks. A silver streak in his black hair gave him what some might call a distinguished appearance. To me, he looked and acted like a skunk.

All of the madness going on in my dining room was ironic, if that's the right word. We planned to be celebrating Daisy and Eric's twentieth wedding anniversary, and here they were tangling like two alley cats. I tried my best

1

to host a happy occasion, but, man, those two made it dang near impossible.

"You do nothing but spend money and accuse me of philandering," Eric said. His scratchy voice sounded like a parrot with a Jersey accent.

"Your accusation of my infidelity is a reflection of your insecurity," he continued. "You should spend more time on a psychiatrist's couch and less in the beauty salon."

"Don't try and make me out as a crazy bitch," Daisy responded. I thought I heard her fists slam onto the dining room table. "I won't let you embarrass me."

Eric returned fire. "Your whole white-trash family is an embarrassment."

Now the man had gone full steam with his favorite pasttime – badmouthing Daisy's family. I supposed I could've gone back into the dining room and defended the Lyle family honor. But I didn't. I told myself to stay out of their marriage, that it was none of my business.

Yeah, that's what I told myself.

To be honest, I held back because of the place on the Jersey Shore. Eric let me use his beach house rent-free one week each summer. I knew that shouldn't stand in the way of defending my family, but it's such a beautiful place.It overlooked the ocean, had comfy beds, and an expresso-maker in the master bedroom.

I'm not proud of admitting my weakness, but having something was a powerful hold when you grew up with nothing.

"I hate you, I hate you, I hate you," Daisy screamed, adding for good measure, "I hate you."

My sister had a volatile temper, and it sounded like she could get physical any second. I had to do something, even if Mandy Simmons, my foster mother, had always said, "Blessed are the peacemakers."

I stepped back into the dining room with a big smile splashed on my face and a basket of breadsticks in my hand.

"The eggplant is almost ready," I said in the style of a grand announcement. "And here is the new kind of breadsticks that Daisy brought with her."

Daisy and Eric, their faces dark with fury, appeared stunned. Maybe the thought of my delicious eggplant parmesan knocked them off their rage rails. Anyway, they both quieted and sat in their chairs, their jaws clenched.

"Now isn't this nice," I said, cooing like a dove, "here we sit celebrating your twenty years of marriage."

Daisy bit hard on a breadstick and sprayed crumbs across the table. Her eyes, dark carbon bits drilled into me. She hated it when I tried to cool her anger. She saw my attempts at peace-making as a character flaw and blamed it on my foster mother.

Let me explain our family background.

As kids, Daisy and I had complicated childhoods. Our folks, Walter and Mabel Lyle, had a history in the fine arts of extortion, drug trafficking, and illicit gambling. Sadly, their little criminal enterprises led to their early deaths in a police shootout.

The authorities assumed that the Lyle genetics destined us to a life of crime. They decided to split us up and sent me, Tommy, the ten-year-old, to Mandy and her bible-thumpin' working-class family. Twelve-year-old Daisy went to the Conway household, a wealthy couple living on the better side of town.

I didn't see my sister much after that. We went to different high schools and ran with different crowds. I pretty much became a loner and spent most of my free time in church getting Mandy's values hammered into my head.

Daisy had a more lavish lifestyle, you might say. She adapted to her new family's money and all, you know, the cute clothes, fancy cars, and living in a big house. I didn't know if she thought about me much back then, but I sure missed her. Not having Daisy in my life all those years hurt more than anything.

It wasn't until I attended her wedding twenty-years ago that we reconnected.

"So, Eric, how's the banking business?" I asked, hoping to move the man off ripping the Lyle family and onto his second favorite topic, making money.

"It'd be doing better if I didn't have so many deadbeat customers living in dumps."

Eric drummed his fingers against the tabletop as his gaze checked out the dining room. I knew he'd add up all of its defects, such as the water-damaged

3

ceiling, peeling discolored wallpaper, and a floor of splintered boards. He'd wonder why he ever lent me the money to buy it.

"I'm curious as to when you're going to make your loan payment," he said. "You're late, once again."

"I'll have a check for you on Thursday."

Eric had inherited a small savings and loan decades ago from his father. Even though I hated the idea of asking him for a mortgage when I bought the house, I had no choice. No one else in this crapper of a town would lend me money. I swore he took more pleasure in reminding me of my debt than the outrageous interest he earned.

"You do remember the contract stated payment would be the first Tuesday of each month."

"My sales commission check was late. I only need a few extra days."

Eric shook his head. He had an off-putting way of showing unhappiness. His head would snap back and forth, his mouth closed, as if some lousy smell had floated by his face. It made me feel disgusting and inferior.

"No, that's not how you agreed to make your payments," he said. "I'll have to add on a late penalty."

My stomach muscles constricted. Any other man would've busted his butt to get out from that humiliating burden of owing Eric money. But a shoe sales clerk living on commission could sell only so many boots and sneakers.

"Punctuality is the hallmark of a civilized society," my brother-in-law continued, picking up a breadstick and waving it like a baton. "Tardiness is the sand in the gears of an efficient enterprise, whether it's business or a family."

I heard a rumble come from Daisy. The noise sounded like I imagined centuries-old magma made pushing its way up the throat of a volcano.

"What do you know about family, you cheating bastard," she said, sending the silverware flying as she slammed her fists on the table. "I'm sick of you."

Eric's mouth twisted into a grin, and he chewed off the end of his breadstick.

"Whenever you want a divorce," he said with a chuckle, "I'll help you find

4

an attorney."

Daisy stood from her chair, a nuclear-tipped rocket of disrespected womanhood. I despised what I saw going on in front of me. Daisy and Eric's fighting reminded me of Walter and Mable threatening to kill each other. And they *had* the hardware to make right on their warnings.

"You're a gold-plated ass," Daisy yelled, her fingers balled up into tight white knobs.

Oh my God, could this get violent?

"You've always been a tiny, little man, Eric Pressman. A boy bullied by his father and manipulated by his mother. If you hadn't been born into money, you'd be shoveling elephant shit at the circus."

Eric started vibrating like a washing machine spinning with an unbalanced load. I knew how he hated having his manhood called into question, especially by Daisy.

"The nerve of you," he said. He rose and bared his teeth. His face was the color of the eggplant that now baked in my oven. He started to speak but produced only a wheezing sound. A series of coughs came from deep inside his chest.

"I'm going to make your life miserable," he finally said in a voice choked with mucus. He laid his palms on the green table cloth. Another round of hacking coughs bent him at his waist. He tore at his shirt as if a colony of ants lived under his skin.

"What…what was is in that…," he said, sweeping the breadstick to the floor.

Eric clawed at the hives popping up on his face. I heard wet wheezing coming from his mouth. Good Lord, he was in the middle of a respiratory Armageddon.

I turned to my sister. "What's going on?"

She hunched her shoulders. "Looks like an allergic reaction, but I'm no doctor."

"What should we do?"

Daisy responded with a thin, creepy smile.

"This is insane," I said, my heart beating so wildly I thought it would break out of my chest. "Do something."

She did. She stretched her smile further.

My brother-in-law frantically patted his suit jacket before pulling a small plastic container from a side pocket. He pushed his thumb against a plug at the end of the tube, but his spastic hands failed him. Daisy reached over and slapped the kit away, sending it skittering across the table. She snatched up the container.

"Don't open that EpiPen without checking the expiration date. You don't know whether it's still good."

Eric leaned against the table, his eyes tiny specks buried in swollen flesh. His bloated right hand pawed at her.

"Doesn't he need that thing?" I said. "Come on, don't screw around."

Eric stretched across the table and grasped at Daisy. She pulled away from him, the EpiPen clutched against her chest.

A high-pitched scream came out of me. "Daisy, what are you doing?"

My sister ignored me and smirked at her husband as he made the sounds of a tire going flat. The man fell back into his chair, a bloated tomato in a mound of pinstripe fabric and one hundred percent cotton whiteness.

"Good Lord, Daisy," I shouted. "What's going on?"

"Stay out of it. He's allergic to nuts. He'll be okay, probably."

As I stepped toward my sister, her head snapped around, and she barked at me.

"Don't make me hurt you, Tommy."

I didn't go any further. My feet felt glued to the floor.

Memory can do that to you.

Chapter Two

Over the years, Daisy told me, "Tommy, someday I'm going to come up with a way to kill my husband." I had my doubts, even when Eric had been his most abusive. Nonetheless, I wasn't going to let her kill him. Not at my dinner party.

With my panic stronger than my fear of pissing off Daisy, I stepped up and wrestled the EpiPen from her hands.

"Don't help him," she yelled as I elbowed her aside. "Let him die."

I ran around the table to Eric.

"Where do I stick him?"

Daisy offered nothing but muttered profanities.

I snapped the container open and pulled out the device. Thank God I saw the instructions printed on the label. A quick read gave me the info I needed. Raising the EpiPen to ear level, I stabbed it into Eric's thigh.

"Damn you, Tommy," Daisy said. "You ruined my anniversary."

I didn't bother throwing my sister a well-deserved dirty look for acting so heartless. My mind was too caught up in wondering if Eric would die in my dining room. What had my sister been thinking, anyway? I swore she'd let her husband strangle without a second thought.

"Is one of those shot thingies enough?" I asked. "He doesn't seem to be getting better."

"It usually takes fifteen minutes. This isn't the first time Eric's blown himself up to ruin my party."

"You never told me Eric had allergies."

My sister shrugged. "I didn't want to bore you with all of Eric's issues."

"Oh my Lord, he ate one of those breadsticks before he got sick. You don't think there's a connection."

Daisy flexed her hands. "I got them at an Italian bakery. They looked tasty."

I ran into the kitchen and retrieved the packaging.

"What does Noccioline, uh Grissini, mean?" I asked after stepping back into the dining room.

Daisy gave me another shrug, which seemed to be her response to all my questions.

"I can't read Italian."

Daisy groused, and I palpitated like a grandmother until Eric's breathing eased and his complexion returned to its normal pasty coloring.

"Are you feeling better?" I asked him. He grunted in a way that I swore had a condescending tone to it. I tried to help him sit up, and he batted away my hand.

"I think he's going to be okay."

Daisy walked away from me, spitting words about getting cheated, and her stupid brother.

"What'd I do?" I asked.

She snarled, "You ruined my best chance at being happy."

I pulled Daisy by the arm into the kitchen. Once behind the closed door, I grabbed her by the shoulders and shook her.

"What's wrong with you?" I said. "What were you thinking?"

She pulled away. "I despise him, Tommy. I can't live with him any longer."

"Murdering your husband isn't the way to go."

She shrugged. "I wasn't trying to murder Eric. I mean, it's not my fault his body isn't built to last."

"Oh, come on. Do you want to end up in prison?"

The corner of her mouth curled up. "Being married to that man for twenty years is like being in prison," she said, "I figured if I've done time, I should do the crime."

Daisy's long blonde hair flipped forward as she bent over laughing.

I didn't find her crack funny. In my mind, Daisy acted criminally with her latest stunt. There must've been something he ate that triggered his attack. Was it those new breadsticks Daisy bought? How'd I know they might've had nuts in them?

Maybe Daisy didn't know either. Maybe it was all a big mistake.

But, my sister did keep the EpiPen away from him. That'd look bad. If Eric didn't have her arrested for attempted manslaughter, he'd get her committed to some institution. The man had enough juice in the county to make either one of those happen.

"Why don't you divorce him if you hate him so much?"

Daisy looked at the floor and studied the yellowed linoleum. "Before we got married, his parents insisted I sign a prenup. I'd get nothing if we ended the marriage."

Knowing my sister had zero work skills and she'd be on the streets if she left her husband, I threw out a better alternative than murdering Eric.

"You could come live with me, you know, just like old times."

Her face softened, and she smiled. "Sorry, Tommy, I'll never be poor again."

"I know I don't have much, but it's better than spending your life in a jail cell."

"That's sweet of you," she said in a syrupy whisper. "But after twenty years of hell, I'm going to get what's owed me."

I didn't know what she intended, but if this evening revealed anything, it would get her in a chunky bit of trouble. I couldn't hold back my tears. "I don't want to lose you again."

Daisy patted my cheek and smiled. "And I don't want to lose you, either."

I hoped she was sincere. That girl was the only family I had. Even on her most self-absorbed days, I knew she loved me. My first wife left me after a year. My second marriage lasted a week before my bride ran off with the officiating priest. After Mandy died, my only connection to human affection came from Daisy.

"I have to escape this trap, somehow," she said. "Eric will never change the prenup and let me walk with his money."

We jumped when the kitchen door swung open. There stood the man-of-the-hour, his face covered with red bumps, bracing his body against the doorframe like a punch-drunk fighter.

"Huh, hey Eric," I said. "Are you feeling better?"

His eyes shifted from Daisy to me and back to my sister. My gut tightened enough to hurt. I wanted to know what he remembered about the last ten minutes. Would he recall how Daisy kept the EpiPen from him? Had he heard her demanding, I should let him die?

"Can I get you some water?" I said, hoping to break the silence and tease out what he recalled.

"I don't want any blasted water."

His left hand gripped the door frame, and he wagged his right index finger at his wife.

"I promise that you'll suffer for this."

Eric took two steps into the kitchen and wobbled.

"Sit down, man," I said, taking him by the arm. He shook me off.

"I'm leaving." He took a few more steps before reaching for the wall to keep from slipping.

"This is so wrong, man. You can barely stand up."

Eric grunted, but he didn't move.

"Come on, Eric, stay and talk to your wife."

He shook his head, and a forelock dropped across his face.

"You and Daisy have put too many years into this marriage to walk away over a little health scare."

"I'm going," he said. "Don't try and stop me."

To get to his car, the man had to leave through the kitchen door leading to the back yard. Not wanting to be seen visiting me, Eric parked his BMW behind my house. He hated people knowing our relationship. Eric edged along the blue papered wall toward the exit. The wide-open basement door, however, seemed to intimidate him. He paused to study the gap.

"Eric, listen to me, man. We're supposed to celebrate your anniversary tonight, not fight."

He spat air on the floor. "I've *nothing* to celebrate."

"Awww, you can't mean that," I said. "We can still make it a happy memory if we try."

I waved at Daisy. "Come on, you two, let's hug it out."

My sister walked closer with her fists clenched. I figured she needed a little coaching on the art of hugging, but she'd taken the first steps. I *knew* I could save the evening.

"Okay, Daisy, I want you to remember why you fell in love with Eric."

My brother-in-law snorted. "She only loved my money."

"I bet that's not true."

My sister didn't say anything to support my position, but she did relax her hands.

I turned back to Eric. "Let's recall why you two fell in love and see if we can rekindle those feelings."

I saw a flash of movement out of the corner of my eye. Daisy jumped at Eric and seized his suit lapel. She planted her right foot on the floor and grunted. The man fell backward into the open basement doorway, grabbing for the door frame, but missing. I saw the sparkle of his silver cufflinks and his shoes rising in the air as he tumbled into the darkness.

My heart stopped beating. I swore to God, it did.

Chapter Three

Daisy stared into the stairwell, never flinching when the sound of bones snapping and tissue shredding echoed up from the basement. She placed her hands on her hips and announced, "That sounded like it hurt."

My knees went soft, and I reached for a chair to sit down. I felt like throwing up.

"How many steps do you think he bounced against?" she asked.

"I've no idea," I said so softly she may not have heard me, "maybe fifteen."

I didn't know the exact number, but I knew it had a steep incline of sharp-edged wooden stair steps. No previous owner ever considered adding carpet since the basement often flooded. I shuddered, thinking about Eric landing on his neck, his head, and his backbone.

"Good Lord, Daisy, what just happened?"

My sister laughed and slapped her thigh. "I got a lucky break, that's what happened."

I dropped my head, slowly shaking it. Daisy had to be nuts. The only person alive who cared about me was certifiably insane. How could my life get worse?

"I don't believe your husband falling to his death is lucky."

"Sure it is, Tommy."

I buried my face into my palms and moaned. I wish Mandy still occupied a space on earth so I could call her for help. I had a mess too big for any one quote from Scriptures. I needed a bunch of them.

"How can you say that's lucky?"

"I should get a life insurance payout of at least two million dollars," she replied. "How's that not lucky?"

"Oh, Daisy, please stop talking like that."

My sister moved next to me and stroked my head like she would a frightened dog in a thunderstorm.

"Think about the other possibilities," she continued. "I'll probably take over running the bank."

"I don't know about that."

She snickered. "How hard could it be? I can count."

I looked at her, freaked out by the confident expression on her face. She seemed to sincerely believe what she said.

"And as the bank president, I'd give you a little loan forgiveness."

She ended that pronouncement with a juicy wink.

I rose from my chair and grasped Daisy's hands. I hated to admit it, but I couldn't recall her brown eyes having such sparkle as they did now. Her joy appeared to be genuine. I had no doubt. But man, she just killed her husband.

"Daisy, sweetheart, how are you going to explain away the dead man in my basement?"

She peeled off my fingers and pushed me away.

"I'll tell the truth."

"Oh, dear sister, how can you say that?"

Daisy's head cocked to one side, an expression that made me feel like a dummy. "Eric had an anaphylactic reaction in the dining room, right?"

"Yeah, I guess."

"He recovered but was still unsteady when he tried to leave through the kitchen."

I nodded.

Daisy strolled around me and clapped her hands in a cadence as she spoke. "You tried to stop him."

"I did."

"He *insisted* on leaving the house."

"Okay, yeah, you're right," I said.

"He lost his balance as he walked in front of the open basement door."

I raised my hand in protest. Daisy knocked it down.

"And in a split second, and much to our horror, he fell backward down the basement stairs."

I shook my head. "Oh, sister, I don't think so."

"That's the way it pretty much happened," she said, pushing out her lower lip. "I think we're talking ninety-nine percent accurate."

I turned away, and my eyes drifted toward the oven where my eggplant parmesan bubbled toward perfection. That dish would go to waste. The insides of my intestines were the only thing getting eaten tonight.

"Daisy, please stop talking like that."

She didn't shut up. Nope, she started acting all ridiculous, her words firing off like a string of cheap firecrackers. "Eric was very unstable. He shouldn't have been walking. He insisted on going through the kitchen. We couldn't stop him. It happened in a blink-of-an-eye. What a dreadful accident on my anniversary."

"Stop it, Daisy," I shouted. "You pushed him."

Daisy fell back, her eyes wide and unfriendly, like a cornered wolverine. My hand jumped to cover my mouth, but the words had already escaped. We stared at each other, stunned. I couldn't recall the last time I yelled at her, if ever. As a kid when Walter or Mabel beat on me, Daisy would fight them off. She'd comfort me when I felt afraid. I *never* raised my voice at her. How could I be angry at the only family who loved me?

Daisy closed the space between us and took my hand. Her palm felt cool against my sweaty skin. She whispered, "I think you're mistaken, Tommy."

"Huh."

"I saw Eric starting to fall," she said, stroking my hand. "I grabbed at him to keep him from tumbling backward."

Daisy's finger moved up to my chest, just over my heart. She tapped me hard. "I tried to keep my husband *from* falling. I *didn't* push him."

Hot tears formed in my eyes, and I wanted to believe her. I really, really did. It'd make everything so much better.

"You were confused," she said, "sorely mistaken."

"I, I don't know."

Daisy pinched my cheek. "Don't you love me, Tommy?"

"Of course I do, but..."

"But, what?" she asked.

My chin dropped, and I felt my stomach hurting like it always did when I was scared. What words would Mandy offer at a time like this? I pulled up my memory of her and looked for a piece of advice. I found one of her favorites.

Love each other deeply, because love covers over a multitude of sins.

I reran the words through my mind. The heat in my belly lifted.

"Okay, maybe you're right."

"Of course, I'm right."

I swallowed a hard clump of emotion. I guess I could've missed what happened. The whole thing did catch me by surprise. Maybe in that nanosecond between Daisy snatching at Eric and whiffing, my brain processed it incorrectly. I just wished she had shown the proper reaction when she realized Eric had been killed, like crying or wailing. Her happy little celebration seemed insensitive, even if she had good reason to hate the man.

"I sure hope you're right," I said as if repeating the statement would make it more convincing. "This makes me anxious."

Daisy smiled and gave me a peck on the cheek.

"I love you, Tommy."

"I love you, too."

We embraced, and for a handful of seconds, all seemed good in my world. Unfortunately for me, that would be the last time. A whimpering cry floated up from the basement and ruined my life.

Chapter Four

The auditorium's acoustic ceiling tiles looked yellowed and stained, and the concrete block walls had seen multiple paint jobs. Twenty or so young men and women bunched in the front center seats. I, Detective Nick Bongiovanni, stood to the side of the podium as a woman in uniform bent to speak into the microphone.

"On behalf of the New Jersey State Police Academy and its recruits, I want to thank Detective Bongee-Bond-geevannie."

"Just call me Bongi," I shouted out. "Even my mother did."

My response to the instructor's fumble of my last name made the group of police recruits chuckle. I liked that. Keeping it light was my forte. It made people underestimate me. Besides, after thirty years in New Jersey law enforcement, if you didn't have a sense of humor, you'd burn out. Not much of an issue for me, considering in only twenty-four days I'd be retired.

"Thanks again for speaking to the recruits," the group leader said, offering her hand. I shook it. Women weren't hired as police when I graduated from the academy. They certainly hadn't been instructors. Progress happens, and the old had to make way for the new.

"I understand that you're a short-timer, huh?" she said.

My nod was a faint bobble of my head.

"Are you looking forward to retirement?"

I shrugged. "Sure. Why not?"

I used that response as my standard reply, although no one had explained precisely why I'd be happy not working. Mandatory retirement was mandatory, they explained to me. I had no option.

"Well, good luck," she said. "You'll be missed."

Yeah, they'd miss me, maybe until everyone sobered up the day after my party. I'd seen plenty of well-respected cops drown in teary-eyed farewells and never surface again.

"Happy I could help you with the class," I said. "Talking with those kids was probably the most productive thing I'd done since I handed in my papers."

The woman's smile went soft, and she shuffled her feet like she had something to tell me. After a few more nervous twitches, she proved my hunch correct.

"I'm sorry about your wife."

I nodded like I'd nodded a hundred times in the past two months. "Uh, thanks."

After the group leader and her charges cleared the room, I started walking back upstairs to my desk. Maybe I should check in with the detectives I'd offloaded my last active case to. I believed it to be no more than one gang banger taking out another and some crying mother demanding justice for her little boy. Perhaps the new guys could benefit from some of my insights.

Naw, I better let it go. There's nothing worse than an old busy body.

"Hey, Bongi, wait up."

I knew the man hollering from across the room. We'd worked a few cases over the decades. As his bulk thundered around the rows of desks, I girded my loins for another drive down memory lane.

"I recalled for some of the younger guys the time we investigated the butcher who chopped up his mother."

The man rested his meaty paw on my shoulder, his breathing rapid.

"Remember that one?"

"I sure do."

"We only found part of her in his freezer, remember."

The man slapped his ample stomach, and his face lit up in laughter. "And we assumed the rest was sold as hamburger to his poor customers. Good God, I couldn't touch meat for a year after that."

My old comrade alarmed me when he folded at the waist, crippled by hilarity. You had to go easy on recollections, even the ones that made you laugh.

"You remember that one, Bongi?"

"I do," I answered. "And keep trying to forget."

I lied about a meeting upstairs at the precinct's detective bureau and escaped any more storytelling. I offered a prayer to the Almighty; *please, Lord, don't make every remaining day filled with people recalling stories from the last thirty years.*

It's not that I wasn't proud of my career; it's just that I hadn't gotten my mind around the idea of leaving it all behind. And with Joanie gone, the future appeared to be endless hours of loneliness.

While upstairs, I thought I'd check for messages and kill some time cleaning out my files. I might spend the rest of the day shopping for fishing gear. It'd be better than hanging around with people reminding me my best days had long left me behind.

Ten steps away from my desk, I heard someone call out, "Detective Bongiovanni." Even without looking, I knew it was Tiny Baker, the only person who didn't call me either Nick or Bongi.

"Yes, sir," I said, turning on my heels.

"Please come to my office."

Baker was the Deputy Chief in charge of the detective unit. Unlike most guys nicknamed Tiny, Baker was diminutive. He must have just made the minimum height requirement to get into the academy. His rise in the hierarchy had to do with his brains, not his brawn. He broke some prominent cases because he had a bigger intellect than anyone else in the building.

"Thanks for speaking to those recruits," Tiny said after I stepped into his office. "You know how those rookies love hearing from the old-timers."

My jaw clamped tight. If I heard someone use the word old about me again, I'd punch him.

"I wanted to get some dates and times for your party," he said, "you know, make sure you're happy with it." I suspected Tiny found party-planning beneath his position, precinct tradition be damned. I decided I'd cut him a break.

18

"How about if I talk with your secretary, and we work out the details."

A grin popped up on Tiny's face. "Sure, whatever is good for you," he said. "And don't worry. I won't throw too many new assignments your way this week."

"Oh, don't be too considerate," I said. "I like feeling I'm earning my pay."

"Sure, sure, of course, you do. I feel the same way."

And I knew he did. Tiny had been a decent boss but a stickler for the administrative bullshit. He wouldn't let me slide, even as a short-timer. But hey, twenty-four more days, and I'd never be in this building again. I'd never smell the stink that wafted through the air during the summer or shiver from the inescapable winter chill. I'd be keeping my promise to Joanie, enjoying a life free of the long hours and the mental stress of dealing with the dregs of society.

Yeah, I'd miss it. I'd miss it bad.

Chapter Five

"Help, help me."

Daisy and I spun our faces toward the basement, our mouths unhinged. Then our heads snapped back, and we looked bug-eyed at each other. Could both of us be imagining the same thing? Did we hear a call for help rise from fifteen steps below?

"Help me."

Those two words sandwiched a long moan. Daisy's eyes rolled towards the ceiling, and she cried, "Sweet Jesus, why can't I get a break?"

I didn't have time to explain to my sister how Jesus worked. Running to the basement door, I flipped a wall switch, turning on the stairwell's overhead lightbulb. I carefully climbed down the stairs and noticed a glob of bloody hair on the third step where Eric's head must have first struck. A blood splatter spread further down on the wall, and a shoe rested on the tenth step. At the bottom of the stairs laid my brother-in-law.

For the second time that evening, I wanted to throw up.

"Eric, man, you look horrible."

A groan rattled his chest.

I shuddered at the thought of sharp-edged wooden steps cutting into the back of his head, and then his knees, and then his forehead, and then his shoulders, as he tumbled over and over.

I cupped my hands around my mouth, "Call 911 and tell them to hurry."

Walking around Eric's crumpled body, I noticed that the back of his suit jacket had split at the seam. Dirt spotted the trousers, and three rouge-colored smudges emerged on the front of his white shirt. Dark red blood had already pooled around the back of his head. A spreading bruise covered half his face, and a large gash laced across his right cheek.

Daisy shouted from the kitchen. "How is he?"

"He's a mess. Did you call 911?"

"Is he going to die?"

"I don't know, but judging from the way his legs are splayed, he might be crippled."

Daisy let fly a string of profanity. "That's all I need," she said. "Everything about him paralyzed except his mouth."

"Did you call 911?"

She didn't answer. What's my sister doing up there? Was she frozen in fear or paralyzed by grief? I climbed the stairs, two at a time, and found Daisy walking in a circle, mumbling.

"What's going on with you? We need to get Eric some help."

She stopped and waved her hands in the air. "Not so fast, Tommy, we have to think about this."

"Eric doesn't have time." I moved toward the wall phone, but Daisy pounced on me, pushing me away.

"Tommy, you're sending me to prison."

"Huh."

Daisy grabbed my shirt and jerked my face closer to her. "Listen to me. If Eric survives, he'll tell everyone I pushed him down the stairs."

"What, are you serious?"

She pulled on me. "You heard Eric. He said he'd make my life a misery."

Yeah, yeah, he did say that. Oh man, I *supposed* he might take revenge. What if Eric had been confused by Daisy's attempt to keep him from falling as I had been? He might think she'd pushed him as I did. I mean, why not?

"But you tried to help him. I'll testify to that."

"Use your head, Tommy. Who are the authorities gonna believe, a rich bigshot with a load of money, or Walter and Mabel's kids?"

My fingers intertwined hard enough to hurt. Daisy had it right. No one would believe that we were any different from Walter and Mabel. The acorn doesn't fall far from the tree and all that.

"I'm in big trouble, Tommy, if you don't help me."

What could I do? Mandy used to call this kind of situation a conundrum. When faced with one, she'd say, "Follow the path of the Lord, and you'll always do right."

"I might never see you again," Daisy said, the ends of her eyebrows dipping. "Is that what you want?"

"No, no."

I held my coupled hands to my lips, hoping the Lord would show me the proper path. I said a little prayer but still didn't see any way out of the mess. I started crying. "I don't know what to do."

"Tommy, listen to me. We Lyle kids always got the shit end of the stick. We have to be smart here, or else we'll get it again, big time."

"But I'm trying to live differently, Daisy, follow a righteous path."

She cooed and stroked my face.

"All I'm asking is you to bend the rules a little bit, you understand me?"

Daisy and I probably had differing ideas of what rule-bending meant. Mandy had instilled in me the golden rule. That sucker wasn't supposed to get bent, ever.

"I don't know," I said, my gaze dropping toward the floor, hoping there might be a hole I could escape through.

Daisy placed her finger under my chin and pushed up my face, locking our eyes onto each other. My insides twisted.

"Let's not forget the shit you're capable of doing."

Now my inside burnt like a fire had just ignited. Tears bubbled in my eyes, and my knees went weak. She had me. I nodded and mumbled, "Okay."

Daisy grinned. "That's my little brother."

I wrapped my arms around myself. Daisy had played the guilt card, and I rolled over without resisting. Good Lord, I'm over forty years old, and I still can't forgive myself. And it seemed, neither could my sister.

"I'm working a plan," she said, tapping her forehead as she moved toward the basement doorway. "So don't worry."

Asking me not to worry was a joke. I came out of the birth canal anxious.

"What should I do in the meantime?"

22

I watched the back of Daisy's head drop out of sight as she descended into the cellar. She called out an answer. "Turn off the oven before that eggplant burns."

I had to admit, my sister had a cooler head than I did at the moment. While I got sick to my stomach from worry, she worked up a solution. She even noticed the food five feet from me was overcooking. I smelled nothing. Daisy had always been mentally sharper than me. That's how she got ahead, I guessed.

I pulled the dish from the oven, burning my hands. Man-on-man, I'm so hapless. I can barely earn a decent income selling shoes. I'm up to my neck in debts. And I only wanted tonight to be some family time free of drama and anger. I'd failed miserably on that count, ending up with a brother-in-law with who knows how many broken bones.

"Oh, Lord, what am I going to do?"

"Come down here and help me."

That wasn't the Lord answering me. It was Daisy. I blew on my stinging palms and stepped into the stairwell. My shadow flickered across the walls as I tiptoed carefully down the stairs.

"Should I avoid touching anything?"

"Yeah, be careful," Daisy answered. "If we're going to leave prints, we should do so in a way that supports our story."

What did that mean? I wanted to ask her to explain when the sight of Eric's head distracted me. Daisy had wrapped it in an old bath towel.

"What have you done to him?"

Daisy stood over her husband, her hands on her hips. "I don't want the blood from his scalp wounds to show up anywhere but down here in the basement."

I found it odd that my sister would be concerned about housekeeping at a time like this.

"Say what?"

"Trust me on this, Tommy. Now we need to move quickly. Roll that wheelbarrow over here."

The basement of my house had an entry to the back yard where I stored my wheelbarrow, among other yard tools. Why she wanted me to push it over to her, I didn't ask her to explain. As she said, I had to trust her.

Daisy tested the knotted towel on her husband's head and grunted in satisfaction.

"Now, grab him by his shoulders and help me lift him into this wheelbarrow."

I stepped back, shaking my head. I trusted her, yeah, but not blindly.

"What are we doing, Daisy?"

She straddled Eric and grabbed the man by his ankles.

"Once in the wheelbarrow, we'll roll him through the basement door. Then we can push him up the drive to the back entrance and into the kitchen."

"Why don't we just call 911 and let the EMTs treat him here?"

Daisy's eyes dimmed. "Are you an idiot, Tommy? Don't you think having Eric in this dank, stinking basement makes it hard for him to breathe?"

I shrugged. She had a point. Getting Eric into a dry place with clean air probably made sense. As I said, Daisy usually operated one-step ahead of me.

"Come on, brother. I can't do this alone."

Daisy and I lifted Eric off the concrete floor and quickly discovered the difficulty in getting a two-hundred pound broken ass man into a wheelbarrow. We pushed the load out the basement, across the weedy patch of backyard dirt, and up the gravel drive to the kitchen door. The sun had gone down an hour ago, and the darkness made the task even harder. By the time we got Eric into the house, we'd collapsed on the floor.

"Once I catch my breath," I said, huffing through my open mouth, "I'll call 911."

Daisy dabbed the sweat off her forehead with her sleeve. "Before you do, I have some questions I need you to answer."

My gut, which I thought couldn't twist any tighter, took another turn. "Okay."

"Do you think Eric would be happy living as a head attached to a big hunk of meat?"

"I don't know, probably not."

24

"How likely do you think it is Eric would accuse me of trying to kill him?"

My hand rose to eye-level, hesitated, and then climbed over my head.

"Right," Daisy said. "And would you be happy with me spending the rest of my life in prison?"

"No, I'd hate being separated from you."

"I know, and I'd detest living out my life in prison." She chewed on her bottom lip. "It seems to me that we have only one way out of this situation."

Daisy rose to her feet and grabbed the smooth wood handles of the wheelbarrow. Her teeth clenched as she grunted, pushing Eric toward the basement.

I screamed, "No, Daisy."

My words didn't slow her down. Bending her back, she heaved the handles of the wheelbarrow up over her shoulders. Eric silently slid out and hit the first step. The rumble of muscles, bone, and flesh bouncing down the stairs seemly lasted forever.

Chapter Six

I covered my eyes with my hands, spreading my fingers once the house went silent. The empty wheelbarrow lay on its side by the basement doorway. Daisy stood at the bank of wood counters on the other side of the kitchen.

"Where do you keep the paper towels?" she asked, pulling open cabinet doors. "Ah, here they are."

I continued sitting on the floor, my body shaking. "That was your plan?" I said, screeching like an alley cat in heat. "You shoving him down the stairs *again?*"

Daisy stood over me and tossed a roll of paper towels in my lap. "Here, wipe up any blood and dirt in the kitchen," she said. "We have to get things cleaned up before we call 911."

My head felt like it could explode. I couldn't believe what I'd seen and heard. I jumped to my feet, my arms whirling.

"Wait a minute, just hold on. What did you just do, Daisy?"

The woman's lips curled to one side. "Aren't you paying attention?"

"Huh?"

"You agreed that Eric wouldn't be happy paralyzed, right?"

"Yes, but."

"You said you wouldn't be happy if I went to prison. Do I remember that correctly?"

"Yeah, but I didn't tell you to shove him back down the stairs."

Daisy tapped the end of my nose.

"Exactly," she said, "and now you have no culpability."

26

So that's my sister's plan, the one that she said I needn't worry about. Her solution to everyone's unhappiness involved killing her husband. Oh my Lord, Mandy must be spinning in her grave knowing my connection with such an evil person.

"Daisy, I don't think I can do this."

She sighed and slowly rolled her head. I felt like I did as a kid when she'd ask a favor, one I couldn't refuse to give.

"I need you to be on my side with this," she said. "Can you do that for me?"

"I don't know if I can."

Daisy grabbed my shoulders, her feet wide apart. She took in a big lungful of air. "Do I have to remind you of what I once did for you?"

I shook my head so hard my brain rattled in my skull. She didn't have to remind me of anything. My chin dropped to my chest.

"Okay, now be a good boy and clean up the floor," she said, turning away and entering the stairwell. "I'll take care of the business in the basement."

I followed her to the edge of the stairs and took in the scene below. Eric had landed at the bottom like his first fall, but this time on his face. Daisy climbed over him, untied the terrycloth towel. She pulled it off, and it made a sucking sound as the blood had congealed enough to bond to his head. She rolled him over. He looked horrible with eyelids frozen half-open, a crushed nose, and teeth swimming in blood.

"Hello, Eric, can you hear me?" she asked.

He didn't answer her.

Daisy folded the towel and placed the remaining clean part under his head. She squeezed the left side of his neck with her finger.

"Damn it, Tommy. He has no pulse," Daisy whimpered. "What a terrible ending to a wonderful evening."

Not for a second did I believe her sincerity. Nope, I knew a rehearsal when I heard one, practicing lines before the authorities arrived. Man, how I regretted agreeing to go along with her. We should've called for help after the first fall, taken a chance that Eric wouldn't remember what she'd done. That would've been the right thing to do.

Daisy rumbled up the stairs and rejoined me in the kitchen.

"Have you started wiping up the mess? Chop, chop, Tommy, let's not dawdle."

I dropped to my knees and soaked up any droplets of blood I found on the kitchen floor. I couldn't believe how much there was. Everywhere I looked, I found a drop or a smear. After fifteen minutes, I'd filled a garbage bag with soiled towels.

Daisy had used the time to move the wheelbarrow outside where she said she'd cleaned it of any evidence. As she reentered the kitchen, I held up the garbage bag and proudly announced, "I'm done, Daisy. What should I do with this stuff?"

"Go stash it in the trunk of your car. I don't want anything suspicious out where the cops can find it."

I felt my face grow warm. "Huh, I can't. My car's in the shop."

I didn't like lying to my sister about my car needing repairs. It had been repossessed. I had a terrible sales quarter, and being late on my mortgage was just one of several delinquencies. I didn't want my sister to know how close to the edge I lived. She'd play it to her advantage.

"Oh, okay." Daisy left the room and returned with a fob, tossing it to me. "Put it in the Beemer then."

I snuck outside, grateful for the darkness, and that I never had the energy to trim the hedge bordering my neighbors. I popped open the trunk and lifted the bag, still marveling at how much bloodied waste I'd collected. With all that Eric bled going down the basement stairs the first time, I thought more couldn't have leaked out.

That's when I realized we had a problem.

"I only know what I see on TV," I said to my sister as I stepped back into the kitchen. "But doesn't Eric's second fall create a different set of physical evidence?"

"That's why I wrapped his head in the towel," she answered. "It stopped any new splatters as he nose-dived his way again into the basement."

"But will that be enough?" I asked, unable to still my quaking vocal cords. "On *CSI*, the lab guys always seem to figure out things."

"Well, if you're watching those cop programs, you also know there's

28

nothing worse than a contaminated crime scene, right."

"Yeah, I guess."

"Now, call 911 while I do a little contaminating."

My sister smiled and headed into the basement stairwell. I heard her shoes clomping as she ran back down the stairs, crying, "Eric, my Eric, oh my God, Eric."

As usual, Daisy seemed to know what she was doing. Not me. I felt ashamed for being a part of this nightmare. Mandy would be so disappointed. Good Lord, could I sink any lower?

Chapter Seven

The wailing sirens stopped with a squawk-squawk, followed by car doors slamming. An ambulance pulled into the driveway while a police car hugged the front curb. Two EMTs ran toward me as I stood at the open front door, satchels in their hands and medical gear hanging from their necks.

I stepped aside and pointed toward the kitchen. "He's in the basement."

They rushed through the dining room door connecting to the kitchen, passing Daisy, hunched over in a chair, a mess of tissues in both hands. I heard their thundering footfalls as they headed toward the basement.

The corner of my mouth peaked as I suppressed a grin. Daisy had been right. Those EMT boys stumbling down the stairs would make a further mess of the crime scene. She'd said you didn't want to be in an accident in this town because the EMTs got terrible training. For once, our lousy municipal services might be worth the taxes we paid.

"Hello."

A man's deep voice pulled me out of my internal carping about our town's emergency services. A big guy who looked like the offspring of a slag pile and a landslide drew my attention. His complexion had the same coloring as potato soup, including the small lumps. The close-cropped hair on his head looked more like a shadow.

"I'm Officer Brutkowski."

I swallowed. "Hey, I'm Tommy Lyle."

We didn't bother shaking hands. I was cool with that. He'd wonder why my palms swam in sweat.

The police terrified me. As a kid, my folks never told us to ask a policeman if we ever needed help, as responsible parents taught. Walter and Mabel hated the law, and for a good reason. The cops frequently hassled and jailed them and one afternoon cut them to pieces in a barrage of gunfire. You never got over fearing cops after something like that, trust me.

Brutkowski stepped further into the house, quickly scanning the room before settling his cold little stare on me.

"Are you the owner of this domicile?"

"Yeah, this is my house."

He pulled a notepad and pen from his back pocket. He flipped a few pages. "Would you spell your last name?"

As I gave him what he wanted, a female officer walked in. She wasn't big like Brutkowski but still outsized. Her intimidating feature was her face, a mask of don't-mess-with-me. She headed into the kitchen.

"Can you tell me what happened?" Brutkowski asked.

I gave him the story Daisy hatched. We'd practiced describing the scenarios before the EMTs arrived, taking it through the allergy attack, the recovery, the instability, and the fall. Our versions differed slightly enough as not to sound rehearsed, yet no holes existed to be picked apart by a cop. That's how, as kids, we concocted excuses when Mabel and Walter were on the warpath. It prevented more than one beating.

Daisy played the emotionally crazed wife like a champ. I could hear her now, blathering to the other cop. I knew Brutkowski and his she-cop's M.O., keeping us apart while getting the scoop. They didn't realize my sister and I knew all about that game. As kids, we saw it played numerous times with our folks.

"Can I join my sister?" I said after Brutkowski closed his notepad. "She's pretty upset."

He nodded and followed me into the kitchen.

I gently touched Daisy's shoulder. "How are you doing, honey?"

She looked up at me with eyes like snake pits of inflammation. Good thing her husband wasn't on a burning funeral pyre right now. Daisy might've thrown herself on top of it.

31

One of the EMTs stepped into the kitchen from the basement, his gear secure and stashed. He approached Brutkowski and tried to communicate what I already knew secretly. Nonetheless, I played along.

"Can you do anything for my brother-in-law?" I asked. The man gave me a well-practiced look of sadness. "I'm sorry, sir. He didn't make it."

On cue, Daisy wailed, "Oh no, not my husband."

She jumped up into my arms. After thoroughly soaking my collar with tears, she collapsed back onto the chair. Part of me hoped that maybe she had been sincere, that she felt sad that Eric had died. Having her show some regret for dumping him down the stairs would make it a little easier for me. I mean, how could I trust a cold-stone killer, even if I loved her?

"What happens next?" I asked Brutkowski.

The cop jerked his thumb back at a woman who'd walked in carrying a camera. "After she finishes shooting film of the accident scene, the medical examiner should be here."

My throat went dry. The word "examiner" worried me. It sounded like they'd take a more careful look-see than Daisy assumed.

"He'll do his thing," Brutkowski continued, "and if he has no questions about the accident, the body can be removed to a funeral home."

Wow, Daisy's plan started to unfold as she said it would. If we can get these cops out of here without any suspicion, then we're a few days and a ceremony from putting this all behind me.

I felt Daisy take my hand. "Tommy, I could use some fresh air."

"Sure, sweetie, let's go outside."

Daisy stood, and I took her elbow and guided her to the back door. I half expected Brutkowski to stop us. I looked back at him and his partner. They crowded around the basement door, the photographer's camera flash lighting their faces, being entertained.

The humid night air and the sound of buzzing insects greeted Daisy and I as we stepped outside.

"Do you think they believed our story?" I asked.

Daisy's mouth tightened. "I don't think their nature is to believe anyone. They're like dogs, their noses always close to the ground, sniffing for anything that interests them. We can't give them any stuff that smells noteworthy, you understand?"

My head jiggled, and I kept making promises until she told me to shut up. My babbling distracted her from planning the next step.

"We got a funeral to think about. That means I'll have to deal with Eric's mother."

Oh Lord, I'd forgotten about Daisy's mother-in-law, Eleanor Pressman. I'd only met the woman once, at Daisy's wedding. A nasty woman who made it clear she hated the idea of Daisy marrying her son. I heard over time from my sister that twenty years had only marinated the woman in bitterness.

"I'm going to need your help, Tommy."

"Of course, I'll help you plan the funeral."

My sister's face went hard on me. "No, I mean, you're going to have to step up big time. The old biddy isn't going to let me have Eric's money without a fight."

I didn't like hearing that. I thought we should be more concerned with keeping my sister out of prison than her getting rich. That would be my priority.

Daisy's gaze moved to something behind me. I turned around to see Brutkowski, filling every square inch of the doorframe.

"We'd appreciate it if you two would stay inside. You never know when we might have a question."

"Sure," I said, stepping toward the entrance. "We were just getting some air."

Daisy followed me back into the kitchen. She sat down in a chair and dropped her head. I followed the cop to the basement entrance. He slowly eye-balled me and pointed to my pant leg.

"You got something on your knee there."

I looked at the spot and scraped it with my finger.

"It appears to be blood," he added.

A swallow of air lodged in my throat, and I had to jerk my head to free it. "Yeah, I guess."

Brutkowski continued to stare at me. I suspected he did so, waiting for me to say something that he could pursue. Daisy had it right. They acted like dogs, those cops, always sniffing for something.

I bent my right arm and exposed the backside of my sleeve. Three blood splatters showed in the fabric. I raised my left arm and pointed to a thin streak of dried blood along the elbow.

"I was trying to help my brother-in-law after he fell," I said. "It got a little messy."

"Is that so?"

I raised my hands, offering a "what-are-you-going-to-do" gesture.

"He was bleeding like a stuck pig."

Brutkowski kept staring at me, his lips thick rolls of pink flesh.

"Not that I've seen a pig stabbed," I said. "I guess they must spill a lot of blood."

His pudgy cheeks squeezed his eyes even smaller. "Yeah, I guess they do."

I said nothing else. Being ahead on points, why take a risk and screw up.

"My grandfather broke his neck falling down a flight of stairs," Brutkowski said, gazing down the stairwell. "He didn't bleed as much as your guy, though."

"Those steps are wood, no carpeting," I said. "Probably like falling on knives."

The cop shook his head. "I don't know. That's an *awful* lot of blood."

"Some people are bleeders."

Brutkowski's eyelids dropped like a window shade, uninviting me from further conversation. I liked that. The big, fat dork had done his job, answered the call, and asked the questions. I didn't cave and give him any reason to suspect the fall had been anything more than a tragic accident. That's all I needed to do. Daisy had promised.

The second EMT dude climbed the stairs and chatted with Brutkowski before leaving. The cop with the camera also came up from the basement. She spoke with both of the police, occasionally throwing a sympathetic look at Daisy. My sister sat on the chair, bent at the waist, her back bounced with an occasional sob. I wondered how long she could keep it up before

34

hyperventilating.

Knowing Daisy, I suspected it could be a long, long time.

Chapter Eight

The sound of the front door opening caught my attention, and a thin, older man walked in. He held a medical bag in his left hand and waved with his right.

"Where is it?" he asked.

The cop with the camera answered him. "The victim's at the bottom of the stairs."

I sprung out of my slouch and made an introduction.

"Tommy Lyle."

"Dr. Dewey," the man responded. The strong odor of low-quality gin coming off of his body gave me more insight than any conversation. With a slight nod, he stepped past me and the cops. He had to use the handrail to steady his descent into the basement. I moved closer and wondered if that rickety old man might he be the second stairwell fatality of the evening.

Brutkowski turned to his partner. "I thought he usually kept it together until he was off duty."

She grinned. "Naw, Dewey's like a vampire. Sun goes down, and he attacks the neck of the nearest bottle."

Neither cop noticed me watching over their shoulders as the medical examiner set up operations.

Dewey squatted to get a better look, swayed, and fell backward, landing on his rear. He grumbled while Brutkowski and his partner clucked their tongues. I said nothing, but inside I sang a hallelujah. How lucky that the town's medical examiner, doing our investigation, arrived in the throes of a bender. We might get through the night without any more snooping police.

36

Dewey put on rubber gloves and, as best as I could see, spent about ten minutes prodding and poking the corpse.

"I think I'm done here," he called out, removing his gloves and wiping at the dirt on the seat of his pants. "It looks like the poor man was just unlucky."

A warm flush filled my gut. Dewey had that right.

"What's his name?"

"Pressman, Eric Pressman."

"Pressman, huh," Dewey said, followed by some mumbling. Then his head swiveled, and his eyes focused on the three of us standing at the top of the stairs. "Did you say Pressman?"

"Yeah," Brutkowski said, followed by a grunt. "I said Pressman."

"Oh my, I know of that man. He's a banker and a big kahuna in the local Republican Party." The medical examiner glanced up at the single 60-watt bulb, throwing light in the basement. "I think I need to do an autopsy. I should look at him in better conditions than this."

I heard Brutkowski murmur to his partner. "I think he means *when he's* in a better condition." The woman chuckled.

I found nothing funny about Dewey. He'd taken away my hope and given me a kick to my stomach.

Chapter Nine

The big storm from early in the morning left temperatures cooler than usual. If ever I should take a stroll to the precinct station, enjoy the rare comfortable August weather, it was today. But I drove, anyway. Walking two miles seemed a bit too ambitious with my creaky knees.

"Detective Bongiovanni, may I see you?"

I wasn't surprised to find Tiny Baker at his desk. His energy seemed boundless, and he probably needed a seven a.m. start time to get everything he wanted to be done, done. I ambled over to his office. If he expected a report on my farewell party planning, he'd be disappointed.

"What's up?" I asked as I leaned against the doorframe.

Tiny maintained a focus on the papers on the desk with his head bent down. I smiled, looking at the bald spot atop his skull. If you're losing your hair, it's better to go bare on top where you didn't see it every morning. My hair still looked pretty thick, at least from what I saw in the mirror.

"I need you to do a follow-up on an accidental death last night. Some guy fell down a flight of stairs."

"Ouch."

"The victim," Tiny hesitated as he read from a note, "was a forty-four-year-old White male named Pressman, Eric Pressman."

"Okay."

Baker shrugged and still avoided looking me in the eye. I suspected his favor would be a doosey.

"This Pressman gave generously to several city and county elected officials.

So did his mother."

"I see where you're going with this, Tiny," I said. "What do you need done?"

Baker heaved a sigh and finally looked at me. "If you could just spend a few hours checking out the police report, talk to the Medical Examiner, you know, make sure everything's properly done."

"Sure, I'll look it over," I said, although I wasn't excited being put in such a position. Most people running an accident or crime scene didn't appreciate having their work checked. I'd bet Tiny expected an eventual call from the Chief and his political cronies addressing family concerns. The rich always raised a stink.

Baker handed me a thin folder. I could probably complete this task in a day or two. It'd be an excuse to get out of the office, mingle with people who didn't care about me being a short-timer. Maybe I could run some errands, like schedule the shutting off of my utilities. I had some housekeeping to do before I retired and headed south.

Tiny smiled at me. "You, Detective Bongiovanni, will be sorely missed."

With Baker's compliment in my pocket, I returned to my desk. After organizing my pencils and note pads, I sorted and dumped the second of four cartons of useless records I'd accumulated over three decades. A few more detectives and staff showed up, offering me a greeting, usually an insult buried in a snort. I gave back as good as I got.

About ten, I'd filled four trash bags with the last of my professional history. I figured I needed to kill time to allow the medical examiner staff to get in. If they worked last night, they wouldn't be in anytime much before noon. I'd chat with the supervising officer from the accident scene. He or she, probably another late shift employee, wouldn't be in until after lunch.

Speaking of lunch, I wondered what my wife had packed for me. She'd put me on a diet a few months ago. "You need to lose a good twenty pounds," she said to me. "I'm not having you sit around all day eating and getting diabetes."

I didn't know where in the hell my mind went at that moment, but it surprised me. I guessed the memory of a wife packing a lunch every day, even if you never got around to eating it, just didn't fade from your consciousness.

Chapter Ten

I suspected that an ordinary citizen like Tommy Lyle would find it impossible to get inside the morgue, considering its location in the basement of the police precinct station. I assumed if you weren't staff, you had to be a cop. The security guard at the front desk looked like she loved the authority her job gave her. And charming a female wasn't my strength, especially one wearing a uniform *and* an attitude.

I'd have to ambush Leo Dewey in the parking lot as he arrived for work. Well, maybe ambush was the wrong word. I wouldn't shoot him, good Lord, I'd never do that. I just needed to talk to him.

Last night's craziness exhausted Daisy, so she asked me to contact Dewey. Being uncertain what exactly I'd say without raising suspicion, my sister volunteered a script. Tell him your sister was in immense distress over her husband's terrible death. She wanted to start the healing process. Mention that the thought of her beloved Eric, iced and naked in some stainless steel refrigerator, drove her to tears. Then ask for the body to be released immediately.

"You're a salesman, Tommy," she added. "Close the damn deal."

I thought Daisy's confidence in my sales skills was overblown, but I wanted to try. The sooner we got Eric buried, the sooner I'd be done helping Daisy find happiness. Yeah, it sounded convoluted when I said it that way, but that's the only way I could think about it and do what my sister wanted.

A rusted-out white Subaru entered the parking lot and pulled into the space designated for Leo Dewey, ME. The car pushed inches into the chain-link fence before completely stopping. I jumped from my vehicle when I

40

heard a car door screech open and saw a man step out.

"Hey, Dr. Dewey, may I have a word with you?"

Dewey's head swiveled, swinging ninety degrees back and forth. When he saw me, his eyes grew wide. I guess he wasn't used to being called out in the parking lot. I didn't care. I'd waited for two hours and already called in late for my shift at the shoe store.

"Dr. Dewey, can we talk?"

Dewey's hands rose, and his body tensed as if I was an approaching predator. I felt terrible scaring him.

"Can I help you?" he said, his voice scratchy as if those words were the first ones he'd spoken that day,

"I sure hope so. I don't know if you remember me. I'm Tommy Lyle."

He struggled to focus. "No, I don't know you."

"We met last night at my house."

"No, I can't recall, sorry." Dewey turned and walked away, his untucked shirttail flapping behind him.

"You were there investigating my brother-in-law's accident," I said as I sped up, closing within a few feet of him. "You know the guy who fell down the basement stairs, Eric Pressman."

That comment brought Dewey to a halt. He faced me, standing not much taller than five-six with the heft of a scarecrow. He touched his lip with his finger, his eyelids fluttering.

"Okay, yes, I guess we did meet."

He started walking away. This time his feet moved in a blur as he stiff-legged it across the gravel lot. I picked up my pace as well.

"Could I please ask a favor?" I said. "I only need a minute to explain."

The man ignored me. I matched him step-for-step as he climbed the concrete stairs to the building entrance. My hand slapped against the glass front door, preventing him from opening it. His head snapped back, his eyes tiny angry spots.

"Dr. Dewey, please listen. My sister is upset. She'd like to have a funeral as soon as possible. Could you release her husband's body so we can make that happen?"

Dewey's face tightened, pulling his coppered skin taut against his skull.

"I'm sorry, but I have two other cases before him. I can't show a preference."

"But does he need an autopsy? It was an accident, after all. You even said so last night."

Dewey's eyebrows bunched over his nose. He said nothing. Afraid I'd blown my chance. I tried a different approach.

"My sister's religion requires a funeral within twenty-four hours of death. She's very observant, and I hope you'll be respectful of her beliefs."

The man smiled. "Which religious tradition is that?" he asked, a soft chortle coming up from his throat.

I sagged and blew out a mouthful of air. Dewey had called my bluff. I knew little about religious practices except for what Mandy taught me. When she died, a week passed before her burial.

"Can I appeal to your better nature?" I asked.

Dewey laughed in my face, and his breath stunk.

"You assume I have a better nature."

I hated begging, but Daisy expected results, and I couldn't fail her. "Is there *any* way I can get my brother-in-law's examination moved ahead?"

"Nope, you'll be lucky if I get to it this week."

He pulled open the door, and I pushed it close.

"Please, Dr. Dewey, won't you reconsider?"

I saw the shadow of the security guard moving toward the door. I dropped my hand and stepped aside as Dewey pulled on the door handle.

"Tanqueray or Beefeater's," I said as he passed me.

He paused for half a second before continuing through the door.

The words slipped from the corner of his mouth. "Bombay Sapphire, liter size."

So that was it. Leo Dewey, the Medical Examiner, had his standards. Lucky for me, having a boozehound as a father educated me on how alcohol made a good man do reckless things, and a bad man turn to evil. I could do business with Dr. Dewey.

"Have a good morning," I shouted at the glass, watching as Dewey cleared security with a bobble of his head. I felt terrible using a man's weakness to get what I wanted, but such a man opened himself up for manipulation. Maybe if I delivered the gin this afternoon, Eric's body would be in our hands by the end of the day.

Daisy would be impressed her little brother found a way.

I strolled toward my car and dialed up my sister. She must be eating the wallpaper in anxiety. The girl had to contact Eleanor Pressman that morning to break the news about Eric's accident. I didn't know why my sister didn't do it last night after everyone cleared out. I knew Eleanor scared Daisy, but she'd have to deal with that old viper sooner or later.

"Hey, Sis, it's your brother."

"How'd it go?"

"I'm getting close. I have to grease the skids with some Bombay Sapphire."

"You're bribing him with jewelry?"

"No, not jewelry, it's a gin."

"When can the body be available for the funeral home?" she asked. "They're ready to pick it up with an hour's notice."

"I think I can make it happen this afternoon."

My heartbeat jumped in anticipation of Daisy telling me I'd done a great job.

"Okay, I needed some good news," she said. "Eric's mother acted horribly when I called her this morning."

Ugh, no attaboy for me from Daisy, I guessed.

My sister reported on the conversation. Eleanor responded by being upset and aggressively accusatory. She demanded the details, names of the attending police and medical examiner. How did Eric's allergy get so out-of-control, she asked. Didn't Daisy check the ingredients of what she served? Why did she call her so late after the death?

"I don't trust the police or the staff of the medical examiner to do a proper job," she'd bellowed at Daisy. "They're hacks."

"Eleanor's going to want a careful investigation of the accident," Daisy said. "We must get Eric's body cremated ASAP, you hear me?"

"Alright, I'll call you as soon as I know when the body's available. You buy yourself a black dress."

I lifted my eyes toward the cloudless blue sky—what a beautiful day. Too bad I had to spend it getting my brother-in-law's busted corpse into a funeral home.

"Make it happen, Tommy. I'm counting on you."

"Yeah, I'm working it. But before you go, did Eleanor, like, you know, shed a tear?"

"Nope, not even a sniffle."

Even though I hated the man, I felt bad for my deceased brother-in-law. The two most important women in his life, and neither one could gin up a teardrop. I wondered who'd cry at my funeral.

"Okay," I said, "I'll be in touch."

I slipped the phone into my jacket pocket and wrapped my hand around the stylish metal fob of Eric's BMW. Last night, Daisy asked me to drive her home. She said I could use the car for as long as I wanted. She said sitting in it made her ill because it carried a hint of Eric's aftershave.

I had to admit, having the car made up for most of the bad things from last night. That vehicle was such a sweet ride. It had a brushed nickel exterior with a deep rouge interior. The engine must have been massive because my head snapped back when I accelerated. I called it Baby.

I wasn't the only one admiring that beautiful piece of automotive art.

"That's a nice set of wheels you got there."

I turned around to the voice behind me. That dang cop from last night, Brutkowski, stood there woofing me.

"Thank you," I said, feeling my insides coil. "How are you this morning, Officer Butt-kowski?"

His cheeks flushed, and I saw his jaw quiver. Oh man, my slip of the tongue touched a sensitive spot. I'd better be careful.

"It's Brutkowski," he said, "with an emphasis on the *brute*."

"Oh yeah, I'm sorry."

The big hunk of muscle and bone, sheathed in a blue uniform, stepped closer. The cop gave me the old cold stare, apparently thinking I'd fold like a poker player with a pair of deuces.

My dad gave me little, except for some insights on handling the law. As Walter always told Daisy and me, "you can't get in trouble if you keep your mouth shut."

So I just looked past Brutkowski and kept walking.

"I saw you conversing with Leo Dewey," he said.

I nodded and opened the car door.

"I'm curious why you'd be chatting up the medical examiner responsible for determining the nature of the very recent incident at your house."

"I believe the correct word would be accident, not incident," I said, slipping my rear end into the front seat of the Beemer. "And I was only thanking Dr. Dewey for his excellent public service."

I felt a smile crack on my face. I'd put Brute in his place, and it felt great.

"Might I ask you whose name is on that car's registration? I'm guessing it's not Tommy Lyle."

I closed the door and lowered the window. "You'd be right, Officer. You'd find the name of my sister, Daisy Lyle Pressman on the title along with my deceased brother-in-law's. Since she's too heartbroken to drive, she asked me to run some errands using her car."

"Is that so?"

Brutkowski's come back sounded so weak I felt emboldened.

"You know my brother-in-law was good friends with half the bigwigs in this town. I bet the Chief doesn't want a call from the grieving Mrs. Pressman, complaining about some beefcake with a badge annoying her family."

Brutkowski watched as the car's backup lights came on, but he didn't move. He kept staring at the trunk. My stomach flipped as I recalled the plastic bag filled with bloody rags. I hadn't got rid of them yet. Stay calm, Tommy. The cop didn't have X-ray vision. He also didn't have any cause to stop me, other than being a dick.

"Excuse me, Officer *Blue*-kowski, I have a funeral to plan."

Brutkowski murmured and walked away. I backed up, shifted Baby into Drive, and pressed hard on the gas pedal. I roared out of the lot, rooster-tailing gravel behind me. It felt amazing.

I had a busy day ahead of me. I had to bribe the M.E. at lunch, get Eric to a crematory by midafternoon, and hopefully walk out by sunset with my brother-in-law sealed in a jar.

Oh yeah, I had to get rid of those awful bloody rags.

Chapter Eleven

After I purchased the liter of gin, I drove around the block near the morgue. I figured there'd be several eateries around for the employees working at the police station and the morgue. I skipped the fast food and family restaurants. I needed places that served more liquid fares. I found two joints within walking distance that served lunch. The Republic Tavern offered pastrami sandwiches and pickled eggs. The Bonnie had a similarly limited menu but provided more than beer from the tap. That's where I parked my car and waited for my new friend, Dr. Dewey.

Leo didn't let me down. At 12:10 pm, he hustled into The Bonnie.

The tavern looked like a typical dive you'd find in this town, dark and stinking of grain-based odors. I walked in and found Dewey bent over at the end of the bar, full shot glass in front of him and the second one in his hand. He didn't say anything as I sat on the stool next to him. I knew he felt me placing the green plastic shopping bag next to his foot. I bet the weight of the bottle of gin caused his heart to flutter. I gestured toward the bartender.

"Soda water, please."

Dewey sniffed. I guess he judged me as a lightweight. I never trusted the hard stuff with my brain, not even wine or beer. I saw my old man make too many mistakes when loaded. If he hadn't been drunk back then, he and mom wouldn't have gotten into that firefight with the cops.

Leo broke the silence after the bartender delivered my drink. "Can I call you, Tommy?"

"Sure, Leo, I hate formality."

The man's reflection appeared in the mirror behind the bar. He smiled at me, his skin lizard-crinkly and dry.

"I devoted my morning to your brother-in-law," he said.

"I appreciate that, Leo, I truly do."

"I should have my report written up by mid-afternoon."

"That's great. Do you think it's possible I can have the body picked up before three?"

"I think it's more than possible."

I took a celebratory swallow of bubbly water. I may not know much, but I knew how to work a boozer. Daisy better be ready to do her part and get the cremation scheduled for today. No corpse to re-examine meant no second-guessing on how Eric died. Daisy would score her inheritance, and I'd start working through my guilt.

Then Dewey pooped on my party by opening his mouth. "But, there might be a hitch."

"Oh, I'm sorry to hear that." And a more sincere statement didn't pass my lips that day. I knew the game the dude had in mind before he even continued playing. Give the sucker the excellent news, pull it back, and tell him how much it'd cost him. I'd seen my folks use a similar routine many times before.

"I reread my notes before I came here," Leo said. "You know the ones I took at the accident scene and from this morning's follow-up examination."

I froze every muscle in my body. I figured what the bum had to say wasn't going to make me happy. Dewey turned his head. His eyes with their filmy yellow lacquer finish, locked onto me.

"There were some curious things about that accident."

"Uh huh, and what might those be?"

"The wounds on the body were inconsistent."

"In what way?" I asked. I didn't want to waste my acting talent playing his game. He knew that I knew the situation. We might as well get to the point.

"Certain wounds on the victim's head were congealed differently than others."

"What does that mean?"

"Blood normally coagulates after an hour. I found some wounds where it had dried and in the same general area, others that appeared to have dried later. It seems that there were two sets of wounds, one older than the other."

"Well, that is curious," I said. "How do you think that happened?"

Then the man proceeded to offer his theory on what might have produced such a result. And boy if he didn't pretty much nail it.

"It looked like your brother-in-law twice tumbled down the stairs."

"That's a disturbing accusation, Leo."

Well, ain't that a stick in the eye. Daisy felt so smart about how she handled Eric's second fall, and a drunk saw through her little scheme. But I didn't wonder why he told me and not the police. It wasn't a matter of why, but how much.

"You know something, Tommy, the salary of a medical examiner isn't that great."

I raised the soda to my mouth but didn't drink. The important thing on my mind didn't involve slaking my thirst. I wanted to get Eric to the crematory before the end of the day, and being coy with Leo wouldn't speed things up.

"How much is this going to cost me?" I asked.

"Ten thousand would be a decent down payment," he said, "and another five thousand a month to keep me happy."

My gut flared like a supernova having a bad hair day. I didn't need that complication, and Daisy sure and hell wouldn't like it. I did some arithmetic in my head. The dude wanted sixty thousand a year, like forever. That's a ton of money, regardless of how massive Daisy's inheritance might be. What choice did we have? I guessed she'd have to write it off as a cost of doing business.

"You know it's my sister who has the dough. I'm the deadbeat brother."

Dewey laughed, throwing back his head and swallowing the rest of the gin in his glass. "I know. I saw your house."

"What I'm saying is I'll need time to explain our business arrangement to my sister and raise the cash. But I want the body released today."

The man looked at me. The skin of his face hung from the bone like melted candle wax. "You're assuming I'm a nice guy," he said. "That's a mistake. Only after I get the down payment will I clear Pressman for release. No money, no body."

I took a swallow of my drink with the hope it would keep my mouth from riffing about him jerking me around.

"Okay, I understand. How soon after I pay you will I get the paperwork, you know, the accident report?"

Leo threw down his second glass of gin and stood, patting my shoulder. "The actual crime report is securely stored in my private safe. The document the police will access, assuming they want to pursue something more than accidental death, is deposited in the central filing. You, my friend, hold nothing."

The man reached down and lifted the shopping bag containing my gifted gin. He moved closer to my ear, whispering, "And the next time we meet, you'll have my fee for releasing your brother-in-law, you understand?"

My chin lifted, and I hummed, "Yeah, man, I hear you."

I didn't bother to track Leo's departure out of the tavern. Screw him. I also wasn't wondering how I'd raise ten grand in twenty-four hours. I figured Daisy had access to that kind of cash. The thought working my brain centered on Dewey having an official record that Eric twice fell down the stairs in *my* house. Now that worried me.

I felt my Adam's apple struggle to climb in my throat. I couldn't believe how quickly everything in my life turned to crap. Somehow helping my sister had gone from being inconvenient to immoral to illegal.

Chapter Twelve

I stood at the front door of Daisy and Eric's house, a mansion in a secluded part of town, made out of blocks of different colored stone with a rust-colored slate roof. It stood two stories and went way back on their six-acre lot. They had a huge kitchen, dining room, living room, master bedroom, a second colossal bedroom, four guest rooms, and a maid chamber, and a three-car garage. But the five bathrooms always impressed me the most.

And Walter Lyle always said none of his kids would have spit.

I wasn't but four-years-old when Walter made it known that he thought poorly of me. Being the type of abuser who'd humiliate you when sober, he'd beat on you when drunk. You could say I had a shitload of unresolved issues with him. Now I've never weighed a shitload of anything, but as far as my father issues, it had to be a big number.

My dad treated Daisy only a bit better than me. I guess he liked her spunk. She didn't roll over as I did. Once, she whacked the old man after he slapped her. Of course, he beat her into rubble, but at least she had him sleeping at night with a gun under his pillow.

Our mother, now that's another story. Don't get me started.

"Thank God you're here," Daisy said, grabbing me by the arm and pulling me into the foyer. "What happened with the Medical Examiner? Why didn't you call me?"

"I have good news and bad news," I said. "I thought it best to tell you in person."

Daisy's cheeks flushed. "I got enough bad news. What's the good news?"

"Dewey will release the body to us as soon as this afternoon."

A squeal came from my sister. "That's great, Tommy," she said, hugging me so hard I coughed. "So all it took was a bottle of gin?"

My head slipped to one side.

"Ah, no, unfortunately, that's the bad news."

"What does that mean?"

I fumbled with my belt buckle. I hated sharing bad news.

"Come on, tell me."

"Dewey found two different wound patterns on Eric's head and body. One was slightly older than the other. He pointed out that not many people fall down a set of steps, climb back up, and fall again."

Daisy bent at the waist as if I'd punched her. "Damn," she groaned, "I thought we had it all figured out."

"Yeah, I thought *we* did."

What else could I say? Blaming her wouldn't do us any good. So she miscalculated how long it took to bring Eric up to the kitchen. She'd never hauled a bleeding man up from a basement. Why did I expect everything to go smoothly? Nothing ever did for the Lyle kids.

Daisy clutched my arm. "Oh God, is he going to the police?"

"No, we're catching a break there," I said, although I almost laughed at the idea that we were lucky. "Dewey, as he put it, is a flexible man in need of added income."

Daisy's hands covered her face, and she slowly shook her head. Growing up, she'd seen the bribery game played out many times in many different forms. "How much does he want?"

"He wants ten grand before he releases the body."

My sister slammed her fist into an open palm. "What a bastard, taking advantage of a grieving widow."

Daisy always stunned me when she went off on a self-pitying rant that ignored her selfishness. As much as I wanted a close relationship with her, loving a narcissist took a ton of energy with little return. I hated feeling trapped like that, but I couldn't stop wanting my sister's approval and affection. I guess we both had a few loose screws in our own ways.

"He did promise that the official report would show the fall was accidental," I said, hoping to cool her anger with my last remaining bit of positive news.

"Okay," Daisy said, "that might be worth ten grand."

"But he wants five thousand a month to bury the report showing that Eric's fall *wasn't* accidental."

As I said, I'm not good at delivering bad news.

My sister stomped her foot, cursed, and spun in a circle.

"Five grand a month, are you joking?"

"Nope, I wish I were."

"And he expects us to pay him for how long?"

I raised my shoulders and croaked. "He didn't say."

"I can't believe it," she cried. "Is everyone a crook?"

Daisy continued spinning, profanity flying off her like water from a lawn sprinkler. I'd give her thirty more seconds to vent and then call a halt. We needed to get Eric's corpse to the undertaker, and to do that, my sister had to cough up some big dollars. Acting all self-righteous did us no good.

"That's enough," I said, my voice echoing around the hallway's twelve-foot ceiling. "What kind of cash do you have?"

Watching the blood drain from her face as she pondered my question caused my stomach to tense.

"Not much at all," she said, mumbling. "Eric gave me a weekly allowance of a few hundred dollars."

"Can you get an advance on your credit cards?"

"I suppose, but if I go above the five hundred dollar limit, Eric gets an alert."

That wouldn't be a problem. Old Eric wouldn't be checking his email anytime soon. Nonetheless, the man had reached beyond the great divide to stifle Daisy's escape.

"Are there any jointly held accounts?" I asked. "Any money in a home safe?"

"No, he controlled everything. That's why I hated him."

Daisy's temper caught fire again, railing about Eric's tightfistedness and the misery he caused her. Having my sister flipping out wasn't getting us

53

any closer to putting the money into Dewey's grubby little hands. We'd be in deep trouble if I had to be the sibling with the cool head.

"You have to get a grip, Daisy. Why are you acting so unhinged?"

"Eleanor called me this morning," she said. "The witch wants to hire a pathologist to take another look at Eric's corpse. She's calling the authorities to get the body released to her."

"Can she do that?"

"I don't know. I'll fight her, but she knows a lot of powerful people."

Heck, if an inebriated Leo Dewey noted the discrepancies in Eric's injuries, a competent doctor would easily expose us.

"We're in deep trouble," I said. "Oh man, we have to get the corpse cremated now."

My head felt like a little hammer-wielding demon had taken up shop inside my skull, banging away. I found the living room sofa to fall onto, closed my eyes as I ran my fingers through my hair. Let's see what we got here. Five hundred cash advance on a credit card, maybe twenty bucks in my pockets, and any loose dollars Daisy's hadn't spent. I swore, having ten thousand dollars in hand sure looked impossible for the Lyle kids right now.

As I stared into space, trying to make wads of cash materialize, my sister strolled around the living room, her manic behavior gone.

"How much do you think these are worth?" Daisy said, her finger directing my attention toward the artwork hanging on the walls.

"I don't know."

She stepped closer to study the pieces, mangling the artist names inscribed on each work. "Come to think of it, Eric liked to brag to his friends about them being expensive."

The fearful thickness clogging my head lifted. Daisy, my problem-solving big sister, had returned. We may get out of this mess yet.

"I bet someone would pay good money for those paintings."

"Would you know how to unload them?" I asked. I mean, how the art world operated was beyond me. All I knew I once saw in a heist movie. It seemed you had to wear tuxedos and sip cocktails while standing around in a room full of art stuff.

"Maybe I do know how to move them," she said as her mouth slipped into a grin. "Back in the day, old Walter and Mabel boosted a lot of stolen property."

"Yeah, but I don't know how they did it."

Daisy's grin stretched into a wide smile. "I went with Walter a few times to cash out stuff. It was a dirty place with lots of junk cars."

I bunched up my shoulders. I didn't know what she meant. Even if she remembered correctly, only about a hundred New Jersey car shops and junkyards met that description.

My sister clapped her hands and giggled. "I remember he dealt with a guy with an animal name."

All my childhood memories had Walter slapping me around. I had nothing that'd cause me to giggle.

"I swear, I'm right," Daisy said, rubbing the back of her neck, working hard to pull up a thirty-year-old memory. "Bobcat...Wolf...Badger, something like that."

"I know it's a long-shot," I said, "but maybe an Internet search of area auto businesses would help. We might find something that'll trigger a memory."

Daisy puffed out her cheeks. "Okay, I guess. Maybe we'll get lucky."

Mandy didn't believe in luck. She said if you walked a righteous path, God would reward you. I've tried doing that for years, and my life pretty much stunk. Maybe I should give Lady Luck a chance.

Chapter Thirteen

Two days after her son's death sparked all this nonsense, I stood in awe of Eleanor Pressman's face. It consisted of a ruddy flag of skin folded around her jawline that flapped when she spoke. Her hair looked like thin strands of colorless fishing line, tightly knotted in a bun. She looked embalmed, which I found to be somewhat ironic since I was there to discuss her son's funeral.

"My condolences on your loss," I said, fumbling the pronunciation of condolence. "Eric's in a much better place."

Daisy's mother-in-law claimed to be seventy-five years old, but you'd be a fool to guess her real age. She might be like those Galapagos Island Tortoises, far older than you'd think to still be moving. Not that she acted slowly like that critter. Oh no, she used quick, twitchy motions, like a squirrel crossing a street in traffic.

"Who are you?" she said, standing inside the main entrance to her condo, a joint that looked, from what I could see, like an art museum. Or at least how I imagine they looked since I'd never been in one.

"I'm Tommy Lyle, Daisy's brother."

Her eyes and nose drew into a tight formation, like a racked set of billiard balls, as she gave me the once-over. "I don't recall ever meeting you."

"I was at the wedding."

A thin-lipped smile emerged across her mug. She slashed the air with a crooked finger topped with a nail lacquered in candy apple red polish.

"Now, I remember you. You were the drunk that we threw out of the reception."

She might as well have slapped me in the face.

"I *was not* drunk," I said, "I've *never* been drunk."

The right corner of Mrs. Pressman's lips curled. I felt a shudder roll up and down my spine. She had the same sneer as Eric whenever he lectured me.

"Do you mean to say you were sober when you acted so obnoxiously? Good Lord, it's been twenty years, and I still remember your boorishness."

I swore the woman channeled her dead son. If I didn't have to explain the details of Eric's upcoming funeral, I'd walk out.

"Daisy wanted me to share her plans for Eric's burial."

"Let me stop you there," Mrs. Pressman said. "Before my son is put into the ground, I want a second opinion on how he died."

"Uh, I don't think so."

Typically I might not have been so mouthy, but I had the cards to be aggressive. With a little help from Mister Internet, Daisy learned yesterday that in New Jersey, the wife had the final say on disposing of her husband's corpse. The mother or any other blood relative had nothing to say about it.

"My sister, as Eric's *devoted* wife, was satisfied with the medical examiner's report. Her husband died accidentally. There will be no second opinion."

Mrs. Pressman's cheeks puffed out, but before she could bellow at me, I yapped at her. "Save your breath, Eleanor. The law's on Daisy's side."

Now I imagined no one spoke to her like that before because she fell back, sputtering. But like a champion brawler, she quickly regained her footing. Her next words came out wrapped in a snarl.

"We'll see about that."

I had no interest in arguing with her. The last twenty-four hours had been hectic. Yesterday Daisy searched the Internet and identified six possible junkyards and auto repro operations that might've been the ones who did business with Walter. We called each one, asking if any employee had an animal nickname. All but one of them told us to do unnatural things to our heads and hung up.

We hit pay dirt late last night when an old-timer named Weasel admitted knowing Walter Lyle.

"Hell of a way to die, getting all shot up by the damn cops," he said to us.

This morning we stripped three paintings from Daisy's living room walls and drove over to Snell's Auto Body. Weasel looked bent from years of manhandling car parts for both legal and illegal purposes yet proved to be a tough negotiator when it came to buying fine art. Over the decades, the man must've purchased and sold most everything.

Daisy and I cleared enough cash from that transaction to pay Dewey his ten grand. Then, we met with an undertaker Daisy had found, named Archie London. She liked the guy because he had squishy ethics and offered the desired mortuary services. He had no problem cremating Eric's corpse and adding a cheap casket and a quickie graveside service.

Eleanor would never know she'd be sobbing over a box of cremains.

"I'm also informing you," I said. "That my sister, *Eric's wife*, wants a private, family-only memorial service."

The woman's spine seemed to add a few extra vertebras as she rose, almost towering over me. She arched her back like a cobra in an attempt to make herself more intimidating. Her action reminded me of my mother, Mabel, when she built a cumulous of rage. I braced against the doorframe expecting a profane verbal smackdown, followed by a punch to the face.

Eleanor did neither. She didn't scream or get physical. Instead, she hissed at me, saying, "I will not be denied."

That wasn't so bad.

When Eleanor hadn't struck me, I felt a surprising sense of gratitude toward her. Mandy tried to convince me that not all women acted like my mother. Most mothers wouldn't use their fists and feet to express frustration. Maybe Eleanor wasn't the devil Daisy made her out to be.

"Well, maybe we can open it up a little," I said. "What did you have in mind?"

"We're a well-respected family in the community. I want a funeral that this town will never forget. Let's start with a top-of-the-line casket, flowers cascading from the walls, and a pianist continuously playing Gounod's Funeral March of a Marionette."

There's the downside of cutting Eleanor a break, I realized, a greedy woman used to getting what she wanted only wanted more.

"That'll cost you," I said. "Daisy's not springing for that."

Mrs. Pressman flapped her head to the side, her lips disappearing into a thin red line. "I'll call the bishop about officiating," she said, dismissing my budgetary concerns with a wave of her hand. "I need to get the invitations out and secure a ballroom and a caterer for the wake."

I'd better apply the brakes to this train before it got too far from the station. "We'll have the service in two days at the Redport Funeral Home. The date and time are not negotiable."

Mrs. Pressman crossed her arms and sent a fearsome stink eye my way.

"I was treated like an appendage by my husband for forty-five years, and my son wasn't much better. By God, I will not be deprived of the attention of a first-rate funeral."

I shrugged. "That's fine, but you'd better act quickly."

Honestly, I didn't know why we had to rush the service. What'd we care when Eric got buried. Once they completed the cremation there's no way to do a second autopsy. By tomorrow, Eric should be nothing but a pile of ash. If I didn't have to deal with the wrath of an angry Daisy, I'd probably give Mrs. Pressman the time she wanted.

"I also want an open casket," she said. "The world needs to see what a handsome man my son was."

Oh man, that wasn't good. I'd better smoother the life out of that demand and do it now.

"I have to tell you that an open casket is a bad idea."

She looked at me with that crooked grin again slicing across her face. I suspected the opinions of a guy wearing a t-shirt with an image of a dead armadillo didn't go far with the likes of Mrs. Pressman.

"I don't care what you think," she said. "That's what I want."

The woman gave me no choice but to up the amperage.

"When Eric fell down the stairs, his mug kissed every step. I mean, it was as if someone rode him like a pogo stick. You don't want people to see that."

Pressman's eyelids operated like nautical flags and signaled that she wasn't buying my argument. So I added more details.

"Let me tell you, experienced cops were barfing in my kitchen after seeing Eric's head."

She didn't react. I must be pitching to a brick wall. I had no choice but to draw upon something I hadn't used since Mandy reformed me in my youth—the bald-faced lie.

"I'm afraid the mortician might not be able to get Eric's head untwisted if you know what I mean."

The older woman's body clenched, and a shiver waved across her shoulders.

"Alright," she said, her mouth chewing the word. "The casket will be closed."

I guessed I should've been please I'd tricked her, although I felt ashamed how easily my instinct for cruelty came back.

"Is there anything else," she asked me, her nose riding toward the ceiling. "Otherwise, I have to make phone calls."

"Nope, I think we have an understanding."

The woman stepped behind me and pulled open the front door.

"Good day, Mr. Lyle."

I studied Eleanor's face and wondered if she'd break down into a deeply felt outburst of tears after I left. You know the rockin' and sobbin' kind of unhinged emotion of a grieving mother. After all, she was about to bury her only child.

As I passed her, she sneered, "Don't think your sister is going to get away with this. She'll never have a day of happiness, I swear."

I guessed payback had a more potent pull than grief for that woman. That worried me. I suspected Daisy would have to do some bad things to battle old Eleanor. Somehow I knew that I'd be doing bad things right alongside her. Why couldn't I have had a sister who liked to knit and gossip with her girlfriends? Why'd mine have to be a cold-blooded killer looking to get rich?

Chapter Fourteen

The memorial service kicked off two days later. The rain came down in a drizzle, and a line of visitors stretched out into the parking lot, a river of black umbrellas and dark fedoras. Mrs. Pressman spent big on the event, and it looked like she got the desired turnout.

Inside the Redport Funeral Home's largest chapel, Daisy and I stood by the casket with Eleanor and Archie London, the mortician and owner. The man wasn't much older than me, except he wore a suit better. His glasses rode a flat nose that had suffered from a few breaks. You knew he hated spending time at the beach with his thinning auburn hair, blue eyes, and freckles.

Slowly rubbing his hands, Archie addressed Daisy and Eleanor.

"We'll open the doors to the mourners in ten minutes. Guests will come in and speak to each of you. The Bishop will start the service, saying a few words of prayer. Most likely, he'll permit people to testify to Eric's character."

That'll be short. I caught a slip of a grin on Daisy's face. She thought the same thing, I knew it. We're siblings, after all.

"When the Bishop signals me, I'll escort the widow and mother out to the limo. Once everyone else is in their vehicles, the procession will depart for the cemetery."

"That sounds good to me," I said. Daisy nodded and pulled a dark veil over her face. Mrs. Pressman said nothing as she stepped up to the casket that sat on a riser. She slowly stroked the side of the cold steel box.

"I don't care," she said, the whisper made loud by the room's emptiness.

"Pardon me," Archie said, his hands fluttering as if anticipating an outburst requiring his gentle touch. "Is something wrong?"

Eleanor ignored him and turned her gaze at me. "I don't care what you say. I want to see my son one last time."

Then that lunatic in a dress swept off the arrays of flowers from atop the casket. Eleanor grabbed the lid and grunted as she tried to pry it open.

Too stunned to move, I heard my voice scream, "Don't do that."

And to my amazement, Daisy jumped on top of her mother-in-law and wrapped her arm around the woman's wrinkled neck.

"No, no, no," Daisy hollered. "I can't look at his face again."

The two women rolled up against the casket, one pushing down on the lid and the other pulling up on it. Archie and I joined the fray, but unfortunately, he and I grabbed Daisy, leaving Eleanor free.

A loud sucking noise sounded as the casket lid popped open, followed by an equally loud gasp from Eleanor's throat.

"Oh my god, where's my Eric," she said, grasping the side of the casket to steady herself.

I panted like a catfish bouncing in the bottom of a boat. Why hadn't that dummy Archie secured the casket lid?

Wondering how Archie would explain the pile of cremains came next in my mind.

An explanation, sadly, wasn't necessary.

Inside that blue steel box laid Eric Pressman, almost six days past his expiration date. His mottled skin and a face falling in on itself made for a disgusting spectacle. An overwhelming musty aroma drifted up to my nostrils, causing my eyes to water. No wonder his mother didn't recognize him.

"That's a terrible piece of embalming," Eleanor said, her words coming out in rapid-fired breaths. "That's horrible, an absolute disgrace."

She slammed the casket lid shut and stormed out of the room. Her voice, full of fiery anguish, could be heard through the closed door.

Daisy jumped at Archie, her hands poised to claw the skin off his mug. "What the hell was that?"

"I can explain," he said, whimpering like a mutt after soiling the living room carpet. "My pickup guy had troubles."

"I don't give a damn about your troubles." Daisy grabbed Archie by his suit lapels. "That was not what I paid you to do."

He muttered some nonsense about a malfunctioning refrigeration system before a booming male voice rolled through the room.

"Stop attacking that man."

The person making the demand sounded enough of a threat that Daisy halted any plan to punch flat the funeral director's nose. A towering dude in flowing white and gold robes barreled toward us like an approaching freight train. I had to say if Moses had been Catholic, that's how he'd looked.

Daisy released the squirming ratfink Archie. I stood behind her, my hands on her arms.

"Bishop Curry," Archie said, his voice a squeak wet with gratitude, "how nice to see you."

Curry stopped a few feet from us, a cold stare on a big flat face.

"Good God, people, let's behave for the sake of decorum."

I didn't have time to worry about etiquette because I had to try and contain Daisy's fury. That jackass undertaker had put her and me in a terrible spot. How long before Eleanor recovered from her shock and realized I'd lied to her? She'd have the body exhumed and a pathologist working on it in a heartbeat.

The Bishop pointed his finger at Archie.

"Get those flowers back on top of that casket," he said. "I'll bring Eleanor back in. We'll start in five minutes."

He turned on Daisy and waved the same digit. "*You* behave yourself."

Daisy growled. She wasn't intimidated by the Bishop. If you wanted to waste threats, throw them at my sister. She'd get her hands on Archie's neck before the end of the day, I knew she would. I couldn't blame her, either. She'd paid big bucks for a cremation that never happened.

Once again, the Lyle kids got screwed.

Somewhere in the room, an organ rumbled to life, and music filled the air. I breathed deeply, trying to calm myself. With Daisy so mad, who knew what she'd do. My dinner party from a few days ago proved her capable of doing some horrible stuff.

I pulled my sister off to the side of the slowly filling chapel. "Daisy, we need to talk."

She pushed me away.

"Leave me alone."

"Ah, come on, don't be that way."

"This isn't what I wanted," she said, stomping her foot. "Eric should've been cremated, the service was supposed to be just us, and now I have to spend hours with Eleanor."

I pulled her into me, whispering, "You need to quiet down. You can't act like a crazy woman in front of all those big wigs."

Daisy's eyes turned dark. "Screw them," she said. "And, screw you, too."

My gut, that reliable barometer of my anxiety, flared.

"Listen to me," I said as I squeezed her arm. "You have to act as if you care, or else you'll raise all kinds of suspicion."

Daisy pulled the veil over her face, grunted, and hustled to a seat in the front row. I joined her, feeling poorly about me calling her a crazy woman. Eric used to accuse her of being deranged. She hated that. However, the Lyle kids *did* act crazy when we lost control of our tempers. I know mine had cost me in the past. I just hoped Daisy realized that being on display required an Oscar-worthy performance from her.

Daisy cursed some deity I'd never heard of and started sobbing.

There she goes. That's my big sister. I knew she'd come through.

Chapter Fifteen

The mucky-mucks behaved at Eric's funeral as I'd expected. They marched in and shuffled by the casket, now barely visible beneath cascading lilies, gladiolas, and chrysanthemums. Most of the clowns laughed and glad-handed each other. When their turn to speak to Eleanor came, they turned sad and misty-eyed and whispered well-practiced lines of condolence. She seemed to love it.

Mrs. Pressman showed up dressed in a deep emerald green cocktail dress with matching shoes and a hat the size of a pizza pan. I knew nothing about funeral wear, but it seemed more of a party dress. The jacket I picked up that morning from the thrift shop made me look like a game show host, but at least it looked appropriate for a burial.

Daisy was another story. Her dress, hat, and veil all were the color of ink. The eye-catching part, in my mind, was her performance as a grieving widow. It exceeded her hysterical acting in my kitchen the night the police came over.

Not that it did any good. Neither Eleanor nor the phonies in line seemed to notice Daisy. The jerks didn't even glance at her, let alone offer a look of sympathy. I imagined after twenty-years of Eleanor badmouthing Daisy, people would be reluctant to even fake interest. They must've figured, why bother, the mother-in-law would win any battles over Pressman money.

I felt hot tears forming. My poor sister had a lifetime of mistreatment. First, our mother abused her, and then over two decades at the hands of Eric and Eleanor. I felt terrible. I'd witnessed it all, yet I did nothing. I'd been a terrible brother to her.

I slowly took her hand and gently squeezed it.

"I love you," I said.

A whisper came from underneath her veil.

"Me too."

"Let's pray that the Lord bear witness to a good man's life."

Bishop Curry began the service with that greeting. I didn't hear much of his babbling after that. My mind relived a lifetime of grievances suffered by Daisy and me. Mandy had always argued that punishment would come to evil people in the afterlife. "Let the Almighty settle your scores," she'd say. "They won't escape His mighty wrath."

I always had trouble with that thinking. Sure, I loved the idea of God punishing Walter and Mabel for mistreating me. I hoped He'd smite the cops who killed my folks. I wanted payback delivered to the bosses who'd fired me over the years, the women who broke my heart, and the people walking the streets judging me. I had a problem, however. I didn't want the same retribution dropped on my head.

As Daisy once pointed out, I'd done some grievous shit in my life.

It seemed like forever before the service ended and the room emptied. I followed the Bishop escorting Daisy and Eleanor to a parked limo if you could call a late model sedan a limousine. Within ten minutes, Archie rolled out Eric's casket and slid it into the back of the hearse.

I arrived to the funeral in Eric's BMW, as I'd been in no hurry giving it up, and Daisy didn't ask for it back. Man, I loved everything about that car. The leather used in the Beemer's interior was beautiful, hand-crafted, and soft to the touch. I couldn't stay away from it. I figured my butt deserved something special, for once.

The grin on my face lasted until I pulled my car behind the limo and saw that dang Brutkowski talking with Mrs. Pressman. I lowered my window in enough time to catch the last of the conversation.

"I'll be coordinating the police escort to the cemetery," he said. "It's an honor to be of service to you."

Eleanor held the cop's hand in hers and mumbled something I couldn't make out. As she turned to enter the vehicle, the big lug took her elbow and gently assisted her. He worked the old lady like a grifter. I knew insincere manipulation when I saw it, and I just saw it.

"Thank you, Officer," she squawked. "I appreciate your understanding."

Brutkowski tipped his hat. He closed the limo door, and as he turned, he saw me watching. He had on sunglasses, but I could imagine his beady little cop eyes looking at me. I wondered what he said to Eleanor. As Daisy warned me, like dogs, cops loved sniffing and digging for trouble.

Brutkowski approached my car.

"Hello, Mr. Lyle."

I nodded.

He paused long enough to ensure I heard his question. "Your sister isn't taking long burying her husband, is she?"

"Why do you care?"

The lug's big, fat cop head slowly swiveled on his big, thick cop neck. "It's not me who cares," he said. "But Mrs. Pressman sure feels you're too eager burying her son."

I doubted Eleanor said anything like that to him. He was a street cop, not a detective. He thought he could play me.

"His mother is the one dressed to party," I said. "She doesn't seem overly sorry."

"Oh, I think she's plenty upset."

"We had to bury him. He was only going to smell worse if we waited."

Brutkowski grunted. I guess he thought of me as some sort of smart ass. Maybe so, I cared less and less how I acted around him. I knew the type; he'd shoot up a room just for the hell of it, like those killer police who murdered my folks.

"She said you refused a second autopsy."

I pushed back into the car seat. Whoa there, maybe old lady Pressman did flap her tongue.

"My sister has complete confidence in Leo Dewey's handiwork," I said. "Eleanor is a grieving mother who can't accept the truth."

Brutkowski leaned into my car, his coffee-thick breath causing my eyes to water. "You're not a nice man, Mr. Lyle."

"Aren't there some donut stores you should be investigating?" I said. "I heard that bakery on 15th street shorted the sprinkles."

The officer stood away from my car, menacingly shifting his shoulders. I didn't care. I wasn't letting that guy bully my sister and me.

"I'm watching you, Mr. Lyle."

The big dude turned and lumbered away.

I wanted to call him out, say I wasn't intimidated. But Eleanor telling him she wanted a second opinion on Eric's cause of death bothered me. If she complained to a lowly cop, how soon would she escalate it to the chief or the mayor? I'm sure she had the chits to call in a big favor.

The fingers of my right hand scraped the console's cup holder, searching for the packet of antacids I kept there.

Chapter Sixteen

Eric Pressman's funeral procession wound its way through town and out into the countryside. The last cars passed under the wrought-iron entrance to the cemetery as the recital of prayers started up on a hillside. Padre gargantuan, the Bishop who'd prevented Daisy from repositioning Archie's nose, lead the service.

"Let's have a show of hands," he said. "How many of you found the deceased to be a prick?"

Naw, the Bishop didn't say that. That comment came from the little voice inside my head. The priestly guy said something like "We are all gathered here to witness the burial of Eric Pressman, a good man called to God sooner than anyone of us would want."

Ha, if the Bishop surveyed the crowd, I bet he'd drop that opener. I'd wager that even his mother wasn't particularly upset by her son's early departure, at least judging by her behavior. I mean, Daisy loudly sniffled with an occasional wail while Eleanor stood silent as if her face had been carved from granite.

I hoped people took notes. I worried that they weren't, or didn't care. My anxiety climbed, wondering if Daisy's resentment had grown over the past. hours. I mean, the girl worked her butt off trying to show her grief. Did she get any reward for her effort? Trust me; my sister didn't do well if she felt cheated.

Daisy and I hadn't gotten a chance to talk after arriving at the gravesite, so I couldn't tell her mood. After nearly an hour of riding alone with Eleanor, who knew her temperature? The veil made it impossible to read her eyes and guess what she might be thinking. Heck, I often didn't know her mind's intentions when I *could* see her face.

Daisy and Eleanor stood by the open grave while a cluster of older people, probably Mrs. Pressman's friends, crowded around them. I sat a few rows back. I supposed I should've felt sorry that no one from our family attended the service, but we had none to invite. If any of Daisy's friends had come, I didn't know them. Whatever, once again, the Lyle kids only had each other.

The religious speechifying continued, and the sun heated the morning moisture to create a sauna effect. The sweat stains on my clothing enlarged as the temperature went from uncomfortable to unbearable. I looked at the rich and powerful standing around and failed to spot one droplet of perspiration on any of them.

The heat made me drowsy, so I failed to keep an eye on Daisy. Only when a new bout of her crying caught my attention did I focus on her. I didn't like what I saw. Her wailing grew louder as they lowered Eric's casket into the ground. She slowly edged closer to Mrs. Pressman as the old gal stood on the grave-edge, peering down into the hole. Daisy slipped her right hand into the fold of Mrs. Pressman's left arm. Most people would see that as a kind gesture of solidarity, the deceased's wife and mother bonding over their shared grief. I knew they'd be wrong. The last time I saw Daisy assist someone, he ended up crashing down a bunch of stairs to his death.

Surely she wasn't going to do something insane in front of all those witnesses.

I peeked between the people's legs in front of me and saw Daisy placing her foot next to Mrs. Pressman's shoe. What was my sister thinking? Was she trying to gain leverage, maybe a position that would allow her to trip her mother-in-law headfirst into the pit?

"Let me through," I said, pushing my way past the black-clad dopes in front of me. Like a ninja, except one wearing a brown and blue plaid jacket and not a judo jumper, I slipped behind Daisy. My right hand slithered under her left arm, and I firmly pulled her toward me. She pushed back. I pulled harder, twisting her arm as she dug her nails into my hand.

"No," she cried out, pulling harder. "No, no, no."

The Bishop halted reading in mid-sentence, and he and everyone looked at my sister and me. I stared back at the hundred pairs of judging eyeballs, my brain desperately searching for something to say. After what seemed like forever, the words found their way out of my mouth. "My sister is overcome with grief. Stand back."

Then with a nifty maneuver, I used my weight to pull Daisy off balance. She lost her grip on Mrs. Pressman and fell back into my arms.

"She's fainted," someone shouted. "Give her some air."

As if on cue, people behind us parted, and I pulled a squirming Daisy out of the crowd. I passed one man, his right eyebrow curved high on his head, staring at my kicking and muttering sibling.

"She's prone to fits when she's upset," I said to him.

He harrumphed like a backfiring car.

I ignored him. What did I care what people thought? If a man dragging his stupid sister disrupted their cozy little prayer circle, so be it. At least they wouldn't witness Daisy pushing another member of the Pressman clan to their death.

Chapter Seventeen

A miserable fifty minutes passed before the last ceremonial shovelful of dirt got dumped atop the casket of Eric Pressman. The crowd quickly dispersed, but not as swiftly as Daisy and me. We quick-stepped it over the hillside and down toward the parking lot. I landed behind the steering wheel of my beloved Baby a second before Daisy dropped into the passenger seat.

"Get me out of here," she screamed, ripping off her veil and sending it flying into the back seat. I did what she commanded, firing up the engine and leaving a trail of burnt rubber on the cemetery parking lot. We'd driven five minutes down the highway before she said another word. And once she started, she didn't stop.

"Eleanor Pressman is the devil. That woman is Satan."

"So, what did Satan say to you?" I asked, curious as to what went down between them. After all, their shared ride might've been the longest those two spent alone together in twenty years.

"When we were a mile from the cemetery, Eleanor turned to me, her eyes red, like the Devil's."

Once my sister locked on a metaphor, she worked it hard. I expected more devil references would follow.

"That old hag said, 'my marriage to Eric's father was hell on earth, but I endured his humiliation up until he died.'"

"So I said, 'I understand your feelings. My marriage to your son wasn't a walk in the park, either.'"

"And then she said, 'well that was your choice, I didn't want you to marry him.'"

"So I said, 'Well, being married to Eric was made harder by the way you treated me.'"

Daisy's eyes grew large, and her hands shook. "Then I swear I could smell sulfur on her breath, and she said, 'One nice thing about my son's death is that I no longer have to look at you, you tramp.'"

Mandy believed the devil showed up in various forms. Demons and their doings always mildly intrigued me, having seen a lot of evil as a kid. So I couldn't help myself. I had to break into Daisy's rant with a question.

"How do you know what the Devil's mouth odor smells like?"

Daisy ignored my interruption and plowed ahead.

"And then I said, 'Well as soon as I get my inheritance, I'm out of this shithole town.'"

"And then she said in a voice that was so unnatural that it had to be Satan talking, 'Well, I'm telling you, honey. I've waited almost fifty years to get my hands on this estate, and I don't intend sharing a single dime with an uneducated floozy like you.'"

My grip on the steering wheel tightened to the point my knuckles stretched white. Everything had grown more and more complicated. Daisy assumed that paying off Dewey would be manageable once she got her inheritance. Eleanor promised to do everything to prevent that. Archie's screw up meant that Eleanor could eventually get her son's body in the hands of an ethical pathologist. Without her share of the estate, Daisy would lack the money to fight the second autopsy.

"Eleanor is going to contest the will. She's going to fight me for every dollar, every piece of property, any investments, the bank, the houses, and the cars."

"Not Baby," I cried. "Please tell me she's not taking Baby."

"Yes, Baby."

"Good God, she *is* the Devil."

Chapter Eighteen

Daisy and I never planned on attending the wake hosted by Mrs. Pressman. I didn't think she invited us, come to think of it. Instead, we drove around town for an hour and tried to blow off steam. Daisy suggested we stop at a tavern so she could throw a few beers down her throat. I didn't like her drinking, but my job was to help her decompress from playing the grieving widow. It had been a difficult five days.

Unfortunately, alcohol and Lyles don't mix well. After Daisy's third beer, she unloaded on me.

"I didn't like the way you jumped me back at the cemetery," she said. "Why'd you freak out like that?"

"What do you mean by me freaking out?" I said, growling. "I stopped you from throwing Eleanor into the grave."

"You're an idiot. I was showing the crowd I was a sensitive and caring person, and you screwed it up."

I felt my jaw drop. "You're kidding me, right?"

Daisy slapped the bar with an open palm. "I was cuddling the old witch, selling the idea I was a caring daughter-in-law. Good God, do you know how hard that was for me?"

"You weren't going to trip her into the grave?"

Daisy bared her teeth.

"You think I'd throw her into a hole in front of a hundred witnesses?"

How could I respond? Yeah, I *did* think you'd push her into an open grave in front of a hundred witnesses. Now I felt like a fool.

"I'm sorry."

"Yeah, yeah," Daisy said, shaking her head before taking another swallow from her glass. "You know, Tommy, you gotta think straight going forward, because we got some serious problems."

"That's an understatement."

"I mean, I'm exhausted right now. I need you to step up, do some of the heavy lifting, if you know what I mean."

"Sure, I can help some, I guess."

Daisy seemed to miss the lack of enthusiasm in my response. My problem wasn't an unwillingness to help. No, I just didn't feel comfortable with my sister's definition of heavy lifting. It usually meant doing things criminal. Then that's when Mandy showed up in my head, warning me about crossing over to guaranteed perdition, as she called it.

"We need to fix some stuff ASAP, you hear me, Tommy?"

Yeah, I heard her. Part of me felt I'd done more than my share. I convinced myself that Eric's first fall had been an accident. I helped get his busted up body to the kitchen. I turned the other way after Daisy sent her husband down the stairs a second time. I'd lied to the police. I'd paid bribes left and right.

Oh my Lord, I was a hundred miles into the darkness. My spiritual destruction was assured if I kept doing the heavy lifting for my sister. I didn't want to do it anymore. Maybe Daisy only needed a day off. If she got a good night's sleep, she'd have the energy to fix her own problems. Yeah, helping my sister get refreshed would work. That'd at least keep my list of sins manageable.

"How about a nice pedicure," I said. "Nothing relaxes a girl like getting her toes prettied up."

Daisy blew out some air and slumped in her seat, too weary, I assumed, to criticize my idea.

"I know a great place not too far from the shoe store."

My sister raised her head, and her brown eyes settled on me. "Okay, I might like that."

With a tipsy Daisy sitting beside me, I raced Baby over to the strip mall in the east part of town. Arriving minutes before the joint closed, the Vietnamese woman behind the counter wasn't too happy seeing us strolling in.

"I'll be outside thinking," I said to my sister. Daisy waved me away, climbing up into the chair for her pedicure.

I went out and stood in the parking lot. The temperature had to be in the nineties, and the humidity high, but my swirling gut bothered me more. Only six days ago, I hosted a dinner to celebrate my sister's wedding anniversary. I willingly tolerated my obnoxious brother-in-law, so I could make Daisy happy. I tried to act like a decent man. Now, I'd become a fumbling accomplice to a murder.

I almost started to cry.

A buzzing cellphone from inside my jacket interrupted my pity party. I pushed a button and raised the phone to my ear.

"Yeah."

It was Archie London. He wanted to see me.

"Why would I want to see you, you jackass," I said.

He answered, "I have something for you."

"Well, it better be a refund."

"Tell me where you are. I'll drive over."

"I'm at the ...," I turned around to read the signage behind me, "Flower Water Nail and Spa. It's the one at the Jepsen Mall."

Twenty minutes later, and my feeling of failure had grown into a brew of bitterness and anger. Old emotions, ones Mandy helped me beat into submission years ago, ran strong in my head.

I wanted to punch somebody, anybody.

A silver Chrysler sedan braked hard before pulling into the parking lot. Archie London sat behind the wheel. Perfect, once he handed over Daisy's cash refund, I'd smack his stupid face. That'd make me feel better.

I walked up to the driver's side window, balling up my fist.

The window rolled down. A smiling Archie London held up a silver vase the size of an overinflated football. "Here's your urn, Mr. Lyle."

"What's that, you incompetent jerk?"

Seeing my cocked fists, the man sputtered. "It's your brother-in-law's cremains."

"Do I look stupid?" I asked, reaching inside the car and shoving the vase into Archie's puss. "Tell me, do I look stupid?"

"No, no," he said, readjusting the glasses I'd knocked off his nose. "I cremated your brother-in-law, as we agreed."

"Get out of that car," I said, taking a step back, pulling my right fist behind my ear. "So, I can properly beat the crap out of you."

Archie was about my size, but even if the dude had been bigger, I felt so angry I'd fight him. Tommy Lyle wasn't going to be played *and* bullied.

"I did what you paid me to do," Archie said, the words riding on a whiny cry. "Why are you mad at me?"

"I saw Eric in that casket, and I saw that casket put in a hearse, and I saw that casket lowered into the ground." I grabbed the car door handle, hoping to drag him out of his seat. Lucky for him, the door was locked. "So don't tell me that Eric's ashes are in that urn."

Archie's face had the same color as a street mime, and he was about as articulate. "Let...let me talk and, and if you're unhappy, you, you can punch me."

I found it satisfying to see him afraid of me. I decided to let Archie quake a little longer. "You have two minutes to make me happy."

Archie proceeded to tell his story. His regular pick up man took yesterday off, so he had to retrieve Eric's body from Dewey's morgue. Then his vehicle broke down on the way back. By the time he got to the funeral home, it was almost midnight. He figured he would have enough time in the morning to cremate the body if he got to work early. Of course, the doofus overslept.

"The more you tell me, Archie, the more I want to clobber your thick head."

The man's Adam's apple bobbed. "When I saw how late it was, and people would be arriving within an hour, I knew I didn't have time to get the crematory hot enough. And I just couldn't leave the body unattended, so I quickly dressed it and dropped him into the casket."

"So if Eric was in that casket, what do you have in your jug?"

"As I said, it's your brother-in-law."

I reached into the car and grabbed Archie by his tie. He squealed like a pig about to be butchered.

"Do I look like an imbecile?" I said, screaming at him.

The man pushed off my hand. "Let me finish," he said, gasping for air and rubbing his neck.

"After everyone filed out of the chapel to the parking lot, I pushed Eric's casket into the back room. Instead of continuing out to the hearse, I parked it, grabbed the same model casket, and shoved it outside to the waiting vehicle."

"So you're saying you pulled the old switch-er-roo?"

"Yes, I did," he said, a shaky grin breaking across his face. "And those steel boxes weigh so much that I knew no pallbearer would notice it was two hundred pounds lighter."

"Let me guess," I said. "While we drove to the cemetery and suffered through hours of faked grieving, you were dry roasting the bones of Eric Pressman."

"Yes, you're exactly right," he said, a tint of coloring returning to his face. "And, when you think about how the mother popped open the casket as she did, we were lucky I hadn't cremated the body."

I relaxed my hands, and my breathing slowed. In a way, Archie called it. Who knew how Eleanor might've acted right then, knowing we'd had her son cremated. At least now, we bought some time to prepare any defense, if and when she got an order to exhume the corpse. As Mandy often said, "God works in quirky ways."

"Okay, man, I'll admit that was quick thinking on your part."

Archie chuckled and handed me the vase. "It's heavier than it looks, and the ashes are pretty hot, so don't burn your hands."

He called that one. I immediately placed the urn on the ground.

"I guess we're done here," I said. "Now, get lost."

The grin on Archie's face lasted about a second longer before morphing into a frown. He rolled up the car window, leaving enough space that I could hear him but not reach my hand inside the car.

"There's a minor problem," he said.

My head dropped so hard that it hurt my neck. Of course, there's a problem. Doesn't everything I touch eventually have some kind of problem?

"Okay, let me hear it."

"We're required by law to submit to Trenton data on any funeral we do."

"So, why is that an issue?"

"My administrative assistant, Phyllis, had a concern."

I stared at him, my stomach stewing in hot juices, anticipating the worse.

"Phyllis is very efficient."

I nodded.

"She was unsure about how to submit the required report for Mr. Pressman's funeral."

He paused again. I realized he was one of those slow talkers. The fact that I held my hands as fists probably slowed him down further.

"She saw that a high end, steel casket had been used for the funeral, yet she heard the incinerator roaring away later that morning."

I muttered various curses.

"As I said, Phyllis is very efficient and was curious why we sold Mrs. Pressman a fancy casket with embalming charges while cremating the body."

"Can't you just tell her to submit the report as a burial and stay out of it?"

"Well, that's the problem. Phyllis is both efficient and ethical."

Ugh. I hated hearing that. Why couldn't the woman be a sleazy bum like her boss?

"Can't *you* submit the report?" I said. "Why does Phyllis need to be involved?"

"She runs everything in my office. I can't get anything past her."

Archie shrugged, his palms open. "She prides herself on being accurate, and, as I said, she's very ethical."

"So, what will we have to do to unethical Phyllis?"

Archie grinned. I suspected he felt happy that I smelled the endpoint of our discussion and jumped ahead.

"I believe a little financial incentive could alter Phyllis's thinking, so she'd feel less guilty, looking the other way."

Damn, are there *any* trustworthy people in this town? Is every dude crooked, their hands out, expecting some easy cash for keeping their mouths shut? I bet you had to bribe the alley cats to catch a rat.

"So how 'little' does this financial incentive have to be to allow Phyllis a comfortable night's sleep?"

"Since your sister is probably going to secure a decent inheritance from her late husband, I think a thousand dollars would do it."

I intertwined my fingers and placed my hands atop my head, closing my eyes. Did I ever think I'd be the go-between crooked medical examiners and undertakers, and a woman who, at best, committed manslaughter?

"I gotta let you in on a little secret, Archie. The deceased, the guy you burned up today, managed his money so tightly it suffocated. So now, my sister has probably a hundred bucks in her purse and has zero access to her credit cards. And that makes her richer than me."

The corners of Archie's eyes slipped downward, and he slowly shook his head. "Phyllis is required to submit the report within a week. I need to have either a good answer for her or some comfort cash."

My teeth bit hard into my lower lip. The man wasn't granting me any favors.

"Yeah, yeah, I'll see what I can do."

"I'm sure she'll be happy with cash."

I felt a smirk kink my face. "They all do, don't they?"

As Archie drove off, I went into my mind. I pulled open my revenge file and filled out a card for Archie London, the Mortician. I noted his excessive greed, his manipulative nature, and his slow talking. I added a line about Phyllis, the ethical office manager. There'd be a day of reckoning, I swore. The mistreatment of Tommy Lyle wasn't going to last much longer.

"Those bastards will get theirs. I swear they will."

The words barely left my mouth when I felt the presence of Mandy. I imagined her looking disappointed. She'd spent so much time taking an angry, guilt-ridden young Tommy and helping him find salvation in the big old embrace of the Lord. Now I was plotting revenge. All her bible lessons and scripture quoting might have been for nothing. She'd be ashamed of me.

"Leave me alone, Mandy," I said. "Stay out of it."

"Stay out of what?"

I jumped at the sound of Daisy's voice coming from behind me. Her forehead furrowed like a plowed field. It seemed the pedicure did little to lighten her sour disposition.

But I couldn't help laughing.

"What's so damn funny?" she said.

I pointed at her feet. "You don't see too many women dressed in a mourning gown with tissues wedged between their toes."

She was in no mood to talk about her tootsies.

"What's going on?" she asked. "I saw you out here talking to someone in a car."

I puffed out my chest. "I have some good news."

My sister's eyes narrowed. "Oh, yeah."

"That was Archie London. He dropped off a little package."

"It'd better be a refund. That rat ass bastard owes me."

"Oh, it's better than that." I bent down and lifted the urn. "Say hello to your husband."

Daisy leaned back. "Are you serious?"

"Yes, I am, sister. This thing contains Eric's ashes."

I gave Daisy the details of Archie's adventure. Like drinking a magic elixir, her angry face melted into a puddle of joy.

"Oh, Tommy, that's great." Daisy grabbed me by the arms. "We finally got something to go our way."

"And you don't have to worry about Eric's body getting a second look."

"I know," she said, bouncing on her freshly painted toes. "I'm starting to believe everything is going to work out."

Hearing Daisy sounding optimistic was a treat for my ears. Why ruin her happiness by mentioning the thousand bucks due in a few days to Phyllis? I bet I could find something else in Daisy's house to sell to Weasel. Yeah, I could handle that. There was no need to involve my sister.

"We're getting close, Tommy," she said as we walked toward the car, the hot cremains in my hands. "I'll call the insurance company tomorrow and start the process of collecting my payout."

"Maybe I can get some of my hours back at the shoe store," I said, "now that you no longer need me."

I laid the urn on the ground, took the fob from my pocket, and popped open the car trunk.

"And with that insurance cash," Daisy said, "I can lawyer up to fight Eleanor for my share of the estate."

I offered up my spin. "Satan will not win, am I right?"

Daisy giggled, raising her fist in a triumph salute. "She will not defeat me."

The Lyle kid's happy jamboree popped like a cheap balloon when my sister bellowed, "What the hell is that?"

She reached into the trunk and pulled out a black garbage bag, shaking it in my face.

"Don't tell me those are the bloody rags from last week."

My head twisted, and I struggled to answer. Oh man, how'd I forget to burn those things?

"How do you explain that?" Daisy said, rattling the bag harder. "How?"

I mumbled my response. "I've been busy."

I knew it was a pathetic reply, but that's the best my brain could deliver.

"Do I have to do everything?" she cried. "Damn it, Tommy."

Oh man, so close to celebrating a happy ending to a rough day, and I screwed up. Now Daisy's anger boiled up again, and it was my fault. She scanned the parking lot. "Where's a dumpster?"

She spotted one alongside the building. The nail salon owner peeking out her window, however, stopped Daisy in her tracks.

"Put it back in the car," I said. "We can't leave it here."

My sister tossed the plastic trash bag in the trunk and flip-flopped to the passenger car seat. Even with her inside the car, I heard her cussing me. I didn't know why she had to overreact. I'd dispose that bag of rags first thing in the morning. Daisy should be happy. With no corpse to worry about; she could focus on the things most important to her, a ton of money, and the freedom to spend it. Me, I'd start working on my redemption.

Chapter Nineteen

"Good morning. I'm Detective Nick Bongiovanni."

The man didn't look excited to see me. They never did. This Tommy Lyle appeared to be one of those skinny little guys who would rather fill his gullet with cigarette smoke than eat a decent meal. He had shark eyes, large black pupils that didn't seem to blink. They say the eyes are the window to a man's soul. In this case, I didn't care about the man's inner workings. I just wanted to be done with the interview and on my way.

"Come in," he said, slowly stepping back to let me enter his dump of a house. "What can I do for you?"

"I'm here to do a little follow-up from the incident last week," I said, "the one where Eric Pressman died."

"I thought the police were all done with that."

"I only need a few minutes," I said, hoping it would take less time, but knowing it wouldn't. I threw out my first question.

"How did you and Mr. Pressman get along?"

I always surprised them by asking how they got along with the victim. A simple query that somehow unnerved people. My whole interviewing repertoire consisted of tricks to throw people off balance, even if they weren't a suspect. After thirty years of police work, I knew the critical stuff you learned often came as a surprise.

"We did okay," he said. "He wasn't the easiest person."

I smiled. I knew I had a disarming grin, so I always used it right out of the box. Lyle seemed to relax, so I guessed I still had the touch.

"When I hear a person wasn't easy, I suspect that guy was a big jerk."

Lyle laughed, and his head bobbled. "You got me there. My brother-in-law *was* a jerk." His shoulders slumped, and he sighed. "But my sister loved him, so what are you going to do, huh?"

"Yeah, we all have one like that," I said.

Lyle cleared his throat and squirmed as if his pants fit too snugly.

"I'm not clear on why a detective is investigating an accidental death," he said. "I mean, the police officers and the medical examiner agreed it was an accident."

"We like to follow up on any death that isn't due to natural causes, just to dot the 'i's' and cross the 't's.'"

Lyle had it right. This visit amounted to a waste of time. The only reason I'm stuck with the task was that the Pressman family had made significant contributions to the mayor's election campaigns. It's always the same. The guys with money got the attention, even when they're dead.

Tiny Baker also wanted to keep me busy right up until my retirement party. That made sense to me. Better than sitting around thinking of my future. Joanie always said I had to keep moving or I'd get in trouble. I'd fidget even while I slept.

Lyle walked me into the dining room, where we both sat down at a table. I started up again with my questions.

"Did you and the deceased have any financial dealings?"

Lyle's eyebrows arched ever so slightly. That brief, involuntary reaction always amused me. I felt the person had an "ah-ha" moment, realizing I considered them a possible suspect. I expected Lyle's tone and behavior would begin to change, *especially* if everything were innocent.

"I borrowed some money from him a few years ago. I mean, not from him personally, but through his bank. It was a mortgage."

"Were you having any trouble making your payments?"

Lyle shook his head, lips tightly pressed together. "Nope, I haven't missed a payment. And like I said, it was a bank loan, not a personal loan."

"Yeah, I got that point."

I glanced over the room. I'm not an architectural historian, but I suspected the house had probably been built a century ago when most of the houses in this part of town went up. Faded wallpaper, peeling paint—it was a 'fixer-upper' still waiting to be revitalized.

"Can you tell me a little bit about the night of the accident?"

Lyle dipped his shoulders and spoke in a casual cadence.

"I was making dinner for my sister and her husband to celebrate their twentieth wedding anniversary. They arrived at six-thirty no; it was closer to seven. We caught up, ate some snacks, and had a glass of wine, nothing unusual."

"Was Mr. Pressman feeling okay at that time?"

"Yeah, he seemed his usual self."

"There were no heated discussions, he didn't get angry, nothing like that?"

Lyle stared off as he pulled up some memory to share with me.

"We got into a testy exchange over the eggplant parmesan I was making for dinner. He was critical."

"My wife used to make the best eggplant parmesan, I swear."

Lyle puffed himself up. "Well, mine is pretty darn good."

"And your brother-in-law was unhappy about it, huh?"

Lyle wrinkled his nose. "Yeah, but he didn't like anything I did."

The man continued talking as I scribbled notes. He told me how a sudden nut allergy attack knocked the victim to death's front door and how Lyle and his sister pulled the man from the brink. He explained how Pressman, after recovering, insisted on leaving. His brother-in-law had parked the BMW in the back of the house, so he came into the kitchen to go. While unsteady on his feet, Pressman had been insistent that he leave. He lost his balance at the stairwell and fell. Lyle and his sister rushed to help, and then they called 911.

"I'd like to see where Mr. Pressman took his fall. Can you show me the stairwell?"

"Sure." Lyle stood from his chair, stepping quickly towards an adjunct door. "The basement stairs are in the kitchen."

I picked up a brown envelope I'd brought in and followed Lyle into the kitchen. Dirty dishes overwhelmed the sink, and the wastebasket overflowed with trash. Lyle waved his hand over the mess, "I wasn't expecting company. Sorry about the disorder."

"Not a problem."

I pointed at an open door. "Is that where it happened?"

Lyle jitterbugged around a kitchen chair, reached for the inside wall of the stairwell, and flipped on a light switch. "Yeah, that's where he fell."

He lowered his head and pulled in air through pursed lips. "I feel pretty bad thinking if I'd closed the door, none of that would've happened."

I studied the man's performance, although I stunk at deciphering human emotions at times like this. People reacted differently when under stress. I'd seen killers bawl like babies and innocents maintain a stone-cold demeanor.

"I'd like to look at the stairs if you'll excuse me."

Lyle stepped aside. "I have to tell you. I scrubbed those stairs and floor soon after they took away the body. No one told me not to clean it. I hope I didn't screw up."

I waved the brown envelope as I passed him. "Not to worry, I got some excellent accident scene photos with me."

I pulled the glossies from the packet and carefully placed individual photographs on the steps, trying to replicate the accident scene. I counted to the fourth step and dropped a photo down. It looked like the victim's head first impacted there. I placed another photo against the cement wall and guessed that spot once had a big blood spray.

Lyle called out from the kitchen. "What are you hoping to find?"

I didn't look up but spoke loudly to ensure my words would be heard. "There's a science to freefalls. We consider the height and weight of the victim, the number of steps, and whether they're wood, cement, or carpeted. There's the pitch of the stairs to consider, as well. We can learn a lot about an accident."

"Really," Lyle said. "That's interesting."

I *assumed* that such research on how a human body would react to falling down stairs existed, but I wasn't an expert. Hell, nearly three decades of investigating unnatural deaths, and I'd seen maybe only three such incidents of someone dying by tumbling down a stairwell. I found that throwing out an occasional bit of nonsense in an authoritative manner got people to reveal something they might not want to share. You just never knew.

"I don't want you to go down any dead ends, Detective, so I think you should know my sister, and I probably messed up your accident scene."

"How's that, Mr. Lyle?"

Lyle carefully descended the stairs, stopping two steps up from me. "We were in a panic when Eric fell. We immediately ran down into the basement to check on him. I'm sure one of us came back up to call 911. I'm afraid we stepped all over everything. I recall washing blood off my shoes afterward."

I smiled. Well, wasn't Mr. Lyle a helpful little fellow? Usually, guys like that are anxious because they're worried about getting into trouble. That's not to say they did anything criminal. Some folks have overactive consciences that get triggered in the presence of the police.

"I'll take that into consideration," I said, turning back to the photos displayed on the steps.

Let me think this through. I held the police report in my hand as I scanned the stairs. The report said Pressman left the room, woozy from an allergy attack, and lost his balance, verifying Lyle's story. The medical examiner's notes stated that the victim appeared to have a fractured skull and a broken neck.

"I don't know if we told the investigating officers, but we did move Eric. My sister panicked and rolled him to his back. I think she may have tried CPR."

"Okay. That helps me."

Now I'm trying to visualize a man falling backward, hitting the fourth step with the back of his head. The momentum of tumbling would probably bring his legs up and over to where his feet would hit the eighth step. I peered at the photo showing a man's shoe on the tenth step. Okay, that made sense. I guessed as the victim fell over, his face scraped the edge of the steps, probably two or three times. Those wooden steps would do it—no carpeting to cushion the blow or prevent a nasty cut.

"Was Mr. Pressman able to speak when you got to him?"

Lyle appeared confused.

"No, not in any way that made sense," he finally said. "I mean, he was only groaning before the EMTs got here."

I pulled a small flashlight from my coat pocket and bent at my knees. I ignored the popping sound coming from my stretched ligaments. Maintaining my balance with my right hand, I stooped low and shined the beam underneath the wood step. I repeated it again and again, moving up from the bottom step to the fourth. When my arm cramped, I stopped. I'm too old for bending. My knees couldn't do it anymore.

But after decades of looking for small things that appeared out of place, habit demanded I keep going. So I did. And darn, something that didn't make sense caught my eye.

I reached into my side pocket and retrieved a tweezer and an evidence bag. Carefully I pinched the small piece of cloth hanging from a splinter under the fourth step. It made me wonder how good of a job the investigating officers did. I sure hope the medical examiner did a thorough analysis.

"Did you find something?"

"I found something, indeed," I answered.

"What is it?"

Boy, Mr. Lyle *was* a curious little fellow. I looked up at him, a tight smile on my face. "It's probably nothing."

It might be something, but most likely not. It just seemed like an odd place for a shred of cloth material. I'd let the lab determine its relevance.

"I think I'm done here, Mr. Lyle."

"Okay," he said. His voice sounded steady, with no sign of stress. So either he was unconcerned or well-practiced in talking to the police. Maybe it was neither. As I said, not all people act oddly when under pressure.

I climbed the stairs, each step tweaking my right knee. That's the joint I told the retirement board I injured last year chasing some perp. Such a job-related injury would boost my monthly payout by a few bucks. They all were within a decade of being in my shoes, so no one questioned my claim.

"Did you grow up here in the county?" I asked Lyle. He acted surprised. I guess he wasn't expecting me to get all friendly.

"Yeah, I was born here. I never left New Jersey."

"What were your folks' names?"

Now helpful and curious, Mr. Lyle turned mute. My hunch struck pay dirt. I swear my precognitive skills could rival a mind reader.

"Mister and Missus Lyle," he mumbled.

My smile served as a prelude to a chuckle, which turned into a full-blown laugh.

"Come on, buddy. Is there a problem?"

"Walter and Mabel, their names were Walter and Mabel."

I didn't say anything at first because my mind tripped down memory lane right about then. When I started on the force, a husband and wife ran numbers and other stuff over in the south end of town. Their last name had been Lyle.

"Walter and Mabel Lyle, you say."

"Yeah, that's what I said."

"A long time ago, when I was a beat cop, a husband and wife with those names were involved in some illegal business. Is there any chance you're related?"

The question caused an ugly sneer to form on his face. I guessed who could blame him. No one liked being asked if their parents were crooks.

"Yeah, they were my folks."

I tried to keep my feelings controlled. Holy Hell, the odds had to be astronomical? About thirty years ago, as part of a team knocking down a door to arrest Walter and Mabel Lyle, I watched them get gunned down in a shootout. And here I stood, interviewing their kid. Now I knew the source of the man's unease. He must hate the sight of any cop.

Lyle raised his hands, waving them in the air. "I'm not anything like my old man."

"I get it. My dad was a German Literature professor at Princeton, and whenever I hear someone talk about Günter Grass or Alexander Chekhov, I want to barf."

I watched Lyle's eyes for any reaction. I liked using that German Lit line when getting to know people. If they called me out on Chekhov being Russian, I figured they had some brains. I always liked to know how much smarter I might be than the person I interviewed. My old man, a street cop and detective, shared that trick with me.

"I'd like to talk with your sister. Could you give me her address?"

Lyle started chewing his lower lip.

"Do you need to do that?" he asked.

"Why is that a problem?"

"I'm not saying it's a problem, but she buried her husband three days ago, and she's still upset. Could you wait until next week?"

I softened my face and gave him another go-to mannerism that I'd mastered. Even if a suspect was a cold-blooded murderer, they still liked to think you're sympathetic to their feelings. My problem was waiting a week or more might mean I couldn't put this investigation to bed before my retirement party. I hated loose ends.

"Sure, I'll stop by in a couple of days. I know what it's like to lose a spouse."

I wished that wasn't true. Being Wednesday, Joanie and I'd be tipping back a few Peroni's at the Italian American Social Club tonight. Not anymore.

"Thanks again, Mr. Lyle. I'll be going now."

The man stepped out of my way. He seemed relieved. I suspected my presence caused his internals to boil, what with his parents killed by police. He'd be even more upset if he knew my history. The shootout involved a lot of rounds that night. Scared shitless, I just pointed my gun into that room and pulled the trigger until I heard the clicking of the hammer against an empty chamber. I didn't hit anything but walls and windows. At least that was the story I told myself.

Chapter Twenty

We had three medical examiners plying their trade here in the county. Two of them did careful and skilled work. The third, Leo Dewey, had a reputation as the one guy a detective didn't want to work his case. Since the second Bush lived in the White House, he hadn't learned anything new about the field. After chatting up Tommy Lyle, I had a conversation with Dr. Dewey.

"Good afternoon, Leo. How's the old noggin feeling?"

The Medical Examiner gave me a wry smile like he was immune to such digs. I felt a little sting of regret. Peel away any alcoholic's bravado, and you'll find disillusionment and self-loathing—what a terrible disease.

But then again, pity couldn't excuse incompetence.

"What are you doing down here?" Dewey asked. "I thought you retired."

"Not there yet, I'm sorry to say. Two weeks and three days or something like that."

Dewey didn't add fuel to the conversation, so I explained the purpose of my visit.

"I'm looking into a case from last week. I think late Friday? A man named Eric Pressman fell on a flight of stairs and broke his neck."

The man grimaced. "Oh yes, that was a nauseating little accident."

"I was over at the residence this morning, checking it out."

Dewey straightened out of his stoop and leaned in toward me. "Why is a decorated detective doing a follow-up for an accidental death?"

"Oh, you know how it goes. A rich woman wanted a closer look at her rich son's death."

Dewey stuck his hands in his pockets and gave me a high voltage stare. "I did a thorough job," he said. "You're wasting your time."

"Oh, I have no doubt. But I was wondering if you found anything suspicious."

He shook his head. "My observations are all in my report."

Even though I heard him, I still had to ask. "So, nothing strange comes to mind."

If you want to push an incompetent man's button quickly, question his competency. Dewey blew.

"I'm handling, on average, eight cases a week. I go on-site; do a careful examination and collection of data. I make my determination and write an exhaustive report. If anything seems out of the ordinary, I make a note of it. If I see nothing, I write nothing."

"I appreciate your reputation for completeness. Do you have time for one more question?"

"Not really."

"Okay, I'll make it quick. By any chance, was the victim wearing a knit hat or a sweater?"

Dewey whooped so loudly the sound bounced against the basement's concrete walls. "Why would he be wearing a knit hat or sweater inside a house during the summer?"

I couldn't prevent a snigger escaping from my mouth as I thought about the silliness of my question. "Sure, I know it doesn't make sense. I'm asking because I found a small piece of fabric hanging underneath the lip of one of the steps. I wasn't sure if it was part of the victim's clothing."

"Let me look at it."

I flinched. "I'm sorry, but I dropped it off at the lab."

Dewey's eyebrows drew closer. "You know those lab guys are behind by a good month."

"You don't say."

"Unless it's an active criminal investigation, you'll be lucky to get it back in two months."

"That's too bad. I'll be fishing off the Outer Banks long before then."

Leo doubled down on his look of pity, adding a slow rotation of his head. "Why are you wasting your time on an accidental death? You should be making everyone at the precinct buy you bourbon shots to toast your retirement."

I snorted and slapped Dewey on the back. "That's a good point. What the hell *am* I thinking?"

"Yeah, don't be a fool."

I turned away from Leo and walked by the refrigerated units, the dissection tables, and the slop buckets, drains, and rows of saws. That might be the very last time I'd ever be in a morgue unless as a corpse. I felt a flutter in my chest, unsure if it was melancholy or excitement. Maybe old Dewey had it right. I should be spending my days letting people celebrate my career instead of determining whether a shred of fabric held any meaning.

I called out as I approached the exit. "I'll see you around."

The man gave me a shout back. "Don't waste your time trying to prove nothing."

Now I felt terrible for cashing in my chits with the lab guys. They promised to take a look at my piece of fabric by the weekend. Oh well, if they got it done before I left, I'd at least have some insight. I guess I'd never lose the desire to have an answer to every question.

Chapter Twenty-One

Walking down the main hall of the precinct station made me uncomfortable. The guys would bellow out insults and try and shame me for retiring. I'd be disappointed if they didn't treat me that way, yet I hated the attention. The young guys acted the worse, giving me almost god-like status. I don't know why. I only broke a few significant cases in all those years of sleuthing.

"I'm looking for Officer Brutkowski," I said to the sergeant running the floor. "Has he started his shift?"

"He just left. You might be able to catch him in the lot."

"What does he look like?" I said as I turned toward the door leading to the outside.

"You can't miss him. He's the biggest guy on the force."

Darn it. Now I'd have to run. Maybe running was an exaggeration, but I'd be moving faster than either my knees or I wanted. I got lucky. As I cleared the exit, I saw a mountain of a man standing at the open trunk of a black and white.

"Hey, are you Brutkowski?"

The man looked up. He started with a dismissive expression, but then, as if a switch turned on inside his head, he smiled. I stopped my pathetic attempt at sprinting and hobbled up to him.

"Hey Officer, I'm Nick Bongiovanni. Can I have a minute of your time?"

Brutkowski continued grinning, a slight tint of color appearing on his cheeks. "I know who you are," he said. "Every cop in this town knows Detective Bongiovanni."

Great, that's all I needed, a not-so-secret admirer.

"I'm following up on an accidental death that you attended."

"Are you talking about the Pressman incident, the one that occurred seven days ago?"

"That's right. Did you arrive at the scene before the M.E.?"

"Yes, I made the request. I mean, I called for the M.E. on duty, not explicitly asking for Dewey."

"I understand."

"That man's an embarrassment to his profession and law enforcement."

I scratched my neck, where a droplet of sweat trickled from my scalp.

"Can you tell me what you saw when you arrived?"

"I first ran into the brother-in-law, Tommy Lyle."

"How was he?"

"He appeared more nervous than upset, if you know what I mean."

I laughed. "I do know what you mean. I spent an hour with Lyle. He's a jittery little guy."

"And I saw the wife. She was pretty upset, and neither my partner nor I could get much out of her."

"Did you get a good look at the accident scene?"

"I followed the EMTs in, and they were down in the basement, working the victim. It was a narrow fit, and as you can see, I'm not built for confined spaces."

"Did you see anyone cleaning the stairs, maybe wiping up using a towel or rag?"

"I made sure nothing was touched until Dewey finished. I couldn't prevent the EMTs from stomping all over the place, but nobody cleaned up while I was there."

"Okay."

Brutkowski's face drooped. "I never considered it a crime scene, or else I'd kept it more orderly."

"Sure, sure, there was no reason to suspect otherwise."

"Is there now?"

"Nope, no reason, so far."

A twinkle appeared in Brutkowski's eyes, joining the slight grin on his mouth.

"It's rather odd that an experienced detective like you is investigating an accidental death."

"You're an observant young man, aren't you?"

"I once attended training, where you gave a lecture. You always said to keep your eyes, ears, and skepticism open."

I hadn't a memory of ever giving a talk to a group of street cops, but the sentiment was something I might've said.

"The truth is less impressive. I'm a short-timer killing three weeks before retirement. The victim was a big supporter of our mayor. Who knows the Chief's motivation to push follow-up? I'm just doing what the boss asked."

I shook Brutkowski's hand, his big mitt swallowing up mine. "Thanks for the chat."

"Did you know that Tommy Lyle's parents were career criminals?" the officer asked.

"I didn't run into him until this morning, but yeah, I knew of his folks."

"Did you know the wife, Daisy Pressman, was Lyle's older sister?"

I nodded. "I kind of figured that out."

"I think it's odd that the wife, a woman from a criminal family, would end up married to a wealthy man like Pressman. His family money runs back a generation, if you know what I mean."

I liked that Brutkowski had a rare curiosity. Most street cops seldom dug beyond surface observations.

"I also coordinated the funeral procession to the cemetery. I spoke to the mother. She didn't think her son's death was an accident."

"That's good to know," I said, even though I already knew it. After all, that's why I got stuck with this job. "I appreciate the tips, Officer."

"Just observing and reporting."

"If you're not thinking about taking the detective boards, you should."

Brutkowski broke a big grin. "That's my intention, sir."

96

Chapter Twenty-Two

The next morning, I stood at Tiny Baker's office door, tapping on the glass. He looked up, unsmiling. I didn't take offense. He only seemed to use his mouth for giving orders and eating.

"Hello, Boss."

"Hey, what's up?"

"I'm here to get my gold watch or whatever you hand out at retirement."

Baker surprised me when he snickered. "I think you're confused. You should be talking to the guy who likes you."

"That guy is broke, so I'm pushing it up the chain."

Baker's gaze returned to the document on his desk. It looked like our light-hearted banter had ended.

"Have you done anything with that Pressman follow-up?" he asked.

I stepped into his office, far enough to drop a folder on the desk.

"I spent the last few days checking it out."

"What did you find?"

"I visited the scene, talked to a witness, and I examined the stairs. I chatted with Dewey, the M.E. who worked the scene, and followed up with the officer who attended the initial call, a big guy named Brutkowski."

"Did you find any reason to question the Medical Examiner's findings?"

"I can't say, either way. By the time I got to the house, the owner had cleaned up the accident scene."

Like a bolt out of the sky, it occurred to me *that* was probably the source of the cloth remnant. Hell's bells, why hadn't I thought of that before? They probably used a cloth to clean up. Damn, good thing I'm getting out. My observational skills have severely slipped.

"Let me guess," Baker said, "You'll eventually conclude it was probably an accident."

I threw my hands in the air. "I have no choice but to go with the initial findings."

"Good. Can you write me up a little synopsis so I can get the mayor off my back?"

"Of course I can do that," I said, "But, first, I'd like to talk to Pressman's widow."

"Any special reason you want to do that?"

My shoulders climbed around my neck. I didn't want to tell Tiny that Brutkowski pointed out that the widow Pressman was the daughter of Walter and Mabel Lyle. I doubted my boss knew much about the old Lyle family. He probably had still been in grade school when it all went down.

"No, not really," I answered with a grin tickling the corners of my mouth. "But as you once pointed out, I'm still getting paid to do my job."

Baker laughed. "I love hearing that."

"Glad I could make your morning, Tiny." I turned to leave. "I'll try and wrap everything up in the next few days."

"Wait," Baker said, handing me back the Pressman file. "Hang on to this."

"I don't need it." I tapped my index finger against my forehead. "Everything I need to know is right in here."

Tiny looked up. "Keep it until you're no longer working for me. I have the impression that the man's mother isn't the type to take no for an answer."

Chapter Twenty-Three

The rapping on my back door sounded like the attack of a demented woodpecker. Who in the hell kept hammering away on my door this late at night? I flipped on the kitchen light and shouted for the idiot to stop.

"I'm coming. I'm coming. Give it a rest."

Before turning the deadbolt, I peeked out the small window overlooking the back porch. I never had unexpected visitors since I had no friends. And I sure and the heck didn't have people showing up this late. I stared hard at the figure standing there, hugging the shadows. At first, I didn't recognize him. Then I did.

"What does he want?" I mumbled, twisting the deadbolt and pulling open the door. The man rushed past me, paused to scan the room, and stepped to the wall switch, and turned off the lights.

"What are you doing, Dewey?" I asked.

He didn't answer me, moving to the kitchen window that faced the street and hunched down as he looked out.

"Come on, man, answer me."

"I think someone's following me."

Now that wasn't what I wanted to be dealing with at 12:30 in the morning—a hallucinating paranoid.

I stepped to the window to check out the street. I saw nothing: no people, no cars, nothing.

"How loaded are you, dude?"

He didn't reply, but the smell floating off of him suggested a pretty high level of gin consumption.

"I had to see you," he said. "There's trouble."

My heart dropped a beat. How could that be? Wasn't Daisy paying Dewey to avoid trouble? I took him by the arm and guided him to a kitchen chair. "Sit down. I'll brew up some coffee for you."

"No coffee."

Dewey plopped in the chair with a grunt. "I can't stay."

That made me happy. Leo's sudden change in behavior made me very, very nervous. The last time we met, he acted controlling, telling me how things would work. Now here he was all fearful, talking nonsense. He reminded me of my old man with his overwhelming suspicion. That's why we had so many guns in the house. My dad thought everyone had a reason to kill him.

"Okay, what's this so-called trouble we're in?"

"I understand a detective by the name of Bongiovanni visited your house yesterday."

"Yeah, do you have any idea what's behind that?"

Dewey's head bounced as if being dribbled. "Pressman's mother got her powerful friends to push a closer look into her son's accident."

Man, that old biddy couldn't wait a day to start a fight.

"The detective told me he wanted to interview my sister about the accident," I said. "Should I be worried?"

Dewey swiped his hand across his mouth. "If he does meet with your sister, you two better have your story straight."

Keeping our stories straight wasn't my concern. Having Daisy grilled by a detective was the issue. Her hatred of the police could quickly rise to the surface if this guy pushed the wrong buttons. Her memory of the way Walter and Mabel died had a degree of intensity stronger than mine.

"We can handle a police interview," I said. "So, don't lose your head over him."

"I know, but there's more." Dewey rotated in his seat, throwing glances toward the window. "He's been working the crime lab, getting people to run tests on your stuff."

"What do you mean by *my* stuff?"

"Some cloth he found on your stairs."

My memory cranked for a minute before the recollection crystallized. Was Dewey talking about that thing the detective picked from under the step? The item he acted all unconcerned about?

"What was he having the lab look for?"

"I don't know. He wouldn't say. But he asked me whether Pressman was wearing a stocking cap when he fell."

I felt my stomach drop to my knees. Did that piece of cloth come from the towel Daisy tied around Eric's head? The towel she said would keep clues inside Eric's skull and not on the stairs and walls. Was *that* the scrap of material the detective found?

With my nerves now jangled, I dug deeper. "What do you think that means?"

"I don't know. Bongiovanni has a reputation for being a grinder, a guy who doesn't give up." Even in the dark, I could see Dewey's eyes grow larger. "I just hope it doesn't lead to a court order to exhume Pressman's corpse. *That* would be a problem."

I supposed I could have soothed Leo's fevered mind by telling him that the cops would only find an empty coffin. But I didn't trust the dude. His instability scared me. I also wanted some leverage on him, sort of reducing the advantage he had over us.

"I think you might be getting ahead of yourself," I said, trying not to panic a guy who was already over the top. "Let's burn that bridge when we get to it."

Dewey started quaking. "Do you have anything to help settle my shakes?"

"Sorry, Leo, That's your poison."

I wasn't going to give that man any alcohol, no matter how badly he vibrated. I wanted to get him out of my house.

"Is that all we need to cover?" I asked. "It's late."

"Yeah, yeah," Dewey said, slowly rising from the chair. "Just watch yourself around Bongiovanni."

I escorted him to the door, and he stepped out on the back porch and paused. It seemed as if his brain spun in circles, grasping for traction. He blinked several times before speaking.

"Don't forget the egg has to be laid in August."

"Say what?"

Dewey angrily shook his head and loudly whispered. "The egg, the August payment is due soon."

I loudly exhaled. Oh, my Lord, Dewey spouted some silly coded message. Why did he worry that someone in my backyard might overhear us? I wondered if his crumbling mental state might be a more significant concern than a detective with a scrap of a rag.

"Good night, Leo," I said, loud enough to catch his ear as he scuttled toward the alley behind my fence. He turned and spat out a harsh whisper, saying something like, "Don't use my name."

I closed the door and leaned against the wall. I imagined Daisy would flip out when I told her about Dewey's craziness. Maybe I wouldn't say anything to her. We had to deal with that Bongiovanni character, a so-called bulldog, with us a bone between his teeth.

I sensed Mandy standing off in the darkness, her chubby arms folded across those big bosoms. Her eyes looked sorrowful and wet with disappointment.

"Don't confuse bad choices with bad luck," she'd be preaching. "You better make some righteous choices, Tommy Lyle, before you lose your way."

Chapter Twenty-Four

L ater in the morning, long after sunrise, I stood in Daisy's kitchen. My sister wore a blue t-shirt with matching leggings. I complimented her planned cardio workout.

"Are you nuts?" she said. "I'm letting this body go, baby. I sweated and starved for twenty years to please Eric. No more of that crap, no sir, I'm getting fat."

Daisy turned and walked to the refrigerator, pulling open the freezer door. A white cloud of frigid air swamped her head. She squinted, shuffled items around before withdrawing a frosted container of chocolate ice cream.

"I'm only doing what makes me happy," she said, flipping off the lid and grabbing a soup spoon from the drawer. "This is the year of me."

I supposed now would've been a good time to tell Daisy about my midnight visit from Dewey and introduce her to Detective Bongiovanni and all of his complications. But I wanted to make sure more pressing things had been taken care of. Besides, she looked so happy. Why ruin it for her?

"Can we talk about tomorrow's meeting with the lawyer?"

I only heard mumbles as my sister shoveled ice cream into her pie hole.

"The dude's going to do the preliminary reading of Eric's Will, you know."

Her head bobbled as her mouth kept slurping.

"Eleanor will be there as well," I said. "Can you sit in the same room without trying to kill her?"

She snickered. "Hope so."

"I'm serious. You have to prepare for the worst."

"Like what?"

"Regardless of what the will says, you know Eleanor will try and prevent you from getting your share."

She remained silent, scraping the insides of the carton with the spoon.

"Can you be coolheaded and not threaten your mother-in-law?"

She chuckled. "I don't think there's enough Xanax in the world to keep me that calm."

"I'm trying to be serious," I said, not happy with my voice's whininess. "You know you're still a long way from getting away with everything."

My sister squinted. "I'm not worried, Tommy. Eric's life insurance can't be contested. I'm the sole beneficiary. That'll be enough money to hire a lawyer to fight for my share of the estate."

She tossed the empty ice cream container into the trash and reopened the refrigerator door. Bending at the waist, I heard her pushing glass bottles around. "Where's that leftover cherry pie?"

It seemed clear to me that Daisy buried any anxiety about the upcoming meeting in calories and carbs. I was wasting my time trying to prepare her for the interview. I'd better concentrate on knocking off the second most demanding item on my to-do list—paying off Phyllis and Dewey. And to do that, I needed six thousand dollars, pronto.

"Any chance you have some cash available?" I asked as my sister pulled out the pie and slipped a fork into it.

"Nope, I spent everything you gave me from the artwork sale."

"All of it?"

She shrugged. "Who'd thought that a widow's dress and shoes would cost so much."

"Too bad you only wore it once."

She looked at me as cherry filling dribbled down her chin. "I hope to be wearing it soon to my mother-in-law's funeral."

I cringed. Daisy had better not talk like that at tomorrow's meeting with the attorney. My sister could easily say the wrong thing if she got pissed, and her mother-in-law had years of experience baiting her.

"You know, we have a critical expense coming up soon," I said.

"What expense?"

"Leo Dewey. You remember him and our little secret, don't you."

She sure did remember him. Daisy cursed the man's name, his mother's soul, and the horse they rode in on.

"That's not helping. We need five grand to cover August, and we need it this week."

My sister wasted another minute raging about the unfairness of her life before going quiet. Her gaze drifted toward the empty space in front of her face. I could almost imagine the gears in her head cranking, searching for an answer.

"If you need money," she said, pointing toward the back door, "you're welcome to clean out the garage."

Ah, that's my girl. There might be enough stuff in the garage to cover it. As I recalled, I saw two fancy bicycles. They had those super thin tires and all kinds of gears and cabling. Not the type of bike I rode as a kid, but I knew they cost a bundle. A new snowblower came to mind. I recalled a bag of golf clubs hanging from the wall and skis with their associated gear. Oh yeah, a big chest of automotive tools.

I felt immediately better. The garage had a bounty of stuff that I could move today. Unlike the paintings, I had a good idea of the value of the things I'd be pushing. I wouldn't be at the mercy of Weasel and his like.

Come to think of it. Maybe I *was* a worrywart. Daisy seemed confident of getting a big, fat insurance payout, and the thought of confronting Eleanor didn't seem to be an issue for her. When push came to shove, she'd quickly found a way to secure the cash for this month's bribes. And she did all of that while gobbling down half of a cherry pie.

My sister acted as stable and confident as I'd seen her in months. She didn't appear to have a worry in the world. I guessed now would be a good time to tell her about the detective, Nick Bongiovanni.

Chapter Twenty-Five

I buried my hands in my pockets as I watched Daisy flick her tongue around the fork, licking off every sugary smudge. "Is there anything else?" she asked.

"Huh, yeah, actually, there's one more thing we need to discuss."

Daisy dropped the pie plate on the table and sat on a stool. "I could tell something else was eating at you. What's up?"

I'd forgotten how easily my sister read my body language. Everyone could tell when something bothered me. Mandy used to read me like a large-print novel.

"Two days ago, I spent an hour with a cop looking into Eric's death."

That remark almost caused Daisy to slip off the stool.

"What?"

"He was some detective."

"Why?"

My sister's face colored. I didn't like the way it looked. I wished she had a cupcake or something to pop into her mouth.

"He gave me some story about how they do a follow-up investigation of every death from unnatural causes."

"Why are they suspicious? The police said it was an accident." Daisy's voice climbed an octave. "What did you tell him?"

"I gave him our story."

Daisy sprung from the stool and pounded a fist into an open palm as she circled me. "You told me that damn Dewey reported the fall as an accident. Why are the authorities keeping the case open?"

106

"It appears that Eleanor pulled some strings."

Daisy cut loose a filthy oath.

"Good God, Tommy, tell me what the detective did when he was at your house."

I told her about Bongiovanni's visit, how he acted all smug and annoying. She didn't care about his personality. She wanted to know what happened while he questioned me. I said, "He spent a long time studying the stairwell. He found something that may be a problem."

When I told her about the scrap of material, most likely from the towel she'd used to wrap Eric's bleeding skull, she rocketed into a rage.

"Why, why, why, does everything you touch turn to shit?"

I fell back a step, my heart racing.

"What, what do you mean?"

Daisy jumped into my face, and her finger jabbed at my chest.

"Why weren't those basement stairs scrubbed clean after the cops left? Why didn't you do that?"

"I thought I did."

Daisy grabbed me by my shirt, jerking me back and forth as tears spritzed from her eyes.

"Damn it, Tommy. You told me Dewey would make this go away if I paid him ten grand. You fouled up the funeral arrangements. You didn't clean up the damn basement as I asked. You're killing me."

Her head dropped, and she heaved a big wet sigh.

"I'm sorry," I said. "I'll fix it. I promise."

Daisy pushed me away, returning to the stool. Her hand flicked the pie plate across the table and onto the floor.

"Is there anything else?"

"He wants to talk to you."

Daisy kneaded her hands. "I don't do well when threatened," she said, a weariness damping her words. "I gotta come up with a plan."

"Threats don't seem to be his style. He's one of those detectives with lots of smooth talk and tricky questions."

Daisy slowly nodded, probably thinking about how she would handle him.

She could be as smooth and crafty as anyone. The interview wouldn't be a problem, not for my sister. I bet she'd come up with an explanation for the piece of towel caught on a basement stair step. She's the brains of the family, after all.

"I'm really sorry, Daisy."

My sister looked at me and growled.

"Please don't hate me," I said.

She twisted her head sideways to avoid looking at me. A half-minute passed, and she waved me over. I stepped up to her, and she opened her arms. I felt like I did all those years ago after Walter or Mabel had smacked me around, and my big sister comforted me. As she held me, I could hear my heart pounding away like a two-cylinder lawnmower engine. She patted my back.

"I'll never hate you, Tommy."

I stifled a whimper.

"But you've created a bigger mess, you understand?"

"I'm *so* sorry."

"Now, for us to get out of that mess, you need to listen carefully to me."

My head bounced against her shoulder. Her request sounded familiar. Then it hit me. She used the same words after the police hauled away the bullet-riddled bodies of our mother and father.

Chapter Twenty-Six

My car, Baby, lacked the space to hold all the gear I pulled from Daisy's garage, so I used Eric's over-sized SUV. It had an all-leather interior and top-of-the-line stereo, but drove like a tank. I tooled across the town's main drag toward the industrial area on its outskirts. My mind chewed away on my morning with Daisy and how I disappointed her. My failure to clean up after Eric's fall had been a blunder of the first order. I swore to all things powerful that I'd do better.

The first test of my resolution came within the hour. I'd arranged a meeting with Weasel to sell the stuff. He came across as disinterested, but I saw his move as an opening negotiation trick. I had to get a great deal, at least clear six thousand dollars. Anything less would be a failure.

I pulled the SUV behind Snell's Automotive and drove it into the garage. Weasel dropped the overhead door and watched as I unloaded the merchandise. The old guy pulled on his whiskered chin and mumbled as he fingered each piece.

"I'll give you four for all of it," he said.

I laughed.

"Man, you're wasting my time." I patted the top of the big metal cabinet. "Just those tools alone are worth that."

Weasel and I went back and forth for another ten minutes, and he'd only increased his offer by a few hundred bucks. I felt sick. Leaving without the full amount would be a disaster. I went with a high counteroffer and hoped we'd eventually reach somewhere close to six thousand dollars.

"I won't let this go for less than ten grand," I said.

Weasel shook his head. "Five thousand take it or leave it."

"I could get that for just the tools and the golf clubs, man."

"Then go sell them to someone else," he said. "I'm going no higher."

I ground my molars so hard my jawbone started hurting. Maybe I should take it. I knew I wasn't a great negotiator. This might be the best I could do. Daisy would be sorely disappointed in me. I couldn't go back and ask her to sell even more of her belongings. I'd have to be bold.

"I guess we can't do business," I said, reaching to lift the tailgate of the SUV. "I'm sorry to take up your time."

Weasel's laugh rang hard against the ceiling of the garage. "You ain't goin' anywhere," he said. "Who else do you know that would buy this much stuff?"

"I'll find a pawn shop, a couple of them if I have to."

"Yeah, sure," Weasel said, snorting. "Let me help you load up your vehicle, Mr. Lyle."

He hoisted the golf clubs, took two steps, and then stopped. The sneer on his mug suddenly disappeared. I turned to look at what had caught his attention. A huge bowling ball of a man stood in the doorway. Judging from the tint of the hair on his head and the creases lining his face, he looked to be in his late fifties. A lime green sweater stretched tight over his enormous stomach.

"Hey, Jimmy," Weasel called out.

The big man waddled over to us. He eyed me and then the merchandise.

"So you're the Lyle kid," he said.

"Yeah, that's right."

"You seem to be asking a lot for this junk."

I shrugged. "It's high-quality stuff, and none of its hot, so I think what I'm asking is reasonable."

Jimmy's dark brown eyes were like periods squeezed between his flat cheeks and bushy eyebrows. They zipped up and down, scanning me from my head to my feet.

"You know, I knew Walter and Mabel."

I nodded and wondered how he knew my folks. I worried he might have a decades-old grudge that he wanted to settle.

"I worked with those two back in the day," he said. "Your old man was something else."

I didn't know what he wanted me to say, so I just stood there trying to keep my imagination from freaking me out. What'd he mean Walter had been something else? That didn't sound like a compliment.

Jimmy looked at Weasel. "Remember Walter, how he'd act like he was a cold-blooded maniac who'd rip your heart out if you cheated him?"

"What a wild bastard," Weasel said, a grin lighting up his face. "And his wife was a hot-tempered woman."

The two men turned to me and chuckled. When they paused, I assumed they expected me to defend the family name.

"I recall them as being lovely people," I said, rolling my eyes.

Jimmy's head tilted back as a deep-throated cackle climbed out of his mouth. He had a kind of laugh that made you feel uncomfortable; like maybe he didn't find what you said funny. Whatever his reaction, it turned out okay for me. He waved a stubby finger over my stuff.

"Give him seven for everything."

Weasel cursed and slowly shook his head as he walked away. I hoped he wouldn't let being overruled by his boss delay getting the seven large ones. I wanted to be on my way. Hanging around Jimmy made me uncomfortable. I didn't know his last name or anything about him, although he sure looked connected to an organization with Sicilian roots, if you know what I mean.

"So tell me, Tommy. One week you're selling artwork, and then it's like a garage sale. Where are you getting this stuff?"

"It's my sister's. She's in between paychecks. I'm doing her a favor."

Jimmy's forehead lifted, and his bottom lip grew fat. "Ah, yeah, Walter and Mabel had a daughter too. What was her name?"

"Daisy. Her name is Daisy."

His gaze swept over the bikes, snowblower, tool cabinet, and the golf clubs. "Your sister must've been doing alright if she owned that stuff."

I kept my mouth shut. I didn't know what quality of merchandise guys like Jimmy and Weasel regularly moved, but I knew Eric only bought the best.

"And those paintings you brought in a while back were snapped up."

I hated hearing that. We should've held out for more.

"That Daisy has done alright," Jimmy said, "all things considered, huh?"

I didn't like the way he talked. Even someone as dense as me could see how his brain connected my sister with some unexpected source of money. I knew he'd be asking how a street rat like Daisy got so lucky.

A cold wave of relief swept up from my gut when Weasel walked back through the open bay, a stuffed paper bag in his hand.

"Thanks again," I said as I palmed the bag and pulled on the SUV door. "Have a good day."

Jimmy's big hand, with the mandatory bejeweled pinky ring, pushed against the car door.

"You know I remember how your folks were killed. I could never figure out why so many cops raided a two-bit hustler like Walter Lyle."

"I was ten years old. I don't have an answer for you."

Jimmy drummed his fingers against the car, his lips twisting. "And I could never understand why he'd shoot it out with them."

"As you said, Walter was something else."

The man stepped back and allowed me to climb into the SUV. I kept my eyes straight ahead after firing the engine, waiting for the garage door to open fully. I hoped we never had to sell another thing to Jimmy. I didn't like his curiosity about our situation, and Daisy and I had enough crooked people in our lives. We didn't need one more helping us out.

Chapter Twenty-Seven

The following afternoon Daisy and I arrived at the offices of Thornton & Associates. The elevator took us up to the top floor of the town's tallest building. A secretary escorted us into a conference room that seemed to be made of nothing but glass and shiny steel. The view from the sixteenth floor might have been impressive if one didn't suffer from a fear of heights. I sat with my back against the windows. Daisy sat to my left.

Already seated across from us, Eleanor Pressman had arrived dressed in a scarlet dress that matched her shoes and lipstick. I nodded at her, but she turned her nose toward the ceiling. Not that I cared. I wasn't there to make friends. I wanted to hear what Daisy inherited, determine the quickest way to get it, and never see a Pressman again.

Two seats from the older woman sat a younger gal. She had short brown hair and dark brown peepers and wore a business suit. I wondered if she'd been a member of the law firm handling Eric's estate. She didn't say anything to anybody.

My attention shifted as a silver-haired man came in with a pile of papers in his arms. His glasses rode halfway down his nose, and he mumbled to himself. He sat down at the end of the table. His hands shuffled the papers like an arthritic Atlantic City card dealer before finally laying them out in front of him.

"Good morning. I'm Seymour Thornton, and we're gathered here as requested by all parties for a preliminary reading of the last will of Eric Pressman."

"What does that mean?" Daisy asked. Good Lord, one minute in, and it became obvious that Daisy didn't know any more than I did about inheritances. The Lyle kids were in over their heads. How could that turn out well?

Thornton cleared his throat. "Mr. Pressman's will is going to go through probate, which will take a few months, considering its complexity."

Daisy whispered, but loud enough that I'm sure everyone heard her. "What the hell. Did he say months?"

The lawyer's eyes narrowed as they rolled over my sister. "Until then, the designated executor will assist the beneficiaries, as the deceased recognized them as being dependent upon his largess."

I reached under the table and squeezed Daisy's hand. I hoped she'd understood what the man had said because I heard she wasn't getting her big payday for a while. And she had little left in the house to pawn off to cover next month's bribe of the Medical Examiner.

Thornton read through a bunch of legal mumbo-jumbo before spilling who would eventually get what.

"Mr. Pressman's life insurance policy lists his wife as the sole beneficiary." Thornton turned to her. "As requested, I was able to expedite the processing of the payment."

He slid a bank check across the table to my sister.

"What the hell?" Daisy screamed, blowing out of her chair like lit mortar. "That better be a misprint."

My sister held the check to her face with trembling hands. Looking over her shoulder, I read the printed amount. Just as I feared, Eric lied about his life insurance and screwed my sister. The amount on the check read twenty thousand dollars, not two million.

Thornton lowered his chin, his mouth wide enough to show his molars. It seemed he wasn't used to wild emotions exhibited by desperate people.

I saw a razor-thin smile appear on Eleanor's face.

"Please compose yourself," he said, then continued reading.

"The bank, Pressman & Sons, is part of Mr. Pressman's trust and will be sold, and all profits will go into the trust's assets. This fiduciary arrangement will return one-per-cent of its value on an annual basis to Eleanor Pressman until her death or until depleted. The trust will also return one-per-cent of its value annually to Daisy Pressman up until her death."

My sister and I looked at each other, our expressions conveying the same cluelessness. What the hell did he say? Was one-per-cent a little money or a lot? How long would it take to sell Pressman & Sons? I didn't know anything about banks. My idea of high finance was carrying around a twenty-dollar bill.

"Mr. Pressman's domiciles will be allocated as follows. The residence on Kingly Road will go to his wife, Daisy. The trust will provide a monthly stipend for reasonable operational expenses."

Thornton cleared his throat before continuing.

"The second property, the townhouse in Majestic Park, will be titled to its current resident, Eleanor Pressman. A monthly stipend for reasonable operational expenses will be provided, as well."

Without looking up, Thornton continued reading.

"The third property, the beach house at Point Pleasant, New Jersey, will be titled to his attorney and loyal employee, Gloria Arbuckle."

Daisy, Mrs. Pressman, and I all shouted out the same words. "Who the hell is that?"

Thornton grimaced at our crude language before bowing toward the woman down the table. She turned a smarmy little smile toward all of us.

"I'm Gloria Arbuckle. I'm the bank's Senior Vice President and a longtime friend of Eric. That's who the hell I am."

Whoa, baby. Could this inheritance mess get any more complicated? Eric having a gal pal on the side didn't surprise me, but that she wasn't some brainless chickee did. This Gloria had the confidence of a shark in a duck pond, and Daisy and I swam like a couple of ducklings.

Eleanor slammed her hand on the tabletop. "This is an outrage."

Thornton growled and rambled on. "The trust will be supervised by Miss Arbuckle. She will have full discretion to render any judgment on the eventual operations of the trust."

"I am quite capable of handling my own money," the older Mrs. Pressman said. "I don't need anyone running my affairs."

It felt good to see her getting worked up instead of just my sister.

Thornton heaved a deep sigh and bunched the documents.

"Mr. Pressman made it clear that he wanted Miss Arbuckle to manage the distribution of his trust. I'm finished here."

The newly minted trustee spoke. "As you read the addendums that Mr. Thornton will make available to you, you'll see what management of the trust means. For example, if either of you remarries, you're out. If either one of you has any outstanding liens to the bank, your share will first go towards paying off those debts."

She turned to Daisy. "Also, I will be the trust executor in perpetuity." Her eyes hardened. "That means forever."

I didn't know where my sister found the strength not to fly across the table and choke out Arbuckle, but I thanked God she had.

The meeting ended soon after Arbuckle staked her claim as the queen of the kingdom. What a rat turd, that Eric. He screwed Daisy, screwed her badly. I felt good knowing that Eric now inhabited a cheap vase rolling around the trunk of a car I drove, and *he* used to own.

My sister, Mrs. Pressman, and I stumbled out of the conference room toward the elevators. Daisy barely held it in. Her life looked to be handcuffed by a monthly stipend so tiny we'd continue to struggle to pay Dewey. The so-called two million dollar insurance check had been one-hundredth in size. Losing access to the beach house felt like a stick-in-the-eye to me, just as the late summer heat kicked in.

I felt lost and didn't know what to do. Mandy would've told me to pray. She believed God heard our prayers when our situation looked most hopeless. I figured I'd only get one chance to beg forgiveness and ask a divine favor. Maybe I should hold off doing it now. I had a feeling that things might get worse, much worse.

Chapter Twenty-Eight

T he next day I didn't feel much better about life. Another sleepless night left me exhausted. I dropped by the Redport Funeral Home and slipped Archie London the thousand dollar hush money for Phyllis. If I had any energy, I might've threatened him again just to watch him shake. I needed some evidence that I wasn't weak and powerless. Just that thought made me feel even more pathetic.

An hour later, Daisy joined me for a late breakfast, which we ate mostly in silence.

"You have to bank that life insurance money," I finally said to her as she stirred her coffee. "We have an ongoing cash suck with Dewey, and God knows what new expenses will show up."

Daisy sipped her joe. "I'm planning to do a little shopping with that money."

I choked on the last swallow of my orange juice. What'd she mean by a little shopping? I'd hoped to avoid a nasty fight with my sister, so I thought I'd give in a little.

"Okay, maybe a hundred bucks."

"I can't buy anything for that amount."

"Are you serious?"

Daisy laid her coffee cup hard on the table. "I told you this was the year I'm going to indulge."

What did I know about the cost of women's clothing? A hundred dollars would be enough to fill my closet with new duds.

"Okay, if you must."

"Damn it, Tommy, I put up with Eric's controlling behavior for twenty years, and I'm not letting you treat me that way."

I sat upright, my chin trembling. How dare she compare me to Eric Pressman? I was nothing like him. I was only trying to keep her out of trouble. She needed to be frugal at a time like this. For a second, I understood why maybe her husband held a firm hand on her spending. Daisy loved to shop.

"Do what you want," I said, "but we have to figure out how to get more from Arbuckle."

"I'm two steps ahead of you, Tommy. I know women like Gloria and how they think. Let's visit her so I can do a little girl talk."

That was my sister, always thinking about the next angle. I swiped a napkin across my mouth and burped. "I'm done. Let's go pay a visit to your new overseer."

And so we did. Thirty minutes later, we parked in a lot next to the Pressman & Son's Savings & Loan.

"I can't believe I won't own this bank." Daisy had a sorrowful catch in her voice. "I really wanted to have that big office."

"I'm sorry as well," I said. Not so much because Daisy's dream of being a bank executive had been snuffed out, but because I'd lose out on her promised forgiveness of my house loan.

Daisy sucked in a breath before barking out an order. "Okay, let's get this over with."

Baby's doors unlocked with a click, and we stepped out and strolled into the bank. An older woman with short trimmed hair greeted us at the door, gently offering condolences to Daisy.

"Mr. Pressman will be missed," she said, her voice choking when her emotions appeared to get the upper hand. As the woman struggled to stop her sniffling, a shadow moved across the entrance. Gloria Arbuckle silently drifted by like some paranormal spirit.

"I'll take care of these two," she said to her distraught subordinate.

The older woman appeared irritated by the intrusion. She clutched her hands and mumbled as she walked away. I hoped Daisy's woman-to-woman approach would work. Arbuckle looked like she could handle herself in a street fight.

Then again, most women intimidated me. Mandy once said if a mother's earliest milk tasted bitter, it'd scar a sensitive child like me. I told her my mother bottle-fed me. She said something about metaphors that I still don't understand.

We trailed Arbuckle into her office. She sat at the desk while we took the two visitor's chairs. I looked at Daisy, who surprised me with her calmness.

"What do you need?" Arbuckle asked.

My sister patiently explained her circumstances and requested her rightful access to any cash in Eric's accounts. Arbuckle responded with equal politeness.

"I'm sorry, Daisy, but as we all heard yesterday, you're on a stringent diet, financially speaking, until the completion of probate."

My sister tensed.

"I'd prefer you to address me as *Mrs.* Pressman."

Arbuckle gave up an empty smile. "Of course, *Mrs.* Pressman, but no matter how I address you, you're still living by Eric's rules as laid out in his final instructions."

"I'd prefer you to refer to my deceased husband as *Mr.* Pressman."

Gloria's grin grew wider and showed her teeth. She looked like a smiling fox at a pen full of chickens. The woman raised her hand and slowly scratched her cheek. The light bouncing off the diamond ring on her finger almost blinded me. No way could her salary afford that kind of bling. I suspected it might have been a bonus from her old boss, the deceased, lying and cheating brother-in-law of mine. It broke my heart, watching her wave that ice in front of Daisy's face.

"Of course, as *Mr.* Pressman stipulated, your allowance will be paid on the second Thursday of each month."

"I need my money today. I have expenses."

"As I recall, you received a healthy life insurance payout yesterday."

"That's none of your business," Daisy said. "And there was nothing healthy about it."

Arbuckle sat for a moment and looked at us. Then her mouth twitched, and I braced for her next move.

"Per Eric's, huh Mr. Pressman's instructions, I do have discretion on all financial matters so I can authorize an earlier payment."

My sister sat back in the chair and smiled.

"Okay. Let's do it."

Arbuckle tapped on her computer keyboard, entering codes and passwords. After a minute, she returned her gaze to Daisy.

"I'll generate a check. It will be in the amount of four hundred and eighty dollars."

Daisy came out of her seat, her fist pounding the desktop. "My husband gave me a thousand dollars a month for spending money."

"I know, but we have to subtract your brother's missed loan payment and late fees."

My sister burst into tears, which seemed to please Arbuckle. A broad smile sailed across her flawless face, and she reached into her desk and pulled out a big book of checks.

"Let me write you a check."

"She wants cash," I said, jumping in as my sister whimpered. "No paper."

The woman stared at me, her eyelids half shut and her lips stiff.

"Of course," she finally responded. "Should I make it all one-dollar bills so she'll feel wealthier with a heavy purse?"

Man, that woman had too much fun toying with my sister. I went mentally into the vault of my mind. I opened my revenge folder and created a new file for Miss Gloria Arbuckle. I noted her nastiness and cruelty toward my sister. Plus, she deprived me of the beach house on the shore. That's all I needed to remember. She'd suffer someday. I promised myself that.

Daisy stopped sniffling enough to protest. "I can't live on that little amount of money. What am I supposed to do?"

Arbuckle's mouth turned down at the corners. "Oh my, you might have to dust off your resume and start looking for a job."

What a dumb idea. Daisy hadn't worked in her adult life. Did Eric intend his wife to live scraping by on handouts? Then it dawned on me that was *precisely* the plan the dude had in mind. Just like when he lived, my sister would be trapped in his hell.

We Lyle kids left the bank, staring at our shoes. We checked into a nearby tavern, and Daisy ordered a beer and a shot and me a ginger ale. Her face looked as soft as putty, and her eyes bloodshot from the crying jag at the bank. She threw down the whiskey and began slowly sipping her beer. Nothing appeared to be going on inside her head, no conniving or plotting.

"I'm feeling overwhelmed by all this," she said, raising her hand at the bartender to secure a refill.

"Yeah, it's been a tough twenty-four hours."

"And it's not getting easier with that detective coming by this later this afternoon."

Yikes, I'd forgotten about that visit. I reached over and held Daisy's free hand.

"If you stick with the plan we discussed, you'll be okay. I promise."

Daisy sighed and zeroed her attention in on me.

"Do you really think I can match wits with that guy?"

"I do," I said. "I really do."

I took a swallow of my drink. Daisy did have one superpower. She could manipulate men to her advantage. When Eric Pressman announced his engagement to Daisy Lyle, they stunned local high society. Eleanor still scratches her head, wondering how Daisy convinced her son to marry her.

My sister could seemingly connect with men in a way that made her sympathetic and attractive. Sure, her marriage eventually went south, but even champion thoroughbreds get fatigued. But for one day, maybe a few weeks, if Daisy applied herself, she'd have that Bongiovanni dude eating from her hand.

Chapter Twenty-Nine

Daisy Pressman's physical appearance could be summarized as in two words, short and pretty, which surprised me, considering her brother. Tommy, he looked the same as when I first met him, skinny and jumpy. I'd arrived at Daisy's house a few minutes before four. The place looked like the polar opposite of her brother's house. No doubt she had the money in the family.

"I'm sorry to bother you, Mrs. Pressman, at such a stressful time," I said as an introduction.

She rapidly blinked her eyelashes.

"I'd appreciate it if you'd address me as Daisy," she said. "Mrs. Pressman is my mother-in-law."

Her cheeks pulled in like she'd sucked a lemon.

"Sure, I can do that."

"Thank you, Detective. I appreciate your kindness."

Since the impetus behind this investigation happened to be the mother-in-law, I had to ask.

"So, how do you and Mrs. Pressman get along?"

Daisy shook her head. "She never liked me."

"That makes it tough."

I tried connecting with Daisy, you know, come across as a nice guy, not some detective bent on ruining her afternoon. But I'd been sincere. I knew that having a mother-in-law who didn't like you made life harder. My mother adored Joanie.

Daisy blinked back a tear. "Yes, Eleanor has made my life difficult."

I decided that Daisy needed some special handling, so I asked about her mood, her sleep, stuff like that. Then I got into my questions.

"I'm curious as to what happened immediately after your husband landed at the bottom of the stairs."

The woman shuddered. "It was horrible."

"Do you have to do this?" the brother asked. "It was an accident, after all."

The little fellow started to annoy me, and I'd been there only a few minutes.

"I know it's disturbing, but certain parties are pushing for some clarification. And the sooner I get the answers I need, the quicker we all can be done with this."

"What exactly do you want to know?" Daisy asked.

I liked her response, and she seemed genuine. I hoped I got her right.

"Did you remember what you might have used to stop the bleeding, if anything?"

She shook her head. "I'm sure I grabbed something. He bled profusely, that's all I recall."

"I'm sure he did. What'd you use?"

She shrugged. "I blindly snatched for anything at hand and applied it against my husband's wounds. It could have been anything."

"How about a towel, or say, a stocking cap, or something like that," I said, hoping I could tip her in the right direction.

She puffed out a breath. "Maybe I used a towel."

The woman kneaded the tissues in her hand. I noticed some grey showing in her hair. I thought rich women would rather die than not look their best. I understood what she might be going through. Why go the extra mile to look nice for someone who wasn't there anymore.

"After they removed the body, did you clean up the accident scene?"

Tommy stood up with a red and twisted face.

"How can she answer that question?" he said, bellowing, spit flying from his mouth. "She was traumatized at the time."

Daisy reached over and patted her brother's arm. "Calm down, Tommy. I can answer his questions."

Mr. Lyle sat back down and grumbled. I had to wonder what hot button

I'd pushed with that guy. Why did he act so over-the-top protective? He behaved a hundred and eighty degrees from what I saw when I met him last week.

Daisy continued talking softly.

"I was in a daze, as you might imagine. I recall asking my brother to clean up the stairs and the basement after my husband's body was removed. No one told us not to."

She closed her eyes and sighed deeply.

"I just switched into auto-pilot, I guess, wanting to wash away any sign of my husband dying in such a gruesome way. Does that make any sense?"

I didn't know how to answer her. My wife died after a long fight with cancer. She just slowly wasted away, slept more, and then never woke up. My panic had been a slow crawl, the inevitable realization that I'd grow old without Joanie.

"Sure, I understand," I said. "My wife died just a few months ago."

Daisy's head dropped to one side. "Oh, I'm sorry."

I didn't want to match grief with Daisy, so I turned to Tommy. "Mr. Lyle, can you tell me about the cleanup?"

He nodded toward his sister. "As she said, we grabbed anything we could to try and stop the bleeding. Afterward, I probably used paper towels, a mop. I don't know. It was a sickening job."

"Yeah, I'm sure," I said, nodding my head. I turned back to the sister. "Daisy, is there anything else you remember?"

"To tell you the truth, Detective, I think after they removed Eric's body, all I did was stand there shaking."

Holy crap! That's it. An old memory climbed out of my dark past from decades earlier. I took part in the raid where Walter and Mabel Lyle got shot up. I remembered the young girl we discovered hiding under the bed. She shook like a leaf blowing in the wind, had wet herself, I think.

Maybe that's why the brother acted like such an overprotective jerk. I was triggering some lousy memory for both of them.

"Daisy, is there anything else you can remember about events following the accident?"

CHAPTER TWENTY-NINE

She hugged herself around her shoulders.

"So much of the last few days are a blur. I remember the funeral service and going to the grave and people I didn't know telling me things I don't remember." The woman gave me a soft smile. "I'm sorry, that's probably not helpful."

No, it wasn't, so I asked one question that might be.

"How was your marriage to Mr. Pressman?"

Daisy's eyebrows climbed up her forehead. I think I surprised her.

"Eric and I had our issues," she said, then blushed and energetically shook her head. "I don't mean to say my marriage was awful. Please don't think that."

I shook my head just as vigorously. "Oh no, I don't think that. Marriage is tough. You do the best you can."

"I miss him terribly." She looked at the floor, and her voice grew even softer. "I'm just trying to get through this as best as I can."

The brother coughed loudly. I sensed he hoped to end my little heart-to-heart chat with his sister. I'd be more than happy to finish up and leave the poor woman alone.

"I found life got better once I wrapped up all the loose ends of dying," I said. "Like settling the estate, boxing up memories, stuff like that."

Daisy looked up with tears in her eyes. "I'm getting there. Once I sprinkle my husband's ashes off the Jersey Shore, I'll feel better. He so loved the ocean."

Tommy Lyle jumped from his chair and stepped between his sister and me. "Okay, that's enough. You're making my sister cry."

I held my palms up, offering my surrender. The sister had a pink flush on her face and mumbled an apology. She looked distraught. I'd better finish up.

Rising from my chair, I closed my notebook. "Thanks again, Daisy, for answering my questions."

"Are we finally done?" the brother asked. "I mean, with this whole follow-up?"

I slipped my notepad into the inside pocket of my suit jacket.

"I'm through bothering you two. I have a few questions for the folks who attended the accident scene. It's all routine procedure."

Daisy seemed to relax, but the runt brother bristled and looked ready to pop off. A second later, he did.

"I know Eric's mother is behind this waste of time," he said. "She'll do anything to cheat my sister. You're being used to do her dirty work."

Hey, what could I say? The little guy pretty much nailed it.

"I promise you I'll be done within a week, maybe in a few days."

"This does nothing but upset my sister," Tommy said. "It's got to stop."

I acknowledged Daisy and strode into the foyer. The brother shadowed me, quickly opening the door and letting me leave without uttering another word.

"Thanks again, Mr. Lyle."

He slammed the door.

As I walked to my car, my mind struggled to sort the factual from the emotional. Perhaps the whole case amounted to nothing more than in-laws hating in-laws mixed in with some childhood traumas. I had to admit Daisy tugged at my heartstrings. Poor thing survived a horrible childhood, apparently dealt with a spiteful mother-in-law, and then witnessed her husband die falling down a stairwell.

Maybe I'd go by the lab and see if they got a chance to examine my mystery cloth. Yeah, if they found nothing, then I'd wrap up this assignment and give Tiny Baker his report.

I mean, why am I harassing a grieving widow?

Chapter Thirty

Shelia Washington had the reputation as one of the best crime lab analysts in New Jersey. She also happened to be one of my favorite people. Smart and dedicated, she spoke in clipped sentences, no wasted vowels for her. She also had a curiosity that made her a frustrating resource at times. With her, nothing ever seemed to be definite.

"Hey, Nick," she called out as I entered the lab.

"Hey, Shelia," I called back. The overhead lighting did nothing to minimize the woman's good looks.

"I took a look at your remnant last night."

"Ah geez, I didn't want you giving up your evening," I said, hoping my insincerity didn't seep through.

The woman sniffed. "I'm sure you felt that way."

Okay, so I couldn't fool her. Thank goodness she liked me.

"Here's what I found," she said, pulling up an image on her desktop computer.

I stepped up close to her, admiring her well-trimmed nails as she stroked the keyboard. I wished Joanie treated herself to a manicure more often than she did. She hated spending the money. I should've insisted.

"The remnant was from a bath towel," Shelia said. "The GSM were somewhere between 400 and 600. I'm guessing you'd find this type of towel at most discount stores."

I gave her my perplexed look while saying, "Huh?"

"Grams per Square Meters, or GSM. It's the standard for classifying towel quality and absorbency."

"So it wasn't from any stocking cap or hoodie."

"No, this was a completely different weave."

"So most likely," I said, "the towel was used to clean up afterward."

"That's one supposition."

Like I said, Shelia Washington didn't feel comfortable with definitive answers.

"What else is possible?"

"Here's where I'm having trouble," she said. "Under the microscope, I saw several features that suggested that might not be an explanation."

"Tell me what you found."

"If they used a towel to clean up blood on the stair step, most likely it would be used in a sweeping motion."

Shelia rotated her hands in a circle.

"Under the microscope, the pattern in the sample didn't indicate that at all. Rather it seemed the blood was absorbed straight on."

"Straight on as if the towel was used as, I don't know, maybe a pillow."

"That's possible."

"But why did I find the remnant hanging under a step a good ten feet from where the victim ended up?"

Shelia stared at me. She wouldn't offer any guesses. She presented the facts, and I had to explain them.

"But there's something more curious," she said, pulling up a color photograph on her computer. Typically, most lab guys would give you a verbal report in a non-criminal investigation like this. My new favorite county employee treated everything like a critical part of a highly publicized murder case.

"Look at this image I copied off the Amscope. See that line in the middle?"

The Amscope was a high-end microscope with a camera attached. It made it easy to share what showed up under the lens. I saw a faint line cutting through the rust-colored blotch on the photo.

Shelia pointed to the picture.

"That line represents an indentation within the dried blood."

"How'd did that happen?"

"That's what's so baffling," she said.

The look on Shelia's face surprised me. I suspected she had an answer, but the darn thing must've stunk too much for her to volunteer. I'd have to pull it out of her.

"What's confusing you?"

"Imagine the force of a blow opening up the scalp, blood quickly seeping from the capillaries, and filling the wound. The victim's head rests on the towel, and the blood is immediately absorbed into the fabric."

"Okay," I said, repeating what I thought I heard. "The cut came first and created an indentation, followed by the blood soaking into the fabric. So what's bothering you about it?"

Shelia arched her shoulders. "I think that the indentation formed *after* the blood was absorbed."

"What are you telling me?"

"I think blood soaked into the fabric *before* the blow to the head."

"So, you're suggesting the man's head was battered twice."

"I don't know. Making sense of it is your job."

So what did we have here? A man fell down the stairs twice. How *did that* make sense?

I learned long ago that nine times out of ten, the obvious answer proved to be the right one. What she suggested sounded too incredible, however.

"Maybe if he fell down half the stairs, laid there for a few minutes while his wife comforted him with the towel under his head, and then tumbled the rest of the way down."

Shelia smiled at me like she thought I'd pulled that guess out of my butt. I felt embarrassed. Maybe I wanted to explain away most anything if I could. I didn't want this investigation to continue, let alone to catch fire.

"I wonder if someone who examined the trauma could provide a clearer understanding," she said. "Who was the M.E. on this?"

"Leo."

The corners of her mouth dipped. "That complicates your effort."

I shoved my hands into my pockets and bent at the waist to again study the image. The lazy, short-timer part of me wanted to ignore the facts.

But, what if Shelia had nailed it and the most obvious explanation had Eric Pressman falling down the stairs twice. And the second time, he had a towel wrapped around his head.

That'd be unbelievable.

Chapter Thirty-One

I had to climb down a flight of stairs from the crime lab to the offices of the medical examiners. If Dewey wasn't out on a call, I knew he'd be there.

I pushed open the door, and the smells made my eyes water. I scanned the room, feeling relieved not to see a body in pieces. On the far wall in a row of desks, I saw Dewey. And as always, he looked spooked upon seeing my face.

"Hello, Leo."

He nodded and quickly returned to his paperwork. He kept his head down even after I sidled up to his desk.

"I'm still trying to understand that Eric Pressman accident," I said.

Dewey mumbled, but I swore he said something like "You're being used."

"When you got there, did you see anything like a bloody towel lying near the body?"

"Did you read my report? Everything I observed, I noted there."

"Yeah, I read it. But sometimes odd things can come to mind after you've recorded your observations."

He frowned, and his eyes turned into slits as he looked up at me. "I have a half dozen cases going on at any one time. I can't recall all the odd minutiae of each investigation."

I had to admit the man might be right. Even with a brain not calcified by excessive alcohol consumption, he'd be hard put to recall such a detail. Of course, that didn't mean I had to stop asking. I hoped something might pop into his head that I could use. Anything that might explain away what

Shelia Washington had just revealed to me.

"Was there anything about the head wounds or abrasions or broken bones that suggested something odd about that death?"

"Why don't you save your fishing for your retirement?" he said, his voice sounding like sandpaper rubbing against fresh-cut lumber.

"I'd love to, but I'm still getting paid to do my job."

The man heaved a sigh and dropped his head. "What *exactly* are you looking for, Bongiovanni?"

"I'm wondering if you observed more abrasions, cuts, and breaks than you'd expect for a guy falling down the stairs?"

I heard an intake of air whistle through Dewey's nostrils. I wondered what answer he might be struggling to form. Had I raised a possibility that gave him pause? He took in more air and looked up at me.

"Nope, I observed nothing unusual."

I allowed a little smile to creep onto my face. I wanted Dewey to be nervous and wonder if I knew something. I'd never tell him what I did know, not until I needed to. Hopefully, keeping him off balance might work in my favor.

"You know, you're right. It's unfair of me to expect you to recall all those details, what with your workload. I'm sorry."

Based on the way his mouth slipped sideways, Dewey indicated he saw through my bull. For the second time within an hour, my fake sincerity failed to work. Maybe I should give it up.

"I wonder how hard it'd be to get a court-ordered exhumation," I said. "What do you think?"

Dewey's raised his middle finger.

I dropped my shoulders and turned to leave, mumbling, "You're right. It's probably pretty difficult."

I could almost feel Dewey's eyes burning through me.

"You're wasting your time," I heard him say, squeezing his words through clenched teeth.

I couldn't argue with the man. After the widow, Daisy Pressman, shared the news of her husband's cremation, I no longer had an autopsy card up my sleeve.

I left and searched for my big buddy, Brute. After experiencing the contempt of Leo, I had a hankering to swim in the praise accorded me by Officer Brutkowski. I found him loading up his cruiser for his shift.

"Hey, Brute, how's my favorite cop?"

No matter how he tried, the big guy couldn't keep the grin off that slab of a face. "I'm good, Detective Bongiovanni."

"Call me Bongi as my friends do."

His grin now extended up to his ears.

"You got a minute?" I said. "I need another favor."

I asked if he would talk to the EMTs who worked the scene from that night. Ask them pretty simple questions, like, did they see anything unusual? Did the victim look more beat up than what they expected? Did they notice any rags or towels under the victim's head when they arrived?

"I'd do it myself, but I'm trying to close out my wife's credit card accounts. I need to get that done before I take off for the Outer Banks in fifteen days."

"Sure, that's no problem. Do you still want me to do another drive-by surveillance of Lyle's house?"

"No," I said. "What you observed the other night was all I needed to know."

Brutkowski shook his head, his shaved dome tilting to one side. "What do you think Dewey was doing over there after midnight?"

I volleyed back the same question. "What do *you* think?"

"I think Leo was being conscientious and wanted to ensure the happiness of his client."

My head kicked back from the force of my laugh. That Brutkowski had a sense of humor.

"You read my mind," I said, slapping the officer's bulging shoulder muscles. "That's how I saw it."

Brutkowski looked relieved. Maybe he feared a joke wouldn't work on me. Whatever his thinking, his willingness to be my errand boy sure served my needs. Two weeks before my farewell party, I didn't have the time or energy to run down every issue about Tommy Lyle that made me suspicious.

And boy, almost everything about Tommy Lyle made me suspicious.

Chapter Thirty-Two

I felt terrible yelling at Daisy, but man-o-man, why'd she tell that detective we'd cremated Eric?

"That interview was a disaster," I shouted as soon as Bongiovanni drove away.

"What do you mean?" she said. "I thought it went perfectly."

"Why did you let him get you into a conversation? I warned you the dude was tricky."

She laughed. "What conversation were you listening to, brother? I played him like a puppeteer working a dummy."

I tried to respond but could only sputter. I needed several seconds to take in enough air to slow myself down.

"Why did you say you wanted to spread Eric's ashes over the ocean? His cremation was a secret."

Daisy's eyes half-closed like she thought I said something stupid. That made me angrier.

"Don't look at me that way. You know that was the story."

My sister waved me off. "Don't be so touchy. It doesn't matter that people know."

"What, since when?"

She shrugged. "At first, we had to lie to Eleanor so she wouldn't pull strings to delay the funeral. Now, I figured it's to our benefit if the authorities know. They could tell Eleanor, no corpse, no second autopsy, and close the case."

I hung my head. That made sense, I guessed. Why hadn't I thought of that?

"Yeah, but," I said, determined to prove her somewhat wrong, "won't that make her mad, knowing we'd tricked her?"

My sister slapped her thighs. "I think she'll be more pissed, having spent thousands on an expensive casket." Her laughter curled her shoulders and brought tears to her eyes. "I wish I could be there when she finds out."

I felt confused by Daisy's cockiness. Why wasn't she still fearful of Eleanor Pressman, the woman she believed to be Satan?

"Besides, Eleanor is no longer in any financial position to badger me with lawsuits and counterclaims. Her son, good old Eric, locked her in the same broke-ass jail as me."

My head bobbled. I hadn't thought about that, either. I guess while I shook in my boots, wondering what would happen next, my sister had figured it out.

Of course, she didn't know everything.

Maybe I should have told her about Phyllis and how I had to slip the woman a grand to buy her silence. Then again, I'd hear her bellowing about me screwing up. I didn't want to listen to that. I'd have to fix that problem on my own.

"I'm going out," I said with a huff. "I need some fresh air."

"Are you going to be mad at me all day?"

I twisted around and waved my finger at her. "Next time, keep me informed when you're changing our story."

Daisy laughed and tapped her forehead. "Even I can't keep up with how quickly my brain moves."

I slammed the door and stepped away from the house. My sister could be so irritating. Sure, I preferred Daisy to feel full of herself rather than defeated, but not at my expense. I had enough pressure with that detective buzzing around us, and worrying about how we'd pay off Dewey. Man, I hated all that stress. I wished Daisy had never pushed Eric down those stairs. I had a simpler life before she did that. A few weeks ago, I knew right from wrong.

Now, I flew through life blind, not sure what I'd smash into next.

* * *

I quickly got out of Daisy's high-end neighborhood and into the funky side of town with the assistance of Baby's thundering six cylinders. I wheeled into the parking lot of the Redport Funeral Home.

I saw only two cars, one being Archie's silver sedan. I sprinted to the front door and went down the hallway. A minute later, I arrived in a small reception area, an office on either side.

I heard a female's voice. "May I help you?"

A woman sitting in the space to my right called out. Her neatly penciled eyebrows hung on her forehead like two quarter moons. I assumed that had to be Phyllis.

"I'm here to see Mr. London," I said, jerking my head toward the other office's closed door. "Is he here?"

"Do you have an appointment?"

I shook my head.

"Let me check his schedule."

I had no patience with her little power play and took three steps over to the other office. After a sharp rap on the door, I walked into a small, windowless space. Right in the center of the room, behind a metal desk, sat Archie. He looked up from a betting sheet, his mouth dropping open.

"Oh, hey there," he said as he slipped the betting sheet onto his lap. "This is a surprise."

I closed the door and sat down. His pupils dilated and I heard his knee bouncing against the desk.

"I'm just checking in," I said. "Did Mr. Pressman's official paperwork get changed as we agreed?"

Archie shrunk into his seat. "Yes, yes, the report listed Pressman's final disposal as a burial."

I threw my thumb toward the other office. "Is your girlfriend satisfied?"

Archie scratched the side of his cheek. "Huh? I'm not dating Phyllis."

I lowered my head, softly squeezing off a profanity. Why did I even try being colorful around such an imbecile?

136

"No, you fool, I'm talking about...oh never mind. Did Phyllis get her money? Will she keep her end of the bargain?"

"You don't have to worry," he said. "She passed her first test about an hour ago."

"What does that mean?"

The man's eyes jittered across the room. He looked like a cornered rat, desperate to find an escape hole.

"A police detective called, looking for me. He asked her whether Pressman was buried or cremated. She assured him there was a burial."

My gut dropped so fast I thought it'd bounced off the floor. That dang Bongiovanni didn't waste a minute. He's now wondering why Daisy told him about a cremation, and the funeral home told him it'd been a burial.

"Did you talk to him yet?"

"Oh no," London answered, shaking his head. "But I'll be ready. You don't have to worry."

I stood up and leaned into him. "Now listen up, Archie, there's two important points you have to get right."

Like an eager-to-please grade-schooler, he rapidly nodded his head.

"When you talk to him, he'll probably ask about the condition of the corpse."

"What should I tell him?"

"Nothing," I said. "Just say you saw nothing unusual. Keep it simple, and don't let Bongiovanni smooth talk you."

The undertaker's head continued to bob up and down. "Yeah, I'll say I didn't see anything."

"When he asks you whether the corpse was buried or cremated, you tell him Phyllis was mistaken, and there was a cremation. Do you understand?"

Archie's mouth fell open.

"I'm confused," he said. "Was he supposed to be buried or cremated?"

"There's a change in the story. Eric was *cremated*, not buried."

"So why did we say he'd been buried?"

"Damn it, man, that doesn't matter."

Archie started shaking. I'd better tone down my voice so he'd relax enough to hear me. He was the kind of guy who could juggle only one ball in the air.

"Okay, I got it. The man was buried, and I saw nothing suspicious about the corpse. You can count on me."

I grabbed Archie by the ear and twisted it as he squealed. "No, you idiot, he was cremated, not buried."

I continued tugging his ear until he repeated three times that it had been a cremation. He fell back in his chair after I let go of him, his ear lobe a throbbing, cherry-red color.

"You have my phone number," I said. "Call me after you talk with the dude."

"Yeah, yeah, I'll call you," he mumbled, fighting to keep the tears from overrunning his eyes."

"Cremation. Hear me, it's a cremation. Don't screw up."

The undertaker slowly raised his right thumb toward the ceiling.

"I got this, Mr. Lyle. You've nothing to worry about."

Sorry, Archie, I wanted to say, but I had a ton of worry. If only Daisy had listened to me and not chatted up that detective, I wouldn't have to hope that an idiot like you could keep straight a simple story.

Chapter Thirty-Three

I stepped out of Archie's office and noticed Phyllis eyeballing me. She wasn't looking at me so much as shooting daggers. I know I should've ignored her, but, man, it bothered me. Why the hate? She had a thousand more dollars than *before* I showed up in her life. Where's the appreciation?

"What do you want?" she asked as I filled the doorway of her office.

"I have to admit your attitude hurts my feelings."

The woman blew a raspberry.

"We worked out a sweet little deal," I said, "and you're treating me like a flea-bitten dog wandering in off the street."

The woman slipped back in her chair, her nose wrinkled. Then she spewed a little more abuse my way.

"I'd rather see a mangy dog walking in here than the likes of you."

Whoa, where did that come from? What'd I do to make her so nasty? I fired back in response.

"What's your problem? Why are you acting that way?"

"It's people like you who are ruining our business," she said, her skin lighting up. "You take advantage of Archie's illness, and I'm the one left to clean up the mess."

"Are you serious? I paid a lot of money to ease your pain."

The skin on her forehead squished.

"I don't know what you're talking about."

"Yeah, you do."

"No, I don't," she said, rising in her chair. "All I know is when I hear Archie

139

whimpering behind closed doors; a rat has to be involved."

Usually, calling me vermin ticked me off, but not that time. Phyllis seemed to have no idea about the bribe, but she was right about a rat. I spun out into the hallway and pushed back into London's office, yelling, "You bastard!"

Archie almost fell out of his chair, pulling the betting sheets against his chest.

I slammed the door shut. I didn't want any witnesses to what I intended to do to Archie's face.

"You made up that story about Phyllis having issues. Her so-called ethics was a big fat lie."

The undertaker looked like he'd soiled himself. I didn't care. I hated being fooled, but swindling me at the same time made my eyes want to pop out of my skull.

"What happened to my money?" I said, throwing my fist at him as he hovered under raised arms. "Give me back my money."

He cried out. "Stop, stop, don't hurt me."

I tried to punch his face, but he dodged my attempt, and my knuckles struck the top of his head. That hurt me more than him.

"Give me back that money, you cheat."

Archie's whining grew louder. "I can't."

"Why not?"

"I, I owed my bookies. I *had* to pay them off. They were going to kill me."

"Huh, you owed people money?"

Archie's shoulders shook and he squeaked a reply. "Yesh."

So that explained the disgust Phyllis had sent my way. Her boss had a gambling problem, and she assumed I had a role in it. Screw her. I didn't care what she thought about me. I just wanted my thousand dollars back.

I grabbed Archie by his shirt and pulled him to his feet.

"You and me are going to your bank, and you're going to withdraw my money from your business account."

"I, I can't do that," he said, his chin trembling. "Only Phyllis can authorize the release of any money."

"You kidding me?"

London hung his head.

"I gave her total control of the finances. I'd be bankrupt if she didn't manage the business."

I couldn't believe that guy.

"You make me wanna puke, you pitiful excuse for a human."

Archie's body collapsed in his chair. He seemed relieved that I found him too pathetic to continue beating on.

"How about I give you a discounted casket?" he said, scraping through the mess of papers on his desk. "Here's a brochure. I'll give you a deal."

I lunged forward, grabbing him by his shirt collar.

"No, you're going to convince Phyllis to release a grand from your business account, or you'll need that deal on a casket."

My open hand slapped the top of his head.

"Okay, okay, don't hurt me."

I again raised my hand, and he started shaking.

"I'm coming back at ten tonight. Have my money, and don't make this unpleasant."

"I...I...I'll have it, I promise."

I walked out and saw wide-eyed Phyllis, the sneer gone from her face.

"What are you looking at?" I snapped. She stepped back into her office.

Once outside, I turned on myself. Damn it all to Hell. Why hadn't I suspected Archie would be a crook from the start? If he lied and cheated Eleanor, why wouldn't he do the same to Daisy and me? Why am I so dense?

Daisy had it right. Everything I touched turned to shit.

I crawled into Baby and sat with my brain boiling in a soup of anxieties. Having a paranoid boozer like Dewey knowing my secrets made me feel insecure enough. Now my life and maybe my freedom rested in the hands of Archie London. If I could easily confuse him, that Bongiovanni would have a field day. I couldn't live with that risk, never knowing who might give me up.

I need someone to kill those two pieces of garbage.

A grin forced its way on my face. Then a chuckle rumbled in my throat before I let loose a hollow cackle. Stop kidding yourself, you fool. With your lousy track record at picking criminal partners, your hired killer would probably shoot off their foot.

I felt my eyes tearing up.

"You're so pathetic, Tommy Lyle," I whispered. "You haven't the guts to fix the messes in your life."

I fired up the car engine and pulled out of the parking lot. As I roared down the street, I felt grateful for having a car like Baby to drive. I loved the sense of power generated with the touch of my foot on the gas pedal. Baby and I raced through town, the broken-down houses and boarded-up storefronts zipped by as I blew through one yellow light after another. For a brief moment, I felt like Superman, indestructible and untouchable.

Mandy used to tell me that you measured a guy's manliness, not by muscles and loud voices, but how responsible he behaved toward his family. I tried to be a dependable man that showed up every day and behaved decently. How'd that work out for me? I had two ex-wives and a sister who saw me as weak and stupid. No one respected Tommy Lyle.

Walter Lyle, on-the-other-hand, didn't behave like a decent husband or father. You never knew how he'd act or when he'd show up. At the same time, no one ever cheated or bullied him. In his crude, brutal way, Walter had respect.

Maybe I should man-up, take control of my situation instead of relying on prayer or my big sister. Yeah, I should stop being that scared little kid hiding under the bed, wetting his pants whenever life got tough.

Sweat dampened my underarms and across my back. My stomach painfully twisted, causing me to grit my teeth.

Could I really shoot someone and kill them in cold blood?

"Stop it," I shouted. "Stop thinking that way."

I slapped the steering wheel as the tears started dribbling down my face.

Why am I so afraid of killing someone? I didn't hesitate when Walter and Mabel needed to die. No, once I made up my mind, I never looked back.

Chapter Thirty-Four

I drove by the Redport Funeral Home. Located in a semi-abandoned industrial park, the joint didn't seem like the kind of operation most people would want processing their loved ones for the afterlife. I wasn't the only one thinking that way. The parking lot stood empty except for one car.

I walked through the front entrance. For a second, an ache made a home in my chest. Three months ago, I sat in a similar place as people came by to pay their respects. I shook my head, rattling my brain enough to snap me free of my melancholy.

At the end of the hallway, I came upon a pair of offices. One looked unoccupied, and a woman of about forty sat in the other. Judging by her expression, my sudden appearance startled her.

"I'm sorry, did I frighten you?"

She blushed. "That front door was supposed to be locked."

"That's a good idea," I said. "You probably don't want to be working alone in this neighborhood."

"I tell Archie that, but he keeps forgetting to lock me in when he steps out."

"I'm harmless," I said, offering an open hand and my world-famous smile. The magic seemed to work on her. I could see her relaxing.

"How might I help you?"

"I'm Detective Bongiovanni from the city police department."

Her face flipped back to the fearful version.

"And you must be Phyllis?"

"Yes, yes, how can I help you?"

"I talked to you a few hours ago about a recent funeral."

She nodded as her lips formed a tight line running across her face.

"It was the Eric Pressman funeral, the one from a week ago."

"I know," she said. "What about it?"

I scanned the woman's office. She looked well organized. She had every piece of paper stapled, stacked, and ordered. I could use someone like her to get my precinct desk organized before I left.

"I imagine that was a big funeral. I heard there were a couple of hundred people in attendance."

"Yes, it was," she replied, her laced hands settling on her desk. "Why are the police concerned?"

I gave her the old song and dance about standard operating procedures, and she didn't seem to buy it. The woman oozed suspicion.

"Can you tell me who made the arrangements?" I asked.

"It was called in by a man identifying himself as the brother-in-law, a Mr. Lyle."

"From what I know of him, that kind of funeral would be pretty expensive for him to foot."

"Oh, he only made the original arrangements," she said. "The mother, Eleanor Pressman, took care of the casket, the embalming, and the service."

There we go, again. I had someone claiming a burial service, not a cremation. I *hadn't* misheard her when we spoke on the phone.

"So, there was a burial, huh?"

"Yes. Mr. Pressman was interned in a SoulMaster 6000, our best stainless steel casket."

"Was that an open casket?"

Phyllis shifted in her chair. "No, apparently the corpse was in such bad shape Archie couldn't make it presentable."

"Is Archie around?"

Phyllis's short bob barely moved as she shook her head. "He left about twenty minutes ago. I don't know when he'll return."

"Okay," I said, the fingers of my right hand squeezing a business card.

"Here, have your boss call me if you could."

Phyllis took the card without taking her eyes off of me. "I'll do that."

I thanked her and stepped out of her office. I waited a beat and stepped back in. She jumped when I reappeared in the doorway.

"Phyllis. Are you *positive* Eric Pressman was embalmed and buried?"

The woman's jawline quivered. I thought I might be getting under her skin.

"Of course, I am. I know everything that goes on here."

"So, you're sure."

I think I pushed her too far, as her voice took on a hostile edge like she could reach over the desk and embalm my fat rear end.

"Absolutely," she said. "If it weren't for me, this place would fall apart."

Phyllis folded her arms across her chest, and her lower lip grew fat. She wasn't a woman used to being challenged. But I couldn't help myself.

"Did you actually attend the preparation and internment of Mr. Pressman?"

The question seemed to rattle her.

"Well, no. I only do administrative and bookkeeping tasks. I didn't come into the office until after the services had concluded."

I nodded and started to walk out again but stopped. There's an art to leaving an interview, almost as important as the questions you asked. You go slow, keeping the other person off guard. You can't rush it. And I thought Phyllis, the woman who kept the Redport Funeral Home operating, might have a few more answers to volunteer.

"Do you have any idea why Mrs. Pressman, the widow, believes her husband was cremated?"

"I have no idea." Phyllis pushed herself out of her chair, her teeth bared. "It wouldn't be possible, anyway."

"Why's that?"

"Our crematory wasn't operating that weekend."

"Are you sure?"

"Absolutely, I'm sure. I saw Archie working on it the afternoon after I came in. He said the system was only burning at 900 degrees."

"That sounds hot to me."

She gave me a look my second-grade teacher used to give me when I offered up an uninformed answer.

"That's about half of what's required to cremate a body properly."

"Is it working now?"

The woman snorted. "We're having a cash flow problem. I don't know when we'll be able to get it fixed."

I felt my mouth wrinkle. I needed a face-to-face with Archie London. As the person in charge of the funeral, I'd like to hear his side of the story. If someone had fooled anyone, I sure in heck didn't want it to be me.

"I appreciate your time, Phyllis."

She pulled a ring of keys from a desk drawer. "I'll lock the door after you leave."

I smiled. "That's smart. You can't be too careful."

Chapter Thirty-Five

The sun had gone down, and I sat at home, looking at a slab of leftover pizza. It contained enough empty carbs to kill my hunger, but since I'd had pizza three meals in a row, including breakfast, the thought of tomato sauce on hard crust made me sick.

After I collected that money from Archie London tonight, I'd go out and find an all-night diner and buy a decent meal. Yeah, I'd get rye bread cuddling a big stack of pastrami and top it off with cake.

My phone buzzed. I glanced at the screen and saw Daisy's number.

"Hey, sis, what's up?"

"Are you still mad at me?"

"No, I'm over that," I fibbed.

"Listen up. I need you to meet me Thursday afternoon."

"What time do you want me to come by?"

"Make it about four, okay?"

"Sure, I'll see you at four. Can I ask why?"

"It's a surprise," she said. "It's a good surprise, so trust me."

I groaned. I hadn't done well with Daisy's surprises, good or bad.

"Speaking of surprises, I have one for you," I said.

"You do, huh? Does it involve lots and lots of money?"

We shared a chuckle, and then I sucked the playfulness from Daisy's voice.

"I've been thinking about Walter."

My sister didn't say a word, but I quickly envisioned her jaw dropping open.

"Dear old Dad has been on my mind a lot lately."

147

I raised the .38 caliber handgun to the overhead light, aiming it with one eye closed. That gun served as my inheritance, you might say. Back when those law enforcement bastards mowed down Walter and Mabel like weeds, they tore the house apart looking for stuff. They pocketed any cash they found and took the guns my parents had stashed. But they missed this one. In all those years since, I hadn't fired it once.

Daisy finally spoke. "Why would you be thinking about that son of a bitch?"

"I don't know. Walter seems to be showing up in my head more and more."

"What's gotten into you, Tommy?"

I didn't want to share my feelings with Daisy. If I did, she'd most likely laugh at me. And in a way, it felt good to have her wondering about me, for once.

"Okay, sister, I'll see you Thursday afternoon."

The call ended, and I wiped the weapon with a napkin and admired the heft of the pistol in my hand. I thought about my return visit to the funeral home. Maybe I wouldn't need to show Archie the weapon at all. The man turned to mush just by me showing up. But that might be his game. You think you've scared him into cooperating, and he fools you.

For all I knew, he might be playing me again. I'd better be ready to get rough. I didn't want to deal with him after tonight.

I stood up to do a little role-playing. Slipping the gun in the back of my pants, I squared my shoulder and furrowed my brow.

"Okay, Archie, you punk, now I'm getting serious."

I reached behind my back, hoping to swiftly grab the pistol, swing it around, and play-acted smacking the mortician in the head. Like most things in my life, it didn't go as planned. The gun barrel somehow snagged the band of my underwear, and as I pulled it out, I gave myself a wedgie.

I started over, doing it again and again and again. By the time I left my house for the mortuary, I'd practiced the gun draw and skull cracking three dozen times. *Ready or not, here I come, Archie.*

The dashboard clock read nine-forty by the time I drove by the funeral home. I saw London's sedan in the lot. I thought I should find another spot to park. Anyone driving by would see just two vehicles, and my BMW 5 Series would be memorable.

Two blocks away, I pulled up to a curb under a busted street light. The walk to Archie's place of business did me good. It gave me time to set priorities. I didn't want to go in there half-cocked. I sorted through the possible scenarios and how I'd react.

One, Archie had my grand, paid me back, and reaffirmed his loyalty. I leave with more money than when I came in, but still doubting whether I could trust him. Do I shoot him or not? No, I show him the weapon to scare him but give him another chance.

In the second scenario, he doesn't have the money; he begs for mercy and swears his loyalty. I leave with no money and a partner who would squeal me out in a heartbeat. What do I do? That's simple, Archie's a dead man.

Number three, he somehow finds a backbone and decides that he has the upper hand. He tells me the thousand dollars would help keep his mouth shut. I leave with zero cash and yet another guy blackmailing me. That's a no-doubter. Archie has a bullet in the brain.

My intestines roiled at the thought of Archie's head exploding.

Maybe instead of killing him, I could pistol whip the dude in all three scenarios. Yeah, cause some damage without ruining my knuckles.

Then again, that might not work. He'd run off scared, get protection, or call the cops. None of those actions made me feel safer. Anyone of them would complicate my already messy life. I didn't need to have another loose threat hanging out there.

I stopped in the shadows when my knees quivered. Was I up for this?

My mind shifted from Archie to Dewey to the detective and then way back to Walter and Mabel. Then I thought of Weasel and Jimmy laughing at me and that big stupid cop, Butt-kowski. I thought about my ex-wives and the bosses who'd humiliated me over the years. No one respected me, not even Daisy. If I wanted to be a tough guy and not some pretender, I'd better prepare to take the ultimate action.

If I had to kill Archie, I had to kill him.

By the time I reached the mortuary's back door, I'd build up my anger and flavored it with fear and self-loathing. I banged on the door and heard a buzz and a click as the lock released. Following a light at the end of the hallway, I found Archie huddled at the desk in his office. He looked like he'd been crying.

"I'm here for my money, Archie."

He pointed at a mound of cash in the center of the desk.

Unless that pile had more than fives and tens in that heap, I'd be very unhappy.

"That's three hundred and eight dollars," he said. "I'll get another five tomorrow and the rest by Friday."

I pulled the gun from my waistband and aimed at Archie's forehead. He closed his eyes, his hands covering his face. Of course, the tears flowed from his eyes before I even opened my mouth.

"I told you not to mess with me. I said not to make me do bad things."

"Please don't kill me, Mr. Lyle."

"I *have* to shoot you. If I can't trust you to pay your debts, how can I be sure you'll keep our secrets?"

"Yeah, you can." The sobs came in threes. "I told that detective what you told me to tell him."

"He talked to you? Didn't I say call me once that happened?"

"Yeah, I guess," he said, his head sliding back and forth. "I lost your number. I was too busy getting your money."

I pulled back the hammer of the .38.

"You're a weak, stupid man. Weak, stupid men are untrustworthy."

Archie opened his eyes and stabbed the air with his finger. "Go into Phyllis's office. There's a laptop and a good printer. You can easily get five hundred dollars for both of them."

"Doesn't that woman need a computer to do her job?"

"Yeah, I guess."

"Isn't she the one who keeps this business going?"

"Yeah, I suppose."

"And you'd be willing to make her life miserable by giving me her computer?"

CHAPTER THIRTY-FIVE

He didn't say another word. He only whimpered.

"Is that the kind of man you are? You repay loyalty by sticking it to your friends."

His suggestion disgusted me, even if I hated Phyllis. I stepped up and pressed the end of the revolver's barrel against his forehead. Tears dribbled down his cheeks. I smelled urine. I just hoped that would be the last disgusting thing he'd do in front of me.

"I'm sorry, Archie, but your days of lying and cheating are over."

I stepped back a couple of feet, not wanting to shoot point-blank. The gun wobbled in my hand. It felt a lot heavier than when I played with it at my house. Man, this was harder than what I expected.

"You're not going to do it, are you?" Archie said, peeking through his splayed fingers.

"Shut up and say your prayers."

Why couldn't I pull the trigger? Maybe only rehearsing pistol-whipping him messed me up. Yeah, that's my mistake. I should've play-acted blowing out his brains. Practice made perfect, right?

A shaky smile snaked under Archie's nose. He lowered his arms.

"I know how to read a man's face. I know when he's bluffing."

I grasped my gun hand with my free one, holding the pistol steady. "Stand up and turn around," I said, hoping not looking at Archie's stupid tear-stained mug would make it easier.

He slowly stood. His face amounted to nothing more than a quivering mouth on a whitewash head. "You'd shoot me in the back?"

"Shut up and turn around, Archie."

I closed one eye, aiming for the spot between the man's shoulders, and then I raised my aim to the back of his head. "You're not going to shoot me," he said. "It's not in your nature, Tommy."

"You don't have a clue about my nature. You know nothing about me."

I pulled the trigger. The gun continued to fire until I'd emptied the chamber.

Chapter Thirty-Six

I ran across the parking lot, searching for the alley that'd take me back to my car. The wad of cash in my pants created an embarrassing bulge, but I had no choice. In my rush to get out of the funeral home, I grabbed the pile of cash off Archie's desk and stuffed it in my pocket. My hands carried the printer and computer. I knew I'd be lucky to get three hundred dollars for the office equipment, but I still felt pretty good. Tomorrow at this time, I'd have at least six hundred bucks in my pocket, a big improvement over zero.

I didn't feel lousy ripping off Phyllis. She'd been ugly with me. Let her suffer a little. More importantly, after she saw what happened to Archie, she'd get the message to zip her lips or risk the same consequences.

The one thing that did bother me was my burning butt crack. After I unloaded the chamber, I stuck the gun into the back waistband of my pants. I didn't realize how hot a pistol would get when firing. I knew now.

I made it through the maze of houses to the street where I'd parked Baby. I loaded everything into its trunk and climbed into the driver's seat. I shook like a twig in a hurricane, even though the temperature must've still been in the eighties. I got pretty hyped up, pulling the trigger, and I guessed the leftover adrenaline gave me the shakes.

I stabbed the starter, and Baby boomed to life. Before I could shift into drive, my hands shook so badly I had to grab the steering wheel to steady them. Sweat flooded from every pore of my skin and soaked my shirt. I looked into the rearview mirror and saw my greasy, bloodless face.

"Oh God," I mumbled. "Now, I'm hallucinating."

I had to be. I mean, how else to explain Mandy in the back of the car. There she sat, those judging eyes, wet with disappointment. That old head with the hairstyle that never changed, slowly rolling back and forth, telling me how I disgusted her.

I slapped the mirror sideways and shoved the stick shift into drive. Baby's tires squealed, and its rear end fish-tailed down the street. I didn't know how long it took me to get home. As I pulled the car in the back of my house, I realized the headlights weren't on.

I pushed open the car door and puked on the ground.

I swore right then and there that I'd never hurt another human being again. After tonight, Daisy had to do her own dirty work. Tommy Lyle had had enough of the thug life.

Chapter Thirty-Seven

The free flow of alcohol numbed the stings from the back slaps. And by free, I mean, someone else paid for my drinks. Even the guys I barely knew offered me congrats and atta-boys as they hoisted a cold beer in my honor.

"How many days you got left, Bongi?" they'd ask me.

My standard answer came easily. "Too many."

One old buddy laughed at me. "I know exactly how many days I have until I retire," he said in a boozy basso. "Four hundred and twenty-six days."

Good for him. He had something to live for. I'm not like that, never had been. I enjoyed being a cop, especially a detective. I thought I was born for that type of work, a natural skepticism, a strong work ethic, and a feeling that I might be able to make the world a little better. Not that I shared those thoughts with my fellow officers. They'd laugh. Within a year of graduating from the academy, most of them became disillusioned and wouldn't understand. I didn't blame them. Seeing what people could do to each other would make God wonder if He'd made a mistake with that creation.

"So what are you going to do with your free time?" my buddy asked.

"I don't know, maybe a little bit of this and a little bit of that."

The man slapped my back once again. "You'll be great at it," he said before lumbering off into the crowd. My body felt grateful to see him move on. I knew my actual farewell party would be the day after picking up my papers, so why did I feel the need to show up every night at our favorite tavern?

I guessed with no one to go home to, I didn't need a reason.

"Excuse me, Detective Bongiovanni."

I turned to the source of my shout out to find Officer Brutkowski. Seeing him surprised me. Most street cops didn't mingle with detectives. Maybe an old desk sergeant might show up, especially if he'd watched the man rise through the ranks. But guys like Brutkowski had their own favorite watering hole, assuming young Brutkowski drank.

"Hey, Brute, what's up?"

He shuffled his size fifteens and muttered an apology.

"Sorry to bother you, but I heard you might be here, and I wanted to share some dope that just went down."

You had to love those eager young guys, always on-duty. I wondered if Brutkowski slept in his uniform. I smiled at the image.

"Sure, what's up?"

"There was a 10-28 called in about thirty minutes ago. A guy named London."

Now that got my attention. Damn, I just spoke with the man that afternoon.

"It might have been a robbery or a burglary gone wrong. Stuff stolen from an office, you know."

"So someone robbed and shot Archie London, huh?"

The officer turned his head to the side. "Oh, you knew the guy?"

"Yeah, a new acquaintance I tried to make today."

I wondered why London would be working there so late. Who'd break into a place like the Redport Funeral Home and shoot a guy over some office gear? But then again, a meth head would do about anything. Nowadays, people didn't need an excuse to kill someone.

"I knew that's where Eric Pressman's funeral was held," the officer said, "and since you had a few questions surrounding his death, I thought you'd like to know."

"Yeah, thanks. What do you make of it?"

"I don't know," he said before launching into a master class of speculation. "As I've said, something about that Tommy Lyle smelled bad from the first time I met him. Add in his late-night shenanigans with Leo Dewey, and

I have to believe they're together on something. The victim's mother is thoroughly convinced her son's death was intentional. Now you tell me you questioned the undertaker about Tommy Lyle's business, and he's shot by a person unknown. It looks to me like Lyle might be the connecting link."

"You can't make every correlation into causation," I said. But I liked his thinking. Sometimes a coincidence was not just a coincidence.

"Yeah, I know," he said. "I'm keeping an open mind. You never know what might fall into it."

I laughed out loud and took a turn at being physical. "I love it," I said as I popped Brute on the shoulder. "That sounds like something I'd say."

"It was. You said it at a lecture you gave at the academy five years ago."

Man, did I suddenly feel old. Here a young pup repeating some quip that I probably heard from a crusty old dick when I was a beat cop. Everything tonight seemed to force me into admitting I'd reached the end of my productivity.

Brutkowski must have noticed the light leaving my eyes because he changed the topic.

"I spoke with the EMTs that attended to Pressman as you asked me. Tony, my buddy, recalled seeing a blood-soaked rag underneath the victim's head."

"Your friend must have a good memory," I said. An accident scene often became chaotic as the EMTs worked to save the victim. Even the good ones got locked in on what they're doing and missed anything unusual.

"He said he remembered because when they moved the victim off his back, the rag was strongly attached to the guy's head."

"Any idea how long he'd been bleeding?"

Brute shrugged. "It's hard to say. I heard the 911 and followed the EMTs to the residence. I'd guess it was no more than ten minutes from the call to them arriving and getting down into the basement."

I nodded. "If you assume that Tommy Lyle called 911 as soon as his brother-in-law tumbled, it should have been no more than fifteen minutes."

Brutkowski's face clenched, and I could tell the man had his mind cranking. "It seems like the bleeding would have started longer than fifteen minutes if the blood was as congealed as Tony remembered."

156

"Yeah, it would seem that way," I said, the barroom noise suddenly muted as my mind focused on the nature of blood.

"Are you *sure* that it was only ten minutes between getting the call and arriving at the scene?"

"Yes, sir, I'm sure of it."

Maybe Brute got his times wrong. Perhaps Lyle and his sister panicked and wasted precious minutes trying to first aid the victim. That's what I would've done. And, who knew whether the temperature and humidity in the basement hastened the drying of the blood? There were so many factors to consider, you just couldn't be sure.

"You know time operates differently when your adrenaline is flowing," I said.

Brutkowski hunched. "I guess, but I always try and stay under control."

"I've been doing this for thirty years, and I still feel my heart kickin' it up a notch."

"I don't know," Brutkowski said, "maybe it *was* closer to fifteen minutes."

I'd never picked up any doubt in the young guy's voice until then. He probably never heard the skepticism in mine.

I looked around me at the laughing, boozing crowd and envied them. Why couldn't I let go of my job when off duty? Why did my curiosity, like a pebble in my shoe, keep digging at me?

"You can go now," I said, brushing him off with a wink. "Thanks for the info."

"Uh, do you need me to check on anything else?"

"Naw, you've been a good scout, Officer. I'm done with you."

"Yes, sir," Brutkowski said, his cheeks coloring. He quickly turned and walked out of the tavern.

I immediately felt terrible at my curtness. I knew I treated Brute like my errand boy, but he sure seemed to enjoy matching wits with me. He probably wanted to be my sidekick as we nailed that Tommy Lyle. But I had to be careful and not get caught up in his enthusiasm. We both might be making a mountain out of a molehill. After all, you couldn't make every correlation into causation.

157

Chapter Thirty-Eight

I arrived at the Redport Funeral Home about eleven-fifteen. I saw about a half-dozen vehicles in the lot, lights flashing like a carnival. It looked to be a well-attended crime scene with patrol, crime scene investigators, a detective, and the local news. I'd have to be careful not to step on anyone's toes. Detectives are prima donnas when it came to their cases. They didn't like being second-guessed. Fortunately, the detective in charge, Chuckie Jones, him and me went way back.

"Hey, Chuckie, what you got?"

The man's sullen expression transformed when a smile sliced across his dark-skinned countenance. "Bongiovanni, my friend, what are you doing out so late?"

"I *was* celebrating my pending retirement at a local pub, and was disappointed you weren't there to buy me a drink."

"So you came *all the way over here* to find me, huh?"

I smiled my world-famous grin, and it worked immediately on him. He laughed harder and longer than reason might dictate. I suspected he recalled some of our adventures over the years. As I said, Chuckie and I went way back.

"The only reason I'm bothering you is that I'm doing an accidental death follow-up for the boss," I said.

"Nice way to finish an illustrious career."

I chuckled. The master of cynicism had nailed it.

"I had a conversation today with your victim, Mr. London, which makes me wonder if there's any connection to my investigation."

"What'd you talk about?"

"I called him about a service he handled last week. It was for the guy whose death I'm investigating."

Chuckie grinned, waiting for me to spill more details.

"I'd gotten conflicting information on whether my guy was embalmed and buried or cremated."

"That doesn't sound like something that'd drive you to murder the mortician."

"Yeah, I know, but the family dynamic involves money and hard feelings."

"Lucky you," Chuckie said, lifting his notepad to his eyes. "What can I tell you? Night security working a warehouse up the block called in a report about ten-fifteen. They heard gunshots, a bunch of them. A street patrol arrived about ten-thirty, and the rest of us came soon after."

"Coming into the building, I noticed a security camera. Does that have anything on it?"

"Naw, I checked the recorder. It was missing the diskette."

I peeked into the room that seemed to be the focus of attention. The crime scene investigator looked busy taking photographs. I saw the top of a man's head but couldn't make him out. He must have been the Medical Examiner, stooped over the corpse.

"The victim was shot in the back of the head," Chuckie continued. He pointed into the room. "See the back wall there. At least six rounds appeared to have entered the plaster in a tight circle. Then we have the blood splatter from the headshot."

"How do you explain that?" I asked.

"I'm not ready to hazard a guess."

I approved of Chuckie's approach. When you have one of those strange situations, you don't want to rush to judgment. It's too easy to get something in your head and waste a lot of time pursuing it. I liked to look and hear before forming an opinion. Yeah, let the clues reveal what happened.

"Can I take a look?"

"Sure, knock yourself out."

"Thanks, buddy."

"Oh, Bongi, when's your party? I want to be there."

"I'll make sure you know, my friend. Just be sure you bring your credit card."

Chuckie chortled and returned to his note-taking. I carefully slipped into the office and took a closer look at the bullet holes in the back wall. It looked like someone aimed and unloaded a clip. I leaned over the desk to check out the action. What I saw made me grimace.

"Well, hello, Leo."

Leo Dewey looked startled. I'm sure he felt more unhappy seeing me than me, him.

"Detective," he said, his gloved hands covered with blood. "What are you doing here?"

I moved around the desk so that I could get a better look at Dewey's handiwork. I also wanted Leo to see me watching him, help keep him on his toes.

"I stopped by because I thought maybe the caskets would be on sale."

The medical examiner didn't react.

"We're all going to need one. Might as well get a good deal," I said. "Am I right?"

Dewey looked down and continued his examination. "You're right. We all need one eventually."

I stepped up to the back wall and eyeballed the bullet holes. A wall made of soft plaster prevented the spent rounds from bouncing all over the place. They'd be easy to find and identify. I turned to look at London, lying face down on the floor. The back of his head a mess of bone shards mixed with hair, scalp, and brains. His hands weren't tied. He'd most likely stood with his back to his killer.

Why would someone create a commotion by firing off a clip and then methodically execute the victim? Did they want him found quickly? It seemed too sloppy for a mob-hit.

"You see anything interesting, Leo?"

"Nope," he said, staying focused on the job at hand. "Doesn't look to be anything other than a shot to the back of the head from, I dunno, maybe four feet away."

Easy guess, I thought. I felt the crime scene told us all we needed to know. Sober or drunk, Dewey wouldn't create more questions than answers this time. Then he surprised me.

"So have you stopped wasting time on that Pressman death?"

The sing-song tone of his voice irritated me. I decided to give some payback.

"Actually, something new has come up."

Dewey's eyes rose up to connect with mine. "You don't say?"

"Shelia Washington identified some odd features on that cloth remnant I found at the scene. Now, I'm wondering if we missed something."

Dewey snapped. "I didn't miss anything. Maybe other people did, but my work was solid."

I smiled and nodded.

"I'm going to petition for the exhumation of Pressman's body."

The man snorted. "Sure, you are."

Dewey surprised me again. Here I threw severe shade on his work, and he thought I was fooling around. What had changed? Maybe he knew about the cremation. As thick as he and Tommy Lyle seemed to be, I wouldn't be surprised.

"So you've decided to give up your retirement, huh?" he asked. "You'll need months, maybe a year to get a court order."

"The mother of the deceased is a wealthy woman with some powerful friends in the city. She wants to make it happen. With her pull, I think I might get Pressman out of the ground in a few weeks."

Dewey blanched and quickly packed his tools. "I'm done here," he called out to Chuckie. He almost tripped over his own feet, passing me.

"Good night, Leo," I shouted. "Be a good boy, now."

Dewey probably cleared the building before my words reached his ears.

I had to admit the more I toyed with Dewey, the more he confused me. If Brutkowski saw Dewey go into Lyle's house and those two were in cahoots, why did Leo flip out when I mentioned an exhumation? Did Lyle not share with him that the body had been cremated, or had Daisy lied to me to throw me off? The dead man lying there at my feet swore he'd cremated Pressman, yet Phyllis had been equally adamant that wasn't possible.

"Did you see anything interesting?"

I looked up and saw Chuckie in the doorway

"I agree with you on the holes in the wall. Why do that, and then deliver a shot to the back of the head?"

"Maybe at first the shooter was delivering a message, didn't get the answer he wanted, and closed the victim out."

I liked that supposition. As the first step in figuring out who did it and why, it made sense. But I couldn't go any further, no matter how much I wanted to dig into it. Chuckie had the lead. I had to step away.

"Good luck to you, my friend," I said. "I'll leave you to solve this one on your own. I'm not doing it for you."

Chuckie laughed and gave me a look of pity. "You're going to miss this, Bongi. I'm worried about you."

"Naw, I'm ready to get out of the crime-busting business."

"You're fooling yourself. What short-timer would be out after midnight, hanging around some other detective's crime scene?"

I laughed, unable to offer my usual retort that since the department paid me for a full day's work, I had to give him the whole day. I told him the truth.

"I don't have anything else going on in my life right now."

Chuckie's face went slack. "Oh man, I'm sorry,"

I waved off his apology, quickly smiling.

"Next month, I'll be rocking out there on the ocean, drowning bait in the sunshine."

"I hope so, Bongi. You deserve it."

I gave my friend a wink and strolled toward the exit, stopping before I hit the door.

"Hey, Chuckie, do me a favor. If you hear any mention of Tommy Lyle during your investigation, let me know."

"You're sick, Bongiovanni."

I sighed and walked out into the humid night air. Let him rib me. You couldn't turn off thirty years of instinct like a light switch. I strolled toward my car, taking in the action around me. Even after all the years of attending to the debris of human behavior, I still got stoked being part of the effort.

I wondered what else I could do to keep from going home.

Chapter Thirty-Nine

I slept in late the next morning and got up around eight. Stumbling down into the kitchen, I heard a stillness I hadn't yet gotten used to hearing. Joanie would've been unhappy I hadn't gotten into bed until way past midnight. It would be one thing; she'd whine if I'd been out drinking with the guys. But to be snooping around on a dead-end accidental death case, you couldn't get more ridiculous than that.

Back before her health started failing her, we had a conversation about my retirement. "Why don't you spend some time looking into a fishing charter?" she said. "You're going to wait too long and won't have one when we get down there."

I responded with my world-class smile, but it didn't impress her. She'd seen it enough in the early years of our marriage that it no longer charmed her.

"If that happens, then I'll fish off the pier."

My darling huffed and puffed and threw her hands in the air. "I don't know what I'm going to do with you," she cried. "I don't want you underfoot and driving me to distraction."

"If I can't fish, I'll spend my days cuddling my honey."

I think the doctor called the next day with the news her cancer had come back with a vengeance.

I wasted about an hour chewing on a cold waffle, drinking some bitter coffee, and reading the sports page. Done with what might be my most significant accomplishment for the day, I went back upstairs to change for work. My knees ached, and when I looked in the mirror, I swore my gut

164

made me look six months pregnant. Maybe Joanie had been right. I should be spending those last days planning my time as a retiree. Who was I fooling? Our precinct alone probably had a half dozen unsolved homicides under investigation. Nobody cared about Pressman's death except the mother. Why should I be working so hard on something that everyone still officially considered an accident?

I flipped open my notepad and turned to the last few pages. I'd started a list of things I needed to do so I could leave town the morning after my retirement party. I wanted to be heading south on Interstate 95 with my car packed with all my necessities.

I'd placed the newspaper stop and mail hold, and the gas and electricity would be off within a day after I left town. I'd terminated the cable a month ago and given the neighbor kid an advance to cut the grass and check on things. An escape from a house full of memories was in the works. I'd make a clean break.

About ten that morning, I got downtown, filled out some retirement paperwork, and tossed insults back and forth with my friends, went out for lunch and stopped by the travel agency, where I took some literature on Italy. Visiting the motherland had been high up on Joanie and my bucket list. I returned to my desk at about two and felt pretty good, like I hadn't completely wasted the day. I spent the next few hours shooting the bull and tossing paperclips into a coffee cup when a phone call saved me from jumping off the roof.

"Hey, Chuckie, do you have something for me?"

"I interviewed the victim's assistant," he said. "Phyllis was her name."

"Did she have any idea why someone wanted to shoot her boss?"

"He had a weakness for all forms of gambling."

"That's never good."

"She mentioned an incident the day of the murder. Some guy stopped by to make a collection."

"You don't say. Did she describe him?"

"She said he was a skinny, vermin sort of guy with a mouth on him."

"My guy is a skinny, vermin-like character. What else did she tell you?"

According to Chuckie, the office manager kept London and the business on the up and up. He'd given her complete fiduciary control, not trusting himself to gamble away the business. He'd come to her after the shakedown begging for an advance on his paycheck. She refused him, having seen it too many times before. Now the woman felt terrible. She thought maybe he'd been shot because he couldn't pay his gambling debts.

"That doesn't sound like my guy," I said. "But, thanks for the call."

I hung up, stood, and grabbed my car keys from the desktop. I passed through the main room of the precinct headquarters. It was crowded and loud as the shifts came and went. I saw a shaved head high above all the rest of tightly trimmed domes.

"Hey, Brute."

The officer looked around, his eyes hooded and suspicious.

"Hello, Detective," he said. His clipped response suggested he still smarted over my treatment of him last night at the bar. For a big fellow, he had the sensitivity of a schoolgirl.

"I told you, call me, Bongi."

"Okay, Bongi."

A smile appeared. Ah, such an easy turnabout. I swear that boy had a major-league man-crush on me.

"I know you're starting your shift, but walk with me. I have something to share with you."

He matched my pace as we strolled across the linoleum floor toward the parking lot.

"You were right," I said. "That 10-28 you turned me onto last night might have a connection to our boy, Tommy Lyle."

"I knew it."

"Easy, big dog," I said. "Now there's an eyewitness who overheard someone fitting the description of Lyle, demanding money from the victim, who, by-the-way, had a serious gambling problem."

"That's interesting," he said. "You think Lyle was running numbers?"

I shook my head as we entered the parking lot. "Naw, he's not that smart. I've seen where he lives. There's no way he has the kind of cash to run an

166

operation."

Brutkowski jumped in. "Plus, most bookies break legs. You kill a deadbeat, and you never get back your money."

I nodded as we reached Brutkowski's cruiser.

"We know Lyle's covering up something," I continued. "I think London might have known what that something was, you know what I mean?"

"I do. I haven't trusted Tommy Lyle from the start." Brutkowski arched his mountain-size shoulders. "But you have to be careful. The worst thing an investigator can do is fall in love with his bias."

I felt my face cringle in a smile. That young guy cracked me up. Here he just called out the old master.

"Don't tell me I said that."

His skin turned the color of a ripe tomato. "Oh, no," he said. "I read that in a Nic Knuckles novel." Then he realized he'd hurt my feelings and quickly recovered.

"But I'm sure you have something just as good."

I laughed and shook my head in denial. But it did kind of hurt my feelings, my protégé quoting something clever he read in a damn pulp fiction novel. I'd better stay focused and forget about pumping up my ego.

"Hey, think you can do me a favor?"

"Of course, I can."

"When you're on patrol today, can you cruise by that strip of pawn shops over on Lincoln Avenue?"

"Sure. What am I looking for?"

"I don't know, some skinny guy trying to pawn office equipment."

The officer snapped a salute. "I'm on it."

I gave him one of my patent-pending smiles. He loved it.

Chapter Forty

About 5:30 in the afternoon, I drove by Lyle's house. I spotted the BMW parked in front, so I pulled my car behind it. The yard, if you could call it that, looked untended since winter. The walk to the front porch was a hazard of broken concrete. I didn't feel comfortable standing on the porch since the flooring gave way a good two inches. I'd seen trampolines with less bounce.

After a minute of pounding my fist on the door, it opened. Tommy Lyle stood on the other side and looked through six inches of space between the door and the frame. He appeared none too happy seeing me.

"Yeah," he said.

"Good afternoon, Tommy. Can you give me a minute?"

"What do you want?" he said, failing to offer me the courtesy of asking me inside the house. Okay, that's good with me. I didn't have time to chat. I wanted to get a confirmation right off, and if I could plant a little seed of worry in Lyle's head, then even better.

"I understand you paid a visit to the Redport Funeral Parlor yesterday."

He sucked in some air but said nothing.

"I understand that you and Archie London had a rather heated discussion about money."

He didn't say a word. He just continued looking at me as if waiting for me to put the statement in the form of a question.

"I was curious about the argument you had with him," I said. "What was that about?"

Lyle blinked his eyelids, his lips turning in.

"I'd ordered an enhanced funeral service package for my sister. An extra thick seat cushion for the graveside, refreshments in the car, stuff like that. She didn't get what I paid for, so I was demanding a refund."

Oh, boy, that's a good one. He's assuming I won't check out whether such a package existed. I'm sure Phyllis would know who bought what.

"Can you tell me where you were last night at about ten?"

"I was here."

"Is there anyone who can verify that?"

"Maybe the cockroaches could tell you," he said. "I live by myself."

"Do you own a gun?"

"No."

"Did you know Archie London had a gambling problem?"

"Why would I know that?"

"One last question," I said. "I talked to Mr. London, and he told me your brother-in-law was cremated. Your sister said the same thing. Yet, according to a witness, the crematory hadn't been working for a month."

He leaned toward me. "I got an urn full of ashes that says your witness was wrong."

I had to admit that answer slowed me down.

"And I was wondering—"

"You said that was the last question, so get off my porch."

The air driven by the slamming door blew the hair back off my forehead. I sighed and walked back to my car. Tommy Lyle had come a long way from our first meeting, where he overflowed with nervous curiosity. I'm guessing that ill-tempered smart ass was the true Mr. Lyle.

My little visit served a purpose. I'd gotten Tommy to admit he fought with Archie London the day of his murder. He knew I thought Daisy lied about the cremation, and my suspicions of her husband's death weren't going away. Hopefully, panic would set in, and he'd get careless.

Now I just had to wait for him to make a move and bring some kind of clarity to my conviction that skinny, whining, pathetic Tommy Lyle had the props to be a cold-blooded killer.

Chapter Forty-One

Thursday came around, and I arrived at Daisy's house at four in the afternoon. She surprised me by waiting outside. Usually, I had to get out of the car and retrieve her.

"Let's go for a ride," she said, climbing into the passenger's seat. My sister had a squirrely expression on her face, which I couldn't read. That made me uncomfortable.

"Where are we going?"

When she answered, "You'll find out," I shook my head. I didn't like her game-playing. The last thirty-six hours had taken a toll on my mood. My angry confrontation with Archie London had fried my nerves. That next morning, when I failed to make it to the shoe store, they fired me. Late in the afternoon, Bongiovanni banged at my front door, pretty much calling us liars. This morning, things didn't get much better. I didn't want to take the risk of pawning Phyllis's' office equipment at a legit shop, so I did something I swore I'd never do, I ended up at Snell's Automotive.

Weasel must've still been irritated that Big Jimmy made him overpay for my stuff the last time. I left with only seventy-five dollars for what should've been three hundred bucks worth of loot.

Of course, I shared none of that with Daisy. I didn't need her piling on about my screw-ups.

For thirty minutes, we drove, Daisy, telling me which streets to take and where to turn. My curiosity spiked when we pulled in front of a rundown café on the north side of town. It looked like the kind of joint old folks with limited budgets went to for the early bird special.

"What are we doing here?"

Daisy pushed open the car door and threw her right leg out. "Come on. We have a meeting."

Once we stepped inside the place, I quickly learned why my sister had been so secretive. If she'd told me that we'd be sitting in a restaurant booth, in an isolated part of the county, with Eleanor Pressman, I would've had her committed to the nuthouse.

But there we were. Mrs. Pressman, dressed all in red and wearing an oversized hat, sat across from me.

"What the heck is going on?" I asked.

Daisy, sitting next to me, turned to Eleanor. "You called me," she said. "Why don't you explain to my brother what's going on."

Sunglasses hid Mrs. Pressman's eyes, but I recognized her thin slice of a mouth. It squirmed before the words came out.

"My situation has become direr since that horrible reading of Eric's Will," she said.

I looked at Daisy. Even without a smile on her face, I knew she loved hearing those words.

"The addendum to the Trust gave that despicable Arbuckle woman the right to review my expenses. Can you believe it? I have to provide receipts and justify every meal, purchase, or entertaining I do."

"That must suck," I said.

Pressman pickled her face.

"Why yes, it does...irritate me." She took a breath and continued with her list of grievances. "If Arbuckle feels I'm spending on what she calls nonessentials, she has the right to trim my stipend. All I can use my money for is groceries, utilities, and weekly maid service. No new clothing, jewelry, travel, nothing. She's confining me to my condominium."

Oh, that's terrible; the poor rich woman hurt for money. I felt so sorry for her. Of course, my sister was another poor, suffering rich woman. But at least she did the dirty work to get her share of Eric's wealth.

"I'm a prisoner in my own home," she continued, her hands chopping the air. "This was not how I envisioned living out my life."

171

"My life isn't much better," Daisy said, enthusiastically joining Eleanor's bitchfest.

I drummed my fingers on the table and hoped the two Mrs. Pressman would finish with their carping and get to the point. I arrived irritated, and they weren't making me feel better. When they started debating who suffered more, I blew.

"Okay, we all agree you two are miserable. But tell me, why are we here?"

Eleanor's jaw clenched, and her shoulders trembled. "Do you know how much the Trust is paying Arbuckle?"

"I'm sure it's more than what she deserves."

"She's getting paid twenty-thousand dollars."

"Oh, that's not so much," I said, figuring an annual twenty grand was a pretty small percentage of the Trust's value.

"A month." Eleanor slapped the tabletop. "Twenty thousand a damn month."

That fact lit up Daisy's temper. "What the hell? That's almost a quarter a million a year."

Eleanor vigorously shook her head. "She could drag this out for years and burn through millions."

Eleanor surprised me by making no mention of her dead son. I wouldn't be shocked to learn he treated her as poorly as he did my sister. Maybe that's a common ground we could build on, you know, let a by-gone be by-gone. Forget about Eric's death. Put it all behind us. That'd take some pressure off if we didn't have to worry about Eleanor pushing for a deeper police investigation.

"Yeah, Gloria's a greedy one," I said. "But what can you do about her?"

Eleanor looked at me and then Daisy. "There are ways of getting Arbuckle's hands out of my, uh, our money."

My sister nodded. I suspected she hoped Eleanor's answer would be a good one because she hadn't yet hatched a solution to the meddling girlfriend.

"If something happened to Arbuckle where she was incapacitated or deemed unfit, as Eric's mother and the wife of the late Mr. Pressman, I'd have grounds to sue for management of the estate."

Daisy snorted. "How does that benefit me?"

"Hypothetically, if you and your brother helped me remove Arbuckle from her position and I gained control of the assets, I'd be beholden to you."

"Hypothetically," Daisy said. "I'd need specifics on which assets you're talking about."

Eleanor shuddered. I imagined being generous toward Daisy required a greater effort than what she intend when we arrived.

"Without that Arbuckle woman, we'd be keeping the trustee fee in our pool of funds."

"I figured that," Daisy said. "What else is there to gain?"

Eleanor pulled off her sunglasses. "I'd find another agent to sell off the bank, one willing to do it at a discounted fee."

"I don't want to sell the bank," Daisy said. "I want to keep it."

I felt my mouth pop open.

Mrs. Pressman chuckled. "If you want to buy my half, then knock yourself out running it."

I regained control of my tongue in enough time to ask Daisy, "What do you know about owning a bank?"

"I watched Eric bungle the business for decades," she said as the flesh under her right eye quivered. "And I think I can do better."

Before I could further question Daisy's sanity, I felt a sharp kick to my shin. I decided to let the argument end.

"The bottom line is simple," Eleanor said. "We eliminate Arbuckle, and we'll have more money and more property to share equitably."

It required ten minutes of back and forth before the two women agreed on a definition of equitable. Once the management of the Trust went to Mrs. Pressman, Daisy would keep her big house; get the bank, the beach property, and five hundred grand in cash. Eleanor would get her condo and the rest of the investments and currency.

"Okay, enough with splitting the loot," Daisy said. "What's your plan to make this happen?"

"That Arbuckle woman needs to be convinced to relinquish control of the Trust. Either because she risks legal jeopardy due to mismanagement or because there are other kinds of threats to her well-being."

The corner of Daisy's mouth tweaked. I sensed she knew Eleanor's thinking behind this conversation, which was more than what I understood.

Mrs. Pressman cleared her throat. "You come from a world where, how should I put it, extraordinary things get done."

I wasn't sure what she meant by her remark. You rarely heard the word extraordinary used when talking about me. Daisy seemed to have a clearer understanding, and it made her angry.

"If you think we're going to kill Gloria Arbuckle, this meeting is over."

Eleanor stiffened, chilling the air around us. "I didn't mention murder," she said, "although that does seem to be part of your skillset."

Daisy slammed her hands on the table and lifted out of her seat. She pitched a few obscenities and yelled at me to come with her. Eleanor's eyes blazed.

"You're still the uncouth ignoramus, Daisy Lyle," she said. "You'll get nothing."

I followed my sister out of the restaurant, and it wasn't until we sat in the car that she stopped cursing.

"Get me out of here," she said.

I fired up Baby, and we hit the streets, driving back toward the center of town. From the corner of my eye, I watched as Daisy's sneer gave way to a smile.

"What's going on with you?" I asked. "What's so funny?"

"I suspected Eleanor was getting desperate when she asked to meet. I went into that joint wondering what she'd be willing to do."

"She seemed pretty anxious to do something."

Daisy giggled. "Yes, she was."

"I liked that she was willing to give you the beach property. But why'd you want the bank? You'd have to work."

My sister slapped the dashboard and laughed. "Oh, Tommy, you're thinking small."

"Huh?"

"I have an idea."

My stomach, the perfect barometer of my fears, tightly clutched.

"I think we can play Eleanor's desperation and get more than just half of the estate."

"What are you talking about?"

"Here's my idea," she said. "Listen carefully."

I listened, and I didn't like her idea. I didn't like it one bit.

"Come on, Tommy. You can do it."

"I don't know. Eleanor thinks I'm an idiot."

"That's why it's so perfect. The woman will think you're keeping me out of it and that she can play you like a fool."

I didn't appreciate hearing my sister confirm that I came across as stupid, even though she'd implied it herself several times these past few weeks. I had to admit Daisy probably guessed right about Eleanor's desperation. But could she use it to trick her ex-mother-in-law? The older woman had already proven to be a crafty and hardened adversary. It'd be like Godzilla versus Mothra, two heavyweight monsters going up against each other.

"My scheme won't work," Daisy said, "if you don't help me."

My sister reached over and squeezed my hand. "We could wrap this up once and for all."

"You promise?"

"Cross my heart and hope to die."

Even though I doubted Daisy's willing to die to make me happy, I needed to hear her say the end was in sight. My mind wasn't built for a life of suspense and dark secrets. Assaulting Archie London proved that to me. The whole incident made me sick and ashamed. My soul had slipped so far from the golden light of redemption that even the ghost of Mandy stopped appearing. I'd do anything to bring this nightmare to a close.

"Okay, I'll help you."

"And don't worry," she said as she patted my hand. "I won't make you do anything to hurt people."

That sounded good to me. The less bad stuff I had to do, the better.

* * *

Eleanor Pressman must've been surprised to see my face showing up on her security system's screen. At ten in the evening, she'd probably be ready for bed. Daisy thought if I showed up late and unannounced, it'd be more believable that I planned everything on my own.

Nonetheless, I felt anxious about meeting with her.

"Just follow the script," Daisy told me, "and you'll be okay."

The intercom to the condo's entrance crackled. "What do you want?"

"I'd like to continue the conversation we were having about that Arbuckle problem."

"Where's your sister?"

"I think you and me can work better without her. You know what I mean."

I guessed she did know what I meant. The entrance lock clicked, and I pulled open the door. It took me two minutes to walk past the security desk and ride the elevator to Eleanor's penthouse. She made me sit on a sofa in her living room. She had some sort of silk nightgown wrapped around her boney body.

"Nice place you got here," I said, rubbing my sweaty palms against my pant legs.

"Get to the point, Mr. Lyle."

I drew a deep breath to calm my nerves. I knew I had only one shot at convincing the woman.

"You mentioned you thought me and Daisy could help you get rid of the Arbuckle problem."

"Yes, but I assumed your sister would be part of the effort."

"I think I'd be a much better partner than Daisy."

Eleanor tilted her head to the side. I felt like she was one of those body scanner machines, slowly looking inside me. When she smiled, I knew she thought there wasn't much there.

"You know something, Mr. Lyle. You *may be* the ideal partner for the job."

Dang, Daisy called it.

I leaned forward, screwing my face into the harshest looking expression I could muster. "I was hoping you'd say that. I have a solid plan that will get us what we want."

Mrs. Pressman blinked a few times before she spoke.

"Well, what is this solid plan?"

"It's best that you don't know."

Eleanor's eyebrow arched high on her forehead. "Why would I want to be kept in the dark?"

I felt moisture in my armpits. My mug may have a gangster look, but the rest of my body quivered like an altar boy at a strip club.

"It's simple. You want to be able to deny everything if our plan goes south."

Mrs. Pressman leaned back, her eyelids narrowing.

"I'm giving you maximum deniability, Eleanor," I said. "It's a good thing."

The woman's face relaxed, and her head slowly moved up and down.

"Alright, that makes sense."

Daisy, had it right again. She predicted Eleanor would fall for that offer. The less the old gal knew, Daisy thought, the better for us. Her ignorance gave my sister flexibility in executing her plan. It would also allow her to put in place certain protections against future blackmailing.

"I need you to use your contacts at the bank to understand Arbuckle's work routine and schedule," I said. "Anything you can learn about her daily doings, the better."

Eleanor nodded. "There's one long-time employee who would be very happy to assist me."

"Good, now listen up."

I drew upon some childhood memories of hearing Walter and Mabel discussing their con games. I ticked off for Eleanor the steps I thought we'd have to take to eliminate possible risks, things like code names and alibis and burner phones. Mrs. Pressman's mouth softened into something that might be called a smile.

"It sounds like you know this criminal business better than I ever will."

I wanted to suggest that she had more natural talent than I'd ever have, but didn't want to blow it by chattering away. It'd be best if I just got out of there while she's still thought of me as a master criminal.

"I think we have a deal."

I offered her my hand. The woman refused the gesture, saying only, "I think so as well."

We stood, and she led me toward the front door.

"I'll call about the next step, so be ready to do your part."

She nodded and smiled. "Good night, Mr. Lyle."

I made one step past the threshold when she slammed the door.

In the elevator, I felt my heart pounding. I couldn't wait to call my sister and tell her how well everything went. We had Eleanor primed and ripe for picking. Daisy would be so proud of her little brother.

I almost skipped across the marble floor of the lobby after the elevator closed behind me. Tommy Lyle played a tough guy far better than being one. Talking old Mrs. Pressman into committing a crime felt so much better than using a pistol to do one. If nothing else, no bloody mess had to be cleaned up.

Chapter Forty-Two

I had the radio playing old-fashioned big band music, you know, the stuff from the forties. I didn't want to hear anything classical. Joanie loved the Beethoven and the Mozart, but I didn't want to be thinking about her. I avoided the old rock-and-roll because it brought back memories of my younger years when my joints didn't ache. Listening to loud music full of horns and drums made me forget how old, tired, and alone I felt.

I stood upstairs, staring at a closet full of Joanie's clothing, wondering what to do with it. I scanned the rows of outfits hanging from the rods on either side of the space. What should I do with all her stuff, some of it still smelling of her perfume?

As a knot formed in my throat, I closed the closet door. I'd deal with it when I got back from the Outer Banks. Yeah, maybe I'd be ready in a couple of months.

I heard my cellphone buzzing like an angry hornet. Damn, it was down on the kitchen table. I cussed every step I took to get to the house's lower level. It must be important because not many people would call me at eleven-fifteen at night.

"Bongiovanni speaking."

"I hope I didn't wake you."

I immediately recognized the voice.

"No, I was awake. What's up, Brute?"

"I had to call you, sir. You're not going to believe this."

"Okay, big guy, what you got for me."

"I was tailing Lyle. You know, liked you asked."

After learning that Tommy Lyle had argued with Archie London hours before the undertaker's murder, I requisitioned a GPS tracker. Brute had been more than willing to do a slap and track, attaching the device to Lyle's BMW, and responding with a tail if the vehicle left Lyle's neighborhood.

"I picked up the signal about nine-forty. He left his house, drove across town, and parked a half block from the Majestic Park condos."

"Okay, go on."

"I got there about ten-ten and parked in an alley where I could catch the action. Sure enough, about ten-forty-five, I see Lyle walking through the lobby of the building and out the front doors."

"I'm not familiar with the place, Brute."

Brutkowski described the residency as a high-end set of condominiums. Not exactly a place a lowlife like Tommy Lyle would visit, he surmised. I agreed with him.

"And guess who lives there?" he said. "Eleanor Pressman."

"How'd you know that?"

"I coordinated the police escort at her son's funeral. We had a conversation, in fact, two of them. She mentioned she lived there."

"Didn't you once tell me that Mrs. Pressman thought her son was murdered by either the wife or her brother?"

"Yeah, that's why I was surprised to see Lyle leaving her residence that late at night."

I expressed a concern that Lyle might've been there to harm the older woman. He admitted Tommy walked out of the building with a bounce in his step, not making an effort to hide anything. Nonetheless, Brute called Pressman's phone number, and she answered.

"I told her I had the wrong number," he said. "I guess Lyle wasn't there to hurt her."

"You sure she was the one he went to visit?"

Brutkowski went quiet for a few seconds. I heard a big sigh, and he spoke, "Well, not a hundred percent."

I doubted Tommy Lyle had friends in that kind of building, but I had to be positive. The idea of him meeting Pressman's mother baffled me. What the hell would they have to talk about that late at night?

"I think I might have to pay Mother Pressman a visit."

Brutkowski asked if he should continue tracking Lyle's BMW.

"If you can," I said. "It seems every time I talk with you, you find something that makes this case even stranger."

Chapter Forty-Three

The familiar roiling heat in my gut started last night after my conversation with Daisy. I'd called her to give her the good news that Eleanor had bought my performance hook, line, and sinker. The conversation didn't go as well as I expected. I thought Daisy would be, oh, I don't know, more appreciative.

"Great. I'll be able to sleep tonight."

That's what she said, no thanks, or good job, Tommy. I'm nothing but a sleeping pill to her.

By late afternoon the next day, my anxiety grew more heated. I had to find a way to raise Dewey's September hush money and I had to do it quickly. Most folks would've assumed with Daisy's $20,000 life insurance payout, that wouldn't be a problem. They didn't know my sister. Once that girl had money in her hands, she didn't easily give it up.

I drove over to Daisy's house with the intention of getting her to cough up the five grand. The sight of a weed-infested front yard heartened my spirit. She obviously had stopped spending money on the lawn service. That could be a sign she'd set some priorities. The front door swung open before I raised a finger to ring the bell. My sister greeted me with a big smile.

"I saw you pull in," she said as she batted her eyelashes. "How do I look?"

I had to admit that Daisy impressed me. She looked so much better from yesterday afternoon. Her hair was cut and colored, and her make-up deleted a decade from her face.

"I guess you're no longer officially a grieving widow."

Daisy laughed and waved me into the vestibule. "I was bored looking sad all the time. I decided to spend some of my insurance money on myself."

"Ah, that's nice," I said, wondering what she meant by *some* of her money.

She kicked her right foot in the air. "How do you like my Manolo Blahniks?"

I didn't know what she showed off, but I suspected her shoes. Since she had given them a name, I assumed they cost a bundle. I called my shoes, *shoes* and they cost less than a hundred bucks.

"Pretty," I said, guessing our plan to protect her insurance haul had gone out shopping that morning.

"And look at this beautiful Helmut Lang jacket. Don't you love the notched lapels?"

"How much did that dude cost?" I asked as she pulled on the leather coat and twirled around in her expensive new shoes.

"If you have to ask, you can't afford it."

Dollars to donuts you couldn't afford it either, sissy, I wanted to say.

"After you called me last night, I was so happy that my plan was in place I figured I could afford to pamper myself. I was there when the mall opened this morning."

So it's my fault she went off the rails, huh. I hung my head and tried to muster up a look of joy for her. I must've failed.

"Don't look at me that way," she said. "I'm not returning anything."

"I'm not suggesting that you take it back. I just think you should probably keep some cash in reserve, you know, for your business expenses."

Her lips pulled taut as she removed the German-sounding jacket.

"What are you talking about?"

"We need five big ones to pay off Dewey, remember?"

"Are you kidding me? What about the money you got selling all my stuff?"

"The ten grand covered retrieving Eric's body and the garage sale five took care of August's bribe. I need five thousand more for September."

My sister sputtered and started circling me.

"You need to do something about him," she said, her finger flicking at me. "I can't afford that big of a bribe every damn month."

When it suddenly became *my* responsibility to eliminate the Dewey problem wasn't explained, and I didn't ask. Right now, my focus was on getting the five grand. We could talk later about eliminating the Dewey issue.

"So, can you give me five thousand or not?" I asked, using a voice harsher than I intended. "I don't want him hanging over my head as I work, Eleanor."

My sibling's unhappy face twisted into a snarl.

"God forbid you could get through a day without asking me for money, Tommy."

I knew it. I knew she'd get nasty if I asked her for the cash. I should remind her that our dreadful situation came about because she pushed Eric down the stairs, not me.

"Besides, I don't have that much money to give you."

That news stiffened my spine.

"Are you serious? You blew through twenty grand on shoes and a jacket?"

Daisy didn't react well to my scolding. Her skin flushed, and she bared her teeth.

"I've waited twenty years to do what I wanted to do. Don't you dare try and stop me."

I grumbled and pawed at my chin. If Daisy didn't want to contribute to the cause, then where were we going to get the money? I'd taken everything in the basement, garage, or attic that I could sell. We had no choice here. Daisy would have to come to her senses.

"Can you at least return those shoes?" I said. "I mean, I can't believe they cost thousands of dollars."

"They didn't."

"I'm confused. So you *do* have enough for the bribe?"

"Nope, I don't."

My sister placed her hands onto her hips and stood a little taller.

"I always wanted to take a grand tour of Europe," she said. "I figured if I were going to be bilked out of my money by Arbuckle, I would at least get my European dream vacation."

My head dropped, and the fingers of my right hand raked my hair. I had to relax and think through what I wanted to say. We didn't have time for a big fight.

"Okay, I understand you want to make a dream come true, but could you just wait until your Eleanor scheme pays off?"

"I'm sorry, Tommy, I paid for the trip. It's non-refundable. I go in less than two months."

I searched hard to find a sign of regret on Daisy's face and saw nothing. My stomach started to hurt.

"You know we're in a tough spot," I said. "I don't know what to do."

I felt tears forming in my eyes. How much more selfish could Daisy act? Couldn't she see that I'd been doing all the heavy lifting to help her? I lied nearly every time I opened my mouth, I'd committed crimes, and I lost my job and my self-respect. How could someone who supposedly loved me treat me that way?

"Come here," Daisy said. "I want to talk to you."

I did as she asked.

"I'm sorry I implied you're a money-sucking incompetent," she said, before laughing as if joking about it would make the sting go away. "I have an idea of how you can solve our Dewey money problems."

I got a sharp pain in my gut, afraid she'd suggest I kill Dewey. What she whispered in my ear sounded almost as horrifying.

"I can't do that."

"Yes, you can."

"No, no, I don't want to."

My sister placed her hands on my shoulders.

"You're not going to cry, are you?"

I blinked twice to keep the tears from flowing.

"Stop it, Daisy, don't make fun of me."

Mandy once told me that behind my angry mask lived a little boy with a good heart, and that explained why I tended to tear up when doing bad things.

My sister slowly smiled. "Listen to me, Tommy. It fixes your problems for two, maybe three months. If you're hard-nosed, we're talking four months, easily."

"Why was this suddenly my problem," I fired back.

Daisy went hard on me. "You made a deal with Dewey. You caved in to him without a fight."

"You don't know that."

Daisy gave me a good shake.

"Come on, who are you talking to, someone who didn't share a bedroom with you for the first ten years of your life?"

I didn't say anything. I wished I had a mouthful of angry words that would make Daisy suffer, but I didn't. It had always been that way. I'm such a loser.

I followed her into a small room off the hall, where she opened a desk drawer.

"Here you go," she said, handing me an envelope. "That's all you need."

I inflated my cheeks and slowly released the air. "Alright, I'll do it."

My sister walked me to the front door and gave me a peck on the cheek.

"I'll call you later about your next meeting with Eleanor. I have some things I need to prepare first."

"Okay."

I looked down at Daisy's feet. "Enjoy your shoes."

"I will."

I had no doubt that she would.

Chapter Forty-Four

Daisy acted surprised when three minutes later, I stood at the front door.

"What'd you forget?"

I lifted an urn to her face.

"Eric's remains have been rolling around in the car trunk. Do you want to keep them in your house?"

Daisy knitted her eyebrows. "Why would I want a reminder of that jerk sitting on my mantel?"

"So, what do you want to do with them?"

"I don't know," she said. Then her mouth flipped from a grimace to a smile. "Wait a minute. He always wanted his ashes spread on the ocean."

"Do you really want to drive to the shore this late?"

"No, no, I have a better idea."

Good Lord, not another Daisy idea. If I had to experience one more of my sister's lightbulb moments, I'd scream.

"I'll grab a flashlight from the kitchen," she said. "Meet me around back by the fence gate."

I stepped through the overgrown grasses surrounding the house, thinking more about some deer tick riding my clothing than what Daisy intended to do with Eric's cremains. Even though it had been only a few weeks ago that my brother-in-law crashed down those stairs, no one seemed to be mourning him. Not his wife, not his mother, and not even his girlfriend. Money appeared to be the only thing that mattered for the three of them.

For a second, I felt sorry for Eric. But the feeling quickly passed.

Daisy threw open the fence gate and took the lead, walking us through the back yard and into the woods bordering the property. She flooded the dirt path in front of us with the light beam. I followed with Eric's receptacle held tightly in my arms. A few dozen steps into the pine trees, and we reached a small clearing.

"That's far enough," Daisy announced as she strobed the light beam across a metal grate buried in the ground.

"How will dumping Eric's cremains in a storm drain spread them on the ocean?"

Daisy chuckled. "The next heavy rain will take Eric through the underground pipes, into the river, and eventually far out into the Atlantic. Mission accomplished."

I groaned. Maybe my sister's disposal of her dead husband's remains matched her feelings about the man, but I still found it disrespectful.

"At least say something nice about Eric as I open the lid, can you?"

My sister bowed her head and muttered some words. She sounded matter-of-fact like we had gathered to empty a vacuum cleaner dust bag. She ended her little speech by getting personal.

"And I hope you burn in Hell for going cheap on that life insurance policy."

Out of a habit instilled in me by Mandy, I mumbled, "Ah-men."

I gripped the round top of the urn and grunted before it gave. Three times around and the lid screwed off.

"What will the cremains look like?" Daisy asked.

I shrugged. "I guess something like powdery grey ash you find in a fireplace."

I straddled the grating and slowly tipped the container. I held my breath and worried that a breeze might blow the ash back into my face. That's the last thing I wanted in my lungs, Eric Pressman's ashes.

"What the hell?" Daisy said. She stuck her hands into the white particles pouring from the urn's opening. "I don't believe this."

I stuck my hand into the flow as well and echoed my sister's question. "What the hell *is* this?"

A cold stream of pure white play sand slipped through my fingers.

Chapter Forty-Five

I only had the appetite for a donut and a cup of coffee. I would've probably selected everything on the menu that I craved if the two errands I did that morning hadn't destroyed my desire to live.

Today had to be one of the worse days in a month of bad days.

Last night, finding Eric's urn filled with sand caused Daisy to go ballistic. I felt agitated as well, more so knowing that I'd have to deal with Archie again. At eight this morning, I called London's office. No one answered. I kept dialing every ten minutes until the message box claimed to be full. Why wasn't Phyllis answering calls?

It must've been about nine when I drove by the building. The empty parking lot bothered me, but not as much as seeing the gate padlocked. I pulled to the curb and rolled down the car window, hoping to figure out the situation.

"Hey, my brother, can you spare some change?"

An older dude startled me, coming up from behind the car.

"Uh, what happened here?" I said, pointing at the Redport Funeral Home. "Did they close down?"

The man lacked some teeth, and his clothing was secondhand, but he came across as a harmless neighborhood local.

"Oh, I don't know that for sure, but they might, what with no undertaker and all."

What did he mean by that? I bet that bastard, Archie, slipped town.

"Do you have any idea where the undertaker went?"

The man's eyes bulged, and his head vibrated. "That undertaker, he went nowhere. He was killed, dead."

I flopped back into my seat. "What? You say Archie's dead?"

The man licked his lips. "I don't know if Archie was his name, but yeah, he's dead."

I felt like my bones all went soft. Without saying another word, I raised the car window and slowly motored a few blocks down the street. I didn't want the old dude, or anyone else, seeing me bent over, crying like a baby.

"Oh my God," I said, sobbing. "How did that happen?"

My mind dug up any memories of my last confrontation with Archie. I remembered telling him to turn around because I couldn't stand looking at his face. He'd mocked me, saying he knew I wouldn't shoot him. He hunched down when I emptied the gun in the wall. It scared him, but I know he wasn't hit.

Then I told Archie that he still owned me, and I'd give him a week to get the rest of my money. After I said that, I slammed the gun butt hard to the back of his head. Yeah, I remembered that because it sounded like I'd whacked a watermelon.

I opened my eyes when I heard him fall on the floor. His scalp gushed blood, and he laid there, out cold. I thumped him, no doubt about it, but not enough to kill him. No way. I swear I heard him breathing.

Or was that *my* breathing I heard?

"What a mess, what a mess," I said over and over again. The burning inside my belly felt so bad I thought it might blister a hole through my stomach.

Then it dawned on me. That detective knew Archie had cheated me, and I'd been determined to get my due. What would it take for his little mind to assume I might've had a hand in killing the man? Oh, crap, as if having Bongiovanni wondering if I had something to do with Eric's death wasn't enough.

I cried out, "Oh, Lord, help me."

I didn't know how much longer I sat sobbing, praying, begging, and arguing with myself. It could've been an hour. I finally got a handle on my runaway wits and called Daisy.

"Did you talk to that snake, London?" she said before I even spoke.

"He's dead."

My sister kept yammering, obviously too mad from the previous evening to listen.

"I said someone killed London."

Daisy paused long enough to process my words. "Oh wow, how lucky is that?"

"Not for Archie."

I didn't like the joy in Daisy's voice as she went on about how the cheater deserved his fate, and she wished everyone trying to rip her off would end up dead. I might've used the opportunity to mention that I probably had a hand in his death and that the police would eventually suspect such. But I didn't. I figured nothing good would come from sharing my troubles with Daisy.

"Don't forget, I made an appointment for you at eleven," she said. "You have to follow through on what you agreed to last night."

"Yeah, yeah, I'm going."

After I hung up the call with my sister, the rest of the morning got uglier. I kept my promise to Daisy, and ninety minutes later, I sat here, picking at a donut and sipping lousy coffee.

"Can I get you more java?"

The waitress, a pot of steaming black liquid in her hand, pulled me from the clutches of my desperate thoughts.

"Uh, no, I've had enough. Just give me the check."

The woman's lower lip rolled, and she wobbled. "You want a box to take that pastry with you? You never touched it."

I nodded, and she dropped off a small foam container with the tab. I scooped in the donut, gave her a twenty-dollar bill, and told her to keep the change. Her mouth twisted to one side, and she walked away, mumbling. She'd be telling her co-workers about the spaced-out dude handing out fifteen dollar tips.

I got up, leaving the glazed donut on the table.

* * *

As I stepped from the restaurant, I saw the second reason for this being the worse day of my life. A ten-year-old Ford LTD sedan with unmatched tires and side panels peppered with rust parked in front of me. Yeah, there sat my new wheels.

I'd sold Baby.

I touched the pocket fat with cash and reminded myself of my much improved financial situation. I now had enough money to cover Dewey's bribe, give a little to Daisy, and pay my utility bills. But that knowledge did nothing to soothe my grief.

After I'd gotten over my early morning Archie-inspired crying jag, I made my way to Chin's Used Cars, where Daisy had made me an appointment. I wasn't in a negotiating mood, so I let those cheats give me fifteen thousand dollars for a car worth twice that.

I couldn't help it. Getting rid of Baby broke my heart. For the two weeks that I drove her, I lived the dream.

Most folks wouldn't understand. It's just an automobile, they'd say. But when you grow up hearing you're worthless, driving around in an expensive car made you feel like you were someone special.

I continued to soak in my guilt and self-pity, even as I met Daisy that evening. My sister appeared quite happy to see me. Why not? Still high from the news that Archie London had gotten his due and me with a wad of cash to share with her, why wouldn't she love seeing her stupid brother. My brain, however, stayed locked in on my troubles.

Daisy twice had to tell me to pay attention to her.

"Your meeting with Arbuckle on Monday is crucial," she said. "You have to crank up your aggression and scare her to death, you understand?"

"Yeah, I hear you."

I heard her, alright. But I had no enthusiasm for scaring the life out of Gloria Arbuckle, or anyone else. Either people laughed at me, or they died by mistake. Then again, maybe it wasn't a mistake. Archie had made me furious, absolutely furious. I *wanted* to kill him. Oh, Lord, what if I had done something so evil that my mind wouldn't admit to it? What if I'd slipped into a darker place and my instincts took over and I murdered him?

CHAPTER FORTY-FIVE

After all, didn't I kill Walter Lyle?

Chapter Forty-Six

An early morning rain had dampened the street, causing me to put my car into a one-eighty in front of Pressman & Sons Savings & Loans. I missed the parking lot entrance because the old Junker I drove had neither of Baby's traction nor sophisticated braking system.

Pressman & Sons Savings & Loans operated in one of those old buildings built when banks served as temples for the rich. The high ceilings made your neck crick from looking up, and the floors felt as slick as an ice pond.

I arrived to execute the next phase of Daisy's plan. She had me going into the bank wearing my meanest, tough guy face. She wanted me to soften up Gloria Arbuckle as part of her grand scheme to secure control of Eric's estate.

"Good morning, missy," I said to the young girl behind the counter. "I'd like a few moments with Miss Arbuckle."

The pixie-like blonde smiled and said, "Who may I say is calling?"

"Tommy Lyle."

Her eyes grew larger, and moisture misted her forehead. I guessed she'd heard of me being Daisy Pressman's brother.

"Uh, okay, Mr. Lyle, I'll let her know you're here."

"That'd be wonderful, doll."

Daisy had suggested I use Edward G. Robinson as my gangster role model. She made me watch one of his movies. I found it somewhat helpful, but I didn't like that for all of his tough guy talk he ended up dead.

I glanced around the reception area, drumming my fingers against the arm of the green upholstered guest chair. I thought about Daisy's desire to take over the bank. Maybe that wasn't such a stupid idea. Sure, she'd probably run it into the ground, but I bet she could make me a bank vice president until that happened. That would show those dudes at the shoe store.

"Ms. Arbuckle is ready to see you now."

I grinned and stood, giving the gal an air kiss. "Thanks a million, sweetheart."

She pointed toward an open office door, and I slowly walked over, stepping inside. Behind a desk the size of an aircraft carrier sat Gloria Arbuckle, dressed to the nines and smelling like peaches.

"Hello, Gloria," I said. "Can I call you, Gloria?"

The woman's eyelids drooped, and I heard a stream of annoyance shoot from her nostrils. "What do you want?"

I closed the door and sat down in the chair across from her.

"I have to tell you; you're making my sister miserable."

Gloria seemed unmoved.

"And a miserable Daisy Pressman can be dangerous."

"Ha, like I'm worried about that doormat."

I guessed Gloria had witnessed first-hand Eric's abuse of his wife. I should've told her how that so-called doormat twice heaved her boyfriend down the basement stairs.

"Maybe you're not worried about my sister, but Eric's mother is a whole different animal."

Arbuckle's flat face broke with a smile. She had beautiful teeth that must have cost a pretty penny. I wondered if Eric paid for them.

"I appreciate your interest in my welfare," she said. "But I've handled a few old battleaxes in my life."

"Oh, I'm sure you have," I said. "But Eleanor's more like one of those constrictor snakes that sneak up on you, wrapping their coils around your body and squeezing the life out of you."

The quiver of her mouth suggested she found my comment silly, but she still had to wonder why I proposed to help her. Or, at least Daisy figured she'd think that way. She suspected a manipulative sneak like Gloria always looked for an advantage.

"I've listened for twenty years about how Eleanor operates, and trust me; she isn't going to let you get away with controlling Eric's assets."

The woman shrugged her padded shoulders. "Let her try. Eric and I had some pretty smart estate lawyers write up that will."

"I'm sure you did. But that's where you don't know who you're dealing with here. Eleanor won't be going after you using the suits. She'd rather employ quicker and more painful means."

Gloria threw her head back as an eruption of laughter filled the room. When she finally stopped, a tear rolled down her left cheek.

"You have to be kidding," she said. "Is that supposed to scare me?"

"I don't know what scares you, honey, but I'm telling you, you'd better listen to me."

"And why, might I ask, are you making it your mission to be so helpful?"

I leaned on my elbow and swung my right leg over my knee, my foot rapidly bobbing in the air.

"Don't fool yourself into thinking Eleanor wants my sister to have one cent of that family money. She'll go after her when she finishes with you. I figured you and me might want to work as a team. You know, two heads are better than one."

She again laughed, only louder.

"From what Eric used to say about you, it'd be more like a head and a quarter teaming up."

I felt the blood rushing to my face and my jaw grinding my molars. All the sting from my brother-in-law's past insults came roaring back. So she and Eric got off laughing about me, huh?

"You better watch yourself," I said. "If you think you can handle Eleanor Pressman without my help, you're in for a lot of hurt."

Gloria leaned to the side and struggled to keep from giggling.

"Are we done here? I have a job to do."

Crap. My threats must've sounded like something you'd hear from a novice in a nunnery.

I walked from the office to my car without the same bounce I felt the other night after visiting Mrs. Pressman. If Daisy thought Gloria Arbuckle would scare easily, she had it wrong. That woman was hard as an airport runway. It would take something more than me talking about Eleanor's nasty side to frighten her. She'd have to experience it.

Chapter Forty-Seven

Eleanor Pressman lived in a condo in the best part of town. It was the sort of location that a homicide detective like me seldom visited. Rich people tended to do bloodless crimes.

After her greeting, the woman directed me into her living room. Joanie would've thought the room's decorations haughty and foreign. She liked stuff made in the good old USA from a hundred years ago.

"So you're the detective that's supposedly working Eric's murder case."

I quickly realized that none of my patent-pending charming behaviors would work with that woman. Not that I felt like being charismatic.

"I'm doing everything possible to make a determination," I said. "So, I appreciate you talking to me."

Mrs. Pressman's cheeks flapped as she shook her head. "I can save you the time and trouble. I'm positive that Eric's wife and her despicable brother caused his death."

"Can you tell me why you suspect your son's death was anything more than an accident?"

The woman reared back, apparently insulted by the question.

"I'm his mother. A mother knows those things."

Now I'm a big fan of mothers. Mine was a saint, let me tell you. Joanie was a great mom to our kid. But sometimes you had to recognize that they weren't always objective about their offspring.

"That's good to know," I said, scribbling her words into my notepad. I wanted to be sure I accurately recorded her remark. I'd share it with the guys at my retirement party. That should be good for some laughs.

But I knew of one issue that wouldn't get me any laughs.

"How was the funeral?"

Eleanor stiffened. "Other than the horrible embalming they did on my son's body, it was a grand affair. The turnout was incredible."

"So, you saw your son in the casket?"

"Yes, it was a hideous preparation. No mother should have to see something like that."

I leaned in toward her. "And you witnessed the casket loaded into the hearse."

"Yes, they pushed it out ahead of us."

"And you saw the casket lowered into the ground?"

Mrs. Pressman looked at me as if I'd spoken Chinese, and I didn't blame her for being confused. "Of course, I saw it lowered into the ground. Three hundred other people also witnessed it."

Okay, another person countering Daisy Pressman's assertion that her husband had been cremated.

"I wanted to be sure I knew everything," I said. "I owed that to you and your son."

Usually, when I fed that line to the bereaved, they at least mumble a few words of gratitude. Not Mrs. Pressman. She crossed her arms and grunted. Now I better understood Daisy Pressman's attitude toward her mother-in-law. The woman chilled me like a cold February wind on the Jersey Shore.

"You should focus not on Eric's burial but his murder," she said, moving closer to me, her hand touching my arm. "I know that woman and her brother killed my son. I just know it."

I crossed my arms and squinted.

"I must say I'm a little confused, Mrs. Pressman. I have a witness who'll testify that Tommy Lyle stopped by your building two nights ago."

I don't claim to know the nature of time, but I'd swear the world stopped moving forward for a solid ten seconds. Mrs. Pressman sat frozen, her eyes open and glaring at me.

"Could you explain why a man you feel had a hand in killing your son would pay you a visit at ten o'clock at night?"

She huffed as if I'd insulted her. Based on years of catching people in lies, I knew she just bought herself time to gin up a plausible answer. I looked forward to hearing it.

"You don't think I know how this town works?" she finally said. "You believe you'd be working my son's case if I wasn't wealthy?"

I couldn't argue with her, so I kept my mouth shut.

"Somehow word got out that my finances were locked up by my son's trustee. Guess what? I can't get the mayor or the Chief to return my calls."

"I'm sorry to hear that," I said. "But how does that explain Lyle showing up at your door?"

"If no one in your department is taking me seriously, then I'll do what I have to do to get justice."

I asked her how doing business with a creep like Tommy Lyle would achieve her objective. She said she thought, with the right incentives, she could get him to confess. She must've thought I just came off the boat from Bologna or someplace. A woman with her life experiences didn't believe in confession. She had something going on she didn't want to share with me.

"Keep in mind that Lyle may come across as a dimwitted clown," I said, "but he's dangerous."

Mrs. Pressman gave me a tight little smile and stood. I guessed she no longer cared to chat with me.

"Please don't play detective. Let me do my job. You'll be safer."

"I'm counting on you to do your job." She turned to lead me to the front door. "But I'm not waiting around for miracles to happen."

* * *

Returning to the precinct building, I made my way to Tiny Baker's office. I thought he'd want to hear about my visit with Eleanor Pressman. It had been nearly a half-hour since I left her condo, and I still couldn't believe what I heard. That case kept getting more tangled with each passing day.

"Hey, boss, you have a minute?"

CHAPTER FORTY-SEVEN

Baker waved me in. "What's up."

I gave him a two-minute summary of the Eric Pressman investigation. He didn't react like I thought he might. He wasn't curious as to why Mrs. Pressman might be hobnobbing with Tommy Lyle.

"I was at HQ a few days ago," he told me. "I saw the chief and brought up your efforts. He laughed it off. No one seems to care anymore."

"What do you mean, no one cares? I have enough unanswered questions to justify further scrutiny."

Baker hunched his shoulders. "You just reported your number one suspect and the mother of the victim were hanging out. It looks like you were right from the start. This case is nothing more than rich people trying to use us to settle their fight over money."

"I don't know if that's true."

Tiny's eyes narrowed as he tried to read me. Then he grinned. "Hey, don't worry about not earning your paycheck. I'll find something else to keep you busy."

I tapped the doorframe with my fist while chewing my inner cheek. Part of me wanted to thank the boss for relieving me of the Pressman case. If upper management no longer cared, why should I? Then I thought about Eleanor's comment. Once the big shots learned she'd gone broke, they stopped taking her calls. That didn't set right with me.

But still, I only had ten days left on the county's payroll. Maybe I should let it go.

"Seriously, Bongi, I want you to drop it."

"But, I think there's more there, a lot more."

Baker gave me an open-mouth smile. "Hey, isn't your party soon? How's that coming along?"

I turned away without answering. I didn't care about a farewell party, not after being jerked around. My mood didn't get better when I found Brutkowski at my desk.

"Hey, Bongi, you got a second?"

"What's up? You got another surprise for me?"

Of course, the big man did share a new twist. He told me Lyle's BMW started moving in the morning, and the GPS Tracker had it eventually parked at Chin's Used Cars. Even though he had hours before starting his shift, Brutkowski investigated. The salesman shared the details of Tommy Lyle's transaction. Daisy Pressman had signed over the title, and Tommy drove off the lot in an eight hundred dollar used car and fifteen grand in his pocket.

"Sounds like he needed the cash," I offered as an explanation.

Brutkowski's hands started shaking. "Here's the kicker," he said. "When they cleaned out the BMW, they found a trash bag in the trunk full of used paper towels, all dried in blood."

Wow, that did sound intriguing. Nonetheless, I quickly stuffed my surge of enthusiasm. Why should I care Tommy Lyle carried bloody rags in his car? Tiny told me to shut down the investigation, and that's what I'd do.

I looked up at Brutkowski and said, "Well, that's something, isn't it?"

The man shuffled his feet. I guessed he expected more of a reaction from me. I fired up the computer on my desk and turned away from him. "I have a report to finish. You'll have to excuse me."

Brutkowski didn't take the hint to leave me alone. "How'd your visit go with Mrs. Pressman?"

I sucked in some air and blew it out loudly. "The old gal isn't who you thought she was."

"What do you mean?"

I described my conversation with Eleanor. When I mentioned that she'd *invited* Lyle to visit, Brutkowski's mouth dropped open. You could've parked a truck on his tongue.

"Maybe I should give her a call," he said. "That seems so out of character for her."

I slammed the desktop with an open palm. "Leave Pressman alone, damn it, it's not your job."

Brutkowski's face flushed. I sensed others in the room looking our way. "Damn it, Brute. Baker told me to shut it down."

The officer nodded. "Yes, sir, I hear you."

Brutkowski knocked aside a four-drawer filing cabinet as he rushed out. When I looked around the office, heads turned away from me. Pounding on the keyboard only frustrated me further. My fat fingers punched multiple keys at once, messing up whatever I'd written. I let fly a stream of obscenities.

Falling back in my chair, I buried my face in my hands. So that's how I'm going out, shit-canning my suspicions and blowing up a young guy who wanted to do the right thing? I'd hit rock bottom.

Maybe I should take sick leave until my retirement date so that I could stay away from people. And screw any party. I just wanted to leave New Jersey and everything associated with it. I wanted to disappear from the face of the earth.

Chapter Forty-Eight

D aisy surprised me when she didn't rip me for failing to intimidate Gloria Arbuckle. She said it had been only the first move and not to worry. What she had me doing later today counted a lot more. That's just what I needed, more pressure.

"Now you have to pay attention, Tommy. This next task is critically important."

"Okay, okay, I'm not some dunderhead."

My sister handed me a sheet of paper, the front side covered with a typed message.

"This is the Apology Letter. You need to get Eleanor to sign it."

"Okay."

She held up the second sheet of paper.

"This is the Screw You Letter."

I nodded, even though I had no clue what she meant.

The third item she showed me was a tissue-thin grey-colored sheet. "Here is a piece of tracing paper."

Daisy laid out what I needed to do. Go over to Eleanor's place, have her sign the Apology Letter, and then transfer her signature to the Screw You letter. Once that's done, fax the nasty-gram off to Gloria Arbuckle.

"It's pretty simple, actually," Daisy said. "All you need to do is get Eleanor's signature and you're good to go."

I swiveled my head, trying to loosen my neck muscles. The task wasn't overly complicated, but I could see how any one part could go wrong. What if she didn't want to sign the letter? What if I messed up tracing her signature? What if I faxed the wrong letter?

I guessed my sister saw a fearful look on my face because she insisted on walking me through the steps two more times.

"You can do this, Tommy. I'm counting on you."

I swallowed on a dry throat and mumbled, "I hope so."

I guess maybe she had good reason to treat me like a dunderhead.

* * *

An hour later, I again occupied a chair in Eleanor Pressman's condominium. She sat next to me, her legs crossed and her arms wrapped around her body. She'd shared what she'd learned about Arbuckle's habits. Gloria arrived at the bank early and stayed late. She took the weekend off, apparently going to the beach house at Point Pleasant Beach.

"Okay, that's good to know," I said, even though the thought of that woman enjoying my favorite place on earth irritated me.

"Now listen up because I'm about to kick off my plan."

Eleanor's eyebrows pulled together. She seemed more skeptical than curious.

"But before I do, we need to make sure nothing gets traced back to you."

Eleanor gently nodded as she appeared to mull my words. A thin smile formed. "Okay, I think that's a good idea, a very good idea."

Just as Daisy predicted, her ex-mother-in-law's powerful instinct for self-preservation had kicked in. Hopefully, it should be easier to slip something by her.

I pulled Daisy's Apology Letter from a folder and handed it to Mrs. Pressman.

"That's a letter to Arbuckle that I typed up and need you to sign."

The woman read it, her face collapsing into a snarl by the time she finished.

"So you want me to say that since she and I both deeply cared about Eric, it would be only natural that we'd be closer?"

"Right, you're reaching out."

"And you want me to admit that I behaved poorly toward her because of

205

my emotional distress."

I nodded. "We're showing your human side."

"And this last part says since Eric loved her so much, I wanted to have the sort of relationship I never had with his wife."

"That's right. This will serve as evidence of your goodwill, so when I apply the old maximum pressure on Arbuckle, even she won't think you had anything to do with it."

Eleanor chilled me with a stare. I held my breath as she chewed the inside of her mouth.

"I won't sign this."

My heart fluttered. That wasn't a good thing. Right out of the gate, and I'd stumbled.

"Why?"

"The grammar you used is atrocious. I'd never write something so poorly structured."

Daisy had given me a few worse-case possibilities and how to respond, but that wasn't one of them. My brain scrambled to think of a way to get Eleanor's signature on that paper.

"Well, feel free to correct anything, and then…uh, sign it, okay."

"That would be too messy." Mrs. Pressman went over to a desk and pulled out several sheets of paper.

"I'll compose the letter using my personal stationery."

Oh nuts, I couldn't let her do that.

"That won't work."

Eleanor huffed. "Why not? Using my stationery will make it look more authentic."

Maybe the woman had a good point, but that stationary wouldn't do. It looked as thick as a pizza crust. I'd never be able to cleanly transfer Eleanor's signature to the Screw You Letter.

"That's a big problem," I blurted out. "That's not gonna work."

Eleanor glared at me. She didn't say anything, but the look on her face demanded I provide an explanation. Unfortunately, I didn't have one, at least not until I remembered my time faxing orders to shoe manufacturers.

"I need to fax your letter to Arbuckle and your stationary would jam up the fax machine."

"Why can't you use the postal service to deliver it?"

"Because, when we fax it, the device prints verification that it was received, as well as a photocopy of what you sent."

"Why is that important?"

"After I make Gloria's pain intolerable, she might try and pin it on you. If the police investigate, you'll have physical evidence that she received your letter making amends. She can't deny you hadn't tried to make nice-nice."

I felt my gut twist another notch. Hearing me explain the reason we needed the faxed letter made it all sound so weak. Eleanor had some brains, after all. I didn't care if Daisy thought the old gal's sense of self-protection would override her common sense.

Eleanor covered her mouth with her hand as she hummed.

"Alright, I understand," she finally said. "I like that approach."

Man, oh man, did Daisy know that woman or not?

"But I must say I'm embarrassed to send such a poorly composed letter. No one would believe I wrote it."

"How about we do this," I said as I flipped over the Apology Letter. "Write your version on the other side, and I'll fax that image to Gloria. Will that make you happy?"

Apparently it did because she sat down at the desk and started to work. I think my heart started beating again when I heard Eleanor say, "There, finished. Now, what do we do?"

"I noticed the lobby had a small business center. Could you call them and ask if they have a fax machine?"

Mrs. Pressman might've thought it lucky that her building had a fax available for residents' use. But I knew the equipment existed there, having caught sight of it during my first visit.

I didn't stop sweating until I got down to the business center, transferred Eleanor's signature to the Screw You Letter, and successfully faxed it to Gloria Arbuckle, in care of Pressman & Son's Savings & Loan.

I smiled, thinking how Gloria might get knocked back a bit, reading

Eleanor's promise of making life miserable and darkly hinting that bad things would happen to her. I doubted she'd notice the poor grammar.

Chapter Forty-Nine

At midnight, with no moon and the clouds blocking out the stars, I waited for Dewey. That's how he wanted it. He preferred moving in the shadows.

I stood at the base of the 5th Street Bridge, as we agreed. The structure crossed over an abandoned channel of the Passaic River that used to flow through town. The street running atop the bridge had little traffic that late at night.

Dewey also suggested it as a meeting point, so he would only have to wobble about a quarter-mile from his favorite saloon. I hadn't seen the dude since his late-night surprise visit to my house, but his phone calls bothered me. God only knew what condition he'd show up in.

The yellow light spreading out from the single operating street lamp gave me enough illumination to catch the uneven movements of someone walking in the middle of the road.

"What are you doing?" I said when the person got within a hundred feet, close enough for me to recognize Dewey. "Get out of the street, you moron."

"Why are you late?" Leo shouted, his words garbled as if he had a mouthful of marbles. "I've been looking all over for you."

"I got here on time. You're the one who's late."

He mumbled a bunch of sozzled nonsense and I understood enough to realize he'd ended up at the wrong bridge. The idiot must have been stumbling around for an hour. How could I trust that guy? His drinking had gotten out of control.

"Come on, Dewey, let's get out from underneath this street light," I said.

I grasped his right arm and pushed him along the pedestrian walkway toward the center of the span. The overhead lights at that spot had been vandalized, and the darkness would give us some privacy to make our transaction. I didn't need some patrol cop driving by and seeing the county medical examiner taking a bribe.

"Come on, walk across the bridge with me."

Dewey pulled against me, but I had the momentum, and we stumbled forward. "Where's my money?" he said. "Do you have my money?"

I patted my jacket. "I got it here."

"You better have it all. You better not cheat me."

I slipped my left hand under his armpit to steady him. I'd never seen anyone so smashed. I wondered what had triggered tonight's binge drinking.

"What happened today? You seem upset."

"They ganged up on me," he answered, the words slurred. "They're going after me."

"Who's going after you?"

Leo's ankle gave way, and he tilted hard to the left, his shoulder striking the bridge railing. I pulled him upright and repeated my question.

"Tell me who's going after you?"

"Washington, she hates me."

Now, what did that mean? I pulled on his lapel, drawing him closer.

"Who's Washington?"

Dewey stepped backward, halted, and burped.

"You're not throwing up, are you?" I asked.

"Nope, nope, nope," he replied, restarting his forward movement, my hand pinched on his upper arm.

"So tell me about this Washington woman. Why was she going after you?"

"She gave me my performance review. She wants me fired. She, she hates me."

"Why does she hate you, Leo?"

I could come up with a dozen reasons why anyone would despise Leo Dewey. But did they give him a lousy job performance rating because they hated him? I sure hoped it wasn't because of a death investigation that occurred at my house.

"Are they looking into any of your recent cases?" I asked. "Like Eric Pressman, maybe?"

Dewey raised his hand and pointed to the wire mesh covering the railing. "I need to stop. I'm going to piss myself."

Oh Lord, halfway across a bridge in the dead of night and I stood with an enfeebled man, as he took a wiz. I couldn't believe I'm giving that dude five thousand dollars to keep his mouth shut.

"Hang on, man," I said. "Get across the bridge before you expose yourself."

Modesty wasn't on Dewey's addled brain.

"Where's my money?" he said, clawing at my jacket.

"I'll give it to you after you answer my questions. Is the department looking into Eric Pressman's death?"

"Yesh."

"Who's behind it?"

He looked me in the eye, bobbing to keep his balance. His index finger thumped me in the chest as he spoke.

"Bongi, Bongi wants to see my notes."

I grabbed Leo and shook him, ignoring his putrid body odor. "You told me your notes were locked up." I gave him another shake. "What the hell is going on?"

Leo's head stopped wobbling, and he bent forward, waggling his finger at me. "No, no, no, the real notes are in my lockbox. I gave them my unreal notes." He started giggling. "My unreal notes."

"Are you going to lose your job?"

"Not yet, but if I am, you, you have to pay me more."

I let go of his arms, and he fell back against the bridge railing. I could smell the urine that I suspected now soaked his pants. I couldn't believe I sold my beautiful car to buy the silence of this piece of human waste. And tonight would be just the second of endless monthly bribes until Leo Dewey passed from this earth.

Daisy had been right. We had to take care of our Leo problem, and the sooner we did, the better.

Chapter Fifty

I didn't like going into hospitals. Joanie had way too many visits to medical facilities that only prolonged her suffering. I'd never come into the sick ward without a good reason.

"I'm Detective Bongiovanni," I said and offered a smile to the nurse sitting at the desk. I'm a sucker for nurses. Who couldn't help but like an angel of mercy?

"How may I help you?"

"I'm here to see Leo Dewey."

"He's in room 18."

It had been two days since Tiny Baker closed down the official part of my Pressman investigation. I admit I was pissed without realizing it. My mind was such a swirl of fearfulness about my future that I both wanted to hang onto the Pressman case and drop it. I'd been grumpy, if not openly hostile to people, so no one told me about Leo Dewey until an hour ago.

"By the way," I said to the nurse, "Has anyone visited Mr. Dewey since he came in?"

"No, no one has been here."

I thanked her and quick-stepped down the hall, and tried not to peek into the open rooms. Who wanted to see sick people with their butts hanging out? The antiseptic smell was enough to make me feel nauseous.

Room 18 was at the end of the hallway. I rapped a knuckle on the door and walked in. A sleeping young man occupied the first bed. Both his arms were in plaster casts and strung from some contraption hooked to the ceiling.

I winced.

Dewey lay in the bed next to the window.

I winced again. He looked horrible.

"Hey, Leo, how you doing?"

"Who's there?" he said, his voice ragged and full of panic.

"It's Nick Bongiovanni. I'm here to find out what happened to you."

Dewey, half his face a deep purple smear of abrasions and contusions, moaned. He looked to be seriously hurting. I suspected alcohol withdrawal played a part in his turmoil. The poor bastard would probably not offer up much insight, but I wanted to try.

"What can you tell me about the other night?"

A sling restrained one of Dewey's arms, but that didn't prevent him from angrily tossing his head back. He started shouting. "No, no, don't do that."

"Don't do what?"

"Please don't," he repeated several times before drifting into a series of moans.

"Hang in there, Leo. Who's hurting you?"

He cried out. "Oh, sweet Jesus, stop it."

"Stop what, Leo? Tell me."

"It's that man with a monkey, momma."

Oh yeah, that's the kind of mental jumble I'd get from him. The man's mind would be spewing nonsense for who knows how long. Then again, what should I expect? They found him nearly drowned, bouncing up against the rocks along the river banks. Based on the busted arm, ribs, and cracked pelvis, Dewey must have gone off the bridge.

I dropped myself into a chair, figuring I should stick around in case he woke. I wondered if anyone from the Medical Examiner's office might send flowers or even a potted plant. Everyone assumed Dewey fell into the river. There'd be no investigation beyond the initial fact-gathering. No one but me thought differently.

"How's our patient doing?"

I looked up to see a nurse with a bucketful of medical gear walking into the room.

"He doesn't look too good to me," I said. "And he's not making any sense,

213

either."

A pair of ruby lips pulled taut across the woman's mouth. "Honestly, we were amazed he made it through the night."

I looked over at Dewey, small in the bed, the white sheets highlighting the copper tone of his skin. "I guess after decades of pickling himself with booze, his body might be immune to dying."

The nurse didn't appreciate my diagnosis.

"Your friend is in a lot of pain," she said, "both physically and psychologically."

I watched the nurse inject some drugs into a port embedded into Dewey's skinny bag of bones. She checked his vitals, murmuring the whole time.

"Have you been on the floor since he came in?"

She shook her head. "I've only been here since six this morning."

"Did you hear him say anything about what happened?"

The woman raised her eyes toward the ceiling, seemingly trying to flush any recollection from her memory. "He did mention a name, someone called Pressman. Otherwise, nothing but gibberish."

Well, isn't that something? Dewey dropped fifty feet off a bridge, smacks hard into the water, somehow keeps from drowning, struggles onto some rocks, is found by a homeless veteran with some scruples who alerts the police. And the only thing on his mind seemed to be Pressman.

"Do you care if I sit here for a while? I'd like to be here when he wakes up."

"Of course, you can stay. But it might be a long wait."

"I got the time."

And that fact disheartened me as well. Here, a week from retirement, and I'm back dogging some accidental death with too many loose ends.

God, why can't I let go of that ridiculous investigation?

I stood and bent over Dewey. "Hey, Leo, did Tommy Lyle do this to you?"

The man didn't say a word. He just whimpered with every breath. He looked pathetic, not much more than a stain on a bedsheet. Is that how it ends for Leo Dewey, delirious, in pain, and all alone?

My life might not end much better. In a few days, I'd be a non-contributing member of society. My brain, well-honed over years of work, would atrophy.

I didn't care how many crossword puzzles I did; my mind would get stale. Instead of putting criminals in jail and securing justice for the aggrieved, I'd be getting seasick, catching fish I'd never eat. I'd probably be one of those sad sacks pulling out his badge in secret and crying over his lost manhood.

"Damn it, Leo," I said. "Don't you wish you appreciated those good old days back when you were living them?"

I chuckled and shoved my depression back into the lockbox of my mind. I'd stay an hour, and if I got nothing, I'd leave. Maybe later today, I could find a sporting goods store open and pick up some fishing lures. Yeah, that'd be a better use of my time. I'd start focusing on the future instead of wasting my energy on all the pathetic losers like Dewey and Lyle.

I had to stop thinking about them. Sometimes it hit too close to home.

Chapter Fifty-One

I couldn't make up my mind. The Dominator looked like it could haul in a Great White Shark, while the Lucky Seven lure sparkled enough that I wanted to bite down on it. Heck, I'd get both of them. The fishing poles also demanded I at least try out half of them. I bought two of those as well. You know, fishing on the ocean might not be too bad. I mean, with all that beautiful gear, how could it not be fun?

That's when I thought of Joanie. I bet she'd raise Cain over me spending almost three hundred dollars on fishing equipment. I'd call it shopping therapy. She'd laugh because that was always her favorite excuse.

I checked out my purchases and walked through the parking lot when my cellphone rang.

"Nick Bongiovanni, here."

It was Shelia Washington calling to say Leo Dewey had died twenty minutes ago.

"That's too bad," I said, wanting to add that I'd failed to get any useful information from him. But I checked my impulse since Shelia seemed too upset to talk business.

"I feel terrible," she said. "I gave him a poor performance review *that* morning."

"I'm sure you were fair."

She tried to agree with me, but the huskiness in her voice suggested otherwise.

"I'm not far from the lab," I said. "Could you use a shoulder to cry on?"

"I'd appreciate that, Nick."

I clicked off the call, thinking I could be decent. I didn't have to be an ass all the time.

* * *

The drive from the shopping center back to the precinct building took thirty minutes. I entered and took the stairs down to the morgue. I found Sheila sitting outside Dewey's cubicle. Her glasses rested atop her head, and she bit on a knuckle, lost in thought.

"How are you doing, kid?"

Shelia went on for five minutes, recapping the foul-ups and unprofessional results that Leo Dewey had produced the past few years. I just nodded as she tried to convince herself that her negative evaluation had been warranted.

I walked past my despondent colleague and dumped my ample behind on Dewey's desktop. "He should've been forced into a program long before your promotion as his supervisor."

She sighed. "I know, I know."

"I mean, I suspected the accuracy of his work on the Pressman case. That alone should've put him on your shit list."

Her eyebrows climbed. "Do you mean the one with the fabric and odd blood pattern?"

"Yeah, and his out-of-office behavior caught my attention as well."

I hoped my testimony might've made her feel better. I think it did, for maybe two seconds.

"I know I was justified, but ten hours after I put him on probation, he jumped off a bridge."

"Oh, come on, you have no evidence that he purposely took a leap. The man was a notoriously unstable drunk. It was probably accidental."

"I suppose you're right," she said, mumbling into her hands. "But still, Dewey had no one in his life. I could've gone easier on him."

One of a million things Joanie taught me over our forty-two years of marriage applied to Shelia. If someone felt guilty, you couldn't convince them otherwise. You could only help by minimizing their self-inflicted beat down.

"You did the best you could, Sheila."

The woman exhaled loudly before returning to gnawing on her hand.

"Do you mind if I look at Dewey's files?" I asked. "I'd like to see if anything is relevant to my case."

Shelia shuddered. "Do you have to do that now?"

I understood why she thought I acted like an insensitive jerk. I mean, her colleague lay dead, barely cold, and here I wanted to clear out his office. But I didn't have the time, and maybe, I might find something that would tip my Pressman investigation one way or the other.

"I won't be long," I said, approaching Dewey's file cabinet. "I'm only interested in one of his investigations."

I quickly pulled the drawers and clawed through the files.

"I'll be quick."

"You know, Leo wasn't always bad at his job," Shelia said.

"You don't say."

I found one folder that belonged to the Archie London homicide. I should alert Chuckie. He wouldn't want that stuff getting lost in the transfer of duties.

"When I first started working here a decade ago," she said, "they held him in high regard."

I turned to the desk and slowly pulled open a drawer. I saw nothing but waste paper and odds tools of the trade.

"What happened to him?"

"His wife died after a long bout with cancer."

My head snapped up.

"I didn't know that."

Shelia rubbed her face with her hands. "First, he lost his wife, and then he was overwhelmed by the bottle. It was sad to watch."

A cold pinch of tension spread across my chest. Yeah, I suppose if anyone could relate to Dewey, it'd be me. But, damn it, just because we lost spouses to cancer didn't mean Leo and I belonged to some sort of brotherhood. I had a job to do, and so did he. You couldn't let your grief crush you.

"Ah, I'll do this later," I said, slamming the file drawers shut. "Come on. Let me buy you a drink."

Shelia shook her head. "I think I'll pass. Maybe I'll be in the mood at your farewell."

I grumbled. I wanted a drink now and not at some lame-ass retirement party.

"I got the memo yesterday," she said. "It's next Wednesday night, right?"

"Yeah, yeah, next Wednesday, I'll see you there, I guess."

I swallowed my disappointment and walked out of the room. I headed upstairs to the main level, thinking I'd get lucky and find someone more enthusiastic about being around me.

* * *

I heard the evening shift assembling as I climbed up from the precinct basement. I looked over at the rowdy men and women in blue, yelling and trash-talking each other. High above the heads and their tight haircuts, I recognized Brute.

I pushed my way through the crowd.

"Hey, Brute, how are you doing?"

Brutkowski saw me and turned away. "I'm good," he said as he clipped his radio's microphone to his shirt.

Oh crap, the big guy was still angry at me. I guess I couldn't blame him. I'd humiliated him in front of a room full of detectives.

"Do you have a minute?"

"Not really."

"It'll take less than a minute. I just wanted to know if you heard about Leo Dewey."

Brutkowski nodded. I stepped into his space and prevented him from completely ignoring me.

"I thought that Dewey, the mortician, Archie London, and Eric Pressman all had two things in common. They had recent interactions with Tommy Lyle, and they're all dead."

Brutkowski laid a pair of dead eyes on me as the words crawled out of his mouth, "That's so interesting."

Damn, the big palooka had the sensitivities of a schoolgirl.

"Come on, Brute. I was having a bad day when I blew up at you."

"My shift's starting," the officer said as he stepped away. "Good evening, Detective Bongiovanni."

As Brutkowski pushed his way through the crowd, I wanted to shout at him, ask him if he planned to come to my farewell party. But I knew it'd sound desperate and pitiful, and I thought it would destroy what little respect Brute still had for the legendry Nick Bongiovanni.

Chapter Fifty-Two

Eleanor Pressman sounded furious. She screamed at me over the phone with an animal vigor.

"I can't believe it. That Arbuckle woman is now demanding an audit of my jewelry."

"What?" was all I could get out before she tore me a new one.

"Is this how your so-called plan is supposed to work, Mr. Lyle? I send a letter asking for reconciliation, and that beast turns on me."

"Gloria isn't going to come around at first," I said. "You gotta be patient."

"Patient, did you say patient? She's ruining my life. You have to do something about her."

Daisy had predicted Gloria would react aggressively to the Screw You Letter. She might've thought it would take a less brutal form than an audit of a woman's jewelry, but she wouldn't be surprised.

"I intend to meet with Arbuckle very soon," I said. "All I need from you and your source is the time Gloria leaves to go to the beach house."

I listened to Eleanor rant for another five minutes before she exhausted herself.

"Call me as soon as you know Gloria's departure for the shore. Got it?"

The older woman whimpered. "Yes."

I hung up and dialed Daisy.

"Gloria didn't react well to the Screw You Letter. Once again, you called it."

My sister chuckled. She loved hearing me brag about her instinct for people's behavior. She saw it as part of the Lyle DNA, honed by our parents' decades-long criminal activity. I had none of those instincts. I never knew how people would act. Heck, I never would've predicted a few weeks ago that I'd have a hand in not one but two murders.

"Come on over so we can rehearse your visit with Arbuckle," she said. "I think we're close to pulling the trigger on this thing."

My heart thumped, hearing Daisy talking about pulling a trigger. I calmed when she put it another way, saying we needed only one more step to finish the job. That made me smile. I'd be relieved when my sister got her share of Eric's fortune and no longer messed with people and made them bleed.

* * *

The drive down to the Jersey shore was a nightmare. Being a Friday, the roads had been jammed for hours, filled with city folks trying to take advantage of the last days of summer. Eleanor called that afternoon with a tip. Our friendly trustee had left the bank early for the beach house. She should be there when I arrived, hopefully with her guard down and a few drinks in her system.

I pulled into the driveway, maybe nine-thirty, if you believed the clock on the Junker's dash. I saw Arbuckle's sedan. I pulled out my cell phone and dialed up the number for the landline in the house. I stayed there enough times to have it memorized.

Looking up through the Great Room's curtained window, I saw a figure approach the counter where the phone sat. The person didn't answer, letting it ring out. I guessed Gloria wouldn't pick up the call because anyone she knew would've used her wireless number.

I redialed. This time she answered.

"Hello," she said in a whisper.

"Hi, Gloria, this is Tommy Lyle."

"What...what do you want?"

The disgust in her voice irritated me. Not that I expected her to be excited, but still, I had feelings.

"I wanted to know if you'd given any thought to our partnership."

"No."

"Has Mrs. Pressman started her harassment? Are you seeing strange dudes hanging around the bank's parking lot and at your condo?"

She said nothing.

"It's okay to be scared. My sister suffered the same treatment while married to Eric. Eleanor tormented her for years."

Again, Arbuckle gave no response. I knew she hadn't hung up because I heard her breathing.

"The only reason Daisy survived was that her husband finally demanded his mother stop. Unfortunately for you, you don't have Eric around to protect you."

Gloria finally responded. "What do you really want?"

I drew in a lungful of salt air to settle my nerves. I had to be persuasive because I needed Gloria to let me into the beach house. She'd probably want to keep me on the phone, maybe talk through an opened door. But I had to be inside so I could see her face and she could see mine. I needed to be sure she got my message.

"I'd be able to explain things better if we could do a sit-down."

"I can't," she said. "I'm not in town."

"I know."

"I'm not going to be back until Monday."

"That's not a problem," I said. "I'm parked right outside the beach house."

Her voice jumped from calm to angry. "Have…have you been following me?"

"No, honey, I knew how to get here. Let me in so I can give you some good advice."

"Leave me alone, you moron."

Gloria and I went back and forth. She made threats, I countered with my own. I tried to scare her. She found bravery. This wasn't going as I hoped. No way was she going to let me into that beach house.

I switched to my back-up plan when she hung up on me.

Climbing out of my car, I walked over to the side of the house. Under a giant fiberglass frog, I found the house key that Eleanor had told me about.

DO IT FOR DAISY

It fit perfectly into the lower level back door. I entered and climbed upstairs, the carpeting muffling my footsteps. Halfway up, I pulled the pistol from my waistband.

Arbuckle's head snapped sideways when I said, "Good evening, Gloria."

She looked indignant and then frightened, probably mad that I got into the house. I guessed having a gun pointed at her head scared her as well. Whatever, now inside, I had to talk some sense into her.

"It's very important that you listen to me, Gloria. I'm only going to say this once."

Chapter Fifty-Three

Gloria Arbuckle sat in a white wicker chair in the middle of the Great Room. I stood over her and tried to build upon the sense of menace the gun gave me.

"Can I pour you a drink?" I said.

She squinted at me, her fingers tightly interlocked, her shoulders hunched. "I don't want a drink."

"You'll have one anyway," I said. "Tell me the code to Eric's liquor cabinet."

Arbuckle did as I asked. A minute passed, and she had in her hands a tumbler half full of one of Eric's better scotch. She still looked as put together as when I last saw her at the bank. I could see why Eric fell for her.

I sat across from her and placed the .38 caliber snub-nosed on top of the small table between us. It wasn't the same weapon I used with Archie London. That thing rested at the bottom of some pond. Daisy had pulled this one from her surprisingly large gun collection.

"I have some disturbing news for you," I said. "Mrs. Pressman has contracted a hired killer to make you disappear."

Her mouth twisted to one side. "How do you know that?"

"I know that because I'm the guy she hired."

Gloria's eyebrows pulled above the bridge of her nose.

"I know for a fact that Eleanor hates you and your sister. I don't believe you're working with that old hag."

I picked up the pistol and aimed it toward her chest.

"Did you or did you not get a nasty fax from Mrs. Pressman, one threatening to hurt you if you didn't ease off?"

Gloria licked her lips. I could tell she struggled hard with that bit of info. She had to wonder how I knew about Eleanor's letter. It took less than a second for her to figure out the obvious conclusion.

"I'll increase your sister's stipend," she said. "I'll give Daisy an extra five hundred dollars a month."

"That's not what I want, so listen up."

"Okay, okay, I think I can get her a thousand. It may take a little longer."

"Stop talking, Gloria, and listen to what I have to say."

I moved the gun barrel closer to her heart.

But she kept on yacking. "Maybe I can guarantee her a bigger profit share from selling the bank."

The rage rose from my gut and exploded out of my mouth. "Shut up and listen to me."

Gloria's hands jumped to her face.

Damn it, why'd she push me? Why do people act like I don't mean what I'm saying? She's behaving the same way as Archie London did, not taking me seriously.

"My sister suffered for the twenty years being married to Eric. He mistreated his mother, as well. They feel they deserve *all of* Eric's fortune because they *earned it*."

I pulled back the hammer of the gun. Gloria flinched. My hand shook, which must've added to her anxiety.

"You did nothing other than sleep with Eric, which, I have to admit, must've been horrible. But, you have no business managing how and when his wife and mother get their money."

Gloria's eyelids fluttered.

"Mrs. Pressman wants me to turn you into a piece of driftwood floating in the ocean. But my sister is willing to give you a chance to keep living, you hear me?"

The woman's hair bobbed up and down as she nodded.

"Daisy wants you to quit as a trustee and move on voluntarily."

A little color started returning to Arbuckle's complexion. I figured a grifter like her saw through my bluff, and killing her wasn't my preferred way to go.

"She's willing to give you severance pay for your troubles, something like fifty thousand. You got that?"

Arbuckle two-handed the glass of scotch and swallowed it all in three gulps.

"Yes, I *got* that."

Maybe the shot of whiskey stiffened her backbone, but the woman's mood changed at that moment. She stared at me, just like Eleanor and that detective did, trying to decide whether to take me seriously or not. My heart thumped harder. Good thing I had Daisy's script memorized, or else I'd probably sputtered into silence.

"We want a letter of resignation in the hands of the estate lawyer on Monday, you understand?"

Gloria's eyes narrowed. She straightened her back and lifted her chin.

"And if I decide not to play along, what happens?"

I jumped up with the pistol raised over Arbuckle's head and started yelling, "Don't mess with me, Gloria. That's a big mistake."

The woman didn't even flinch.

"Now answer me, do you understand what you're going to do on Monday?"

Gloria's lips thinned over her teeth. "Yes, Mr. Lyle, I understand. Now would you please leave?"

I stepped back, feeling uneasy. The woman looked too relaxed. At least I had Archie shaking in his shoes when I threatened him. Gloria appeared bored like I'd been a bank customer asking her to cash in my pile of nickels.

"Okay, I'm glad you got the message."

Her mouth puckered at its corners.

"You'd better do it," I said, taking a step back, waving the gun barrel at her. "I'm not kidding around, Gloria."

That's when all hell broke loose as the heel of my shoe snagged the area rug, and I fell hard on my ass, cracking my head against a pole lamp. The gun flew from my hand, skittering across the floor and stopping at Gloria's feet. She picked it up and aimed it at me.

"A man breaks into my house, threatens my life, and I shoot him," she said.

"I think that's a pretty good story."

Then she started laughing her high-pitched, snooty laugh.

Tears formed in my eyes and my skin felt hot. I didn't know what hurt more, my body from the fall or my sense of humiliation. I'm such an idiot. Could I screw this up anymore? Daisy wouldn't forgive me if I didn't scare Arbuckle into quitting.

I slowly moved to my knees and stood, rubbing the bump rising on the back of my head.

"Give me the gun," I said as I stepped toward Arbuckle. "Come on."

She pulled back.

"I said, give me the gun."

The woman's stern expression broke with a grin. "This thing isn't loaded, is it?"

Damn, Gloria got it right. I'd removed the rounds before I entered the house. I wasn't going to repeat what happened with Archie. There'd be no one getting murdered tonight.

"I'm going to pull the trigger," she said in a sing-song voice, "You better watch out."

"Give me back my gun."

I grabbed the gun barrel and jerked the weapon from her hand. She fell to one side, cackling. "You are such a fraud. Get the hell out of here before I call the police."

"You better do what I said, I swear."

"Tell your sister and her mother-in-law to start looking for cheaper digs because I'm evicting them from those palaces."

I raised the gun butt in the air like a hammer.

"I mean it, Gloria."

The woman spat on the floor. "Get out of here, you moron."

A red hot rage exploded in my brain. Walter Lyle always called me a moron. He loved using that slam.

I started screaming at her.

"So you think I'm a moron, do you? Let me tell you how Eric died. His skull was split open like a cantaloupe. There were blood and brains up and down the stairs. His legs were almost twisted backward."

Arbuckle didn't look cocky anymore.

"Do you think he ended up like that from accidentally falling down the stairs?" I roared, "Well, do you?"

The woman leaned back into her seat, her eyes big and unblinking.

"You may think I'm a clown," I said, my hands trembling, "and you may think my sister is a pushover, but we killed your damn boyfriend. And we're going to get away with it."

Arbuckle's jaw started quivering.

"I'm not so funny now, am I? Laugh at me one more time, and I'll smash your face."

That pretty much ended the conversation. I took the stairs to the back door, got into my car, and sped away. For a second, I worried Gloria might regain her attitude and call the Point Pleasant police. But what would she tell them? She had no bruises or busted furniture to show off. What proof did she have that I ever had been there?

Hopefully, the vision of Eric's cracked skull and broken back would shut her up for good. Maybe knowing she was dealing with people capable of murder would be enough to get her to give up everything and leave town.

Damn her for making me get all crazy.

My anger cooled by the time I drove the thirty minutes to reach the Metedeconk River. That's when tears rolled down my cheeks, and prayers fell from my mouth. I couldn't clear my mind of Gloria's face when I went off on her. She acted like she saw a monster standing in front of her.

Oh, Mandy, please show me the way.

Chapter Fifty-Four

It had to be well past midnight when I pulled up to Daisy's house. She'd rung my phone several times on the way over from Point Pleasant, but I didn't answer. I felt too upset to both drive and tell her I no longer would play the thug again.

"Damn it, Tommy, why didn't you call me?" was her greeting as she opened the front door. She jumped when I shouted back, telling her to leave me alone. My tears also must've convinced her I needed gentle handling.

"Okay, tell me what happened," she said, leading me into the living room.

So I told her what happened, mostly.

Yes, Arbuckle looked frightened when I showed up and pointed a gun at her face.

I didn't mention how she eventually realized it wasn't loaded.

I told Daisy how the woman trembled in fear, sparing the detail of how she later shook with laughter.

My sister nodded when I told her how I laid out our expectations. If Gloria wanted to live, she'd quit her job and move on.

"I was clear, and trust me," I said, "she got the message."

"Did you give her the deadline?"

"Absolutely. I said no later than Monday."

"Good job, Tommy," she said, stroking my arm. "I know it wasn't easy for you."

I leaned my head onto her shoulder. It felt nice to have her comfort me for once. Of course, I doubted she'd be so compassionate, knowing how I'd tripped over my feet and almost knocked myself silly and how Arbuckle ended up pointing the gun at my face.

"How much did you tell her she could take?"

"Fifty."

"You should've said twenty if she was shaking in her shoes."

I knew it. I *knew* Daisy wouldn't resist pointing out how I fell short.

"I don't think so," I said, determined to defend myself. "Even with a gun on her, she was pretty fierce."

Daisy's mouth went crooked, and her head tilted to one side.

"You did scare her, right?"

"Yeah, I sure did."

My gaze followed the seam of my pant leg down to the floor, where I focused on the carpet pattern. I didn't want to look at my sister. I knew she'd root around inside my head and force me to tell the truth.

"Can I go now?" I asked.

My effort to deflect Daisy's mindreading abilities failed.

"Tommy, what aren't you telling me?"

I pulled my head into my shoulders and rubbed my hands on my thighs.

"I...I think I messed up."

Daisy bent her head back and noisily sucked in air.

"What does that mean?"

"Arbuckle, well, at the end, she didn't seem that scared, and I worried that she'd, you know, not follow through. So that made me mad, really angry, you know."

Daisy crossed her arms and drilled me with a heated stare.

"And then she laughed at me, so I told her how messed up Eric looked after his fall. I wanted her to have an idea, you know, a picture of what I could do."

"I don't understand," Daisy said, her voice crackling like a lit fuse. "Surely, you didn't admit to pushing Eric down the stairs?"

"No, no, no," I said, my head vibrating. "But I think I might've mentioned that, that, that his fall wasn't an accident."

Daisy bent at the waist, profanity riding the air she expelled through her grinding teeth.

DO IT FOR DAISY

"I'm sorry," I said. "Don't be mad."

The shrillness of my sister's voice twisted my nerves even tighter. She explained how I'd handed Arbuckle a weapon that she could use to ruin us. Best case, the woman might team up with Eleanor and completely cut out Daisy. In the worse situation, she tells the police, offering to serve as a witness and give that damn detective an excuse to dig up Eric's body.

"You screwed me, Tommy. You truly let me down."

I started sobbing, and the tears spritzed into the air.

"I'm sorry, Daisy, you know I'm not good at that kind of stuff."

My sister snorted. "Yeah, sure, you're a snowflake."

"I told you I couldn't hurt people. You knew that."

Daisy hooted, "Give me a break. You had no problem getting Walter and Mabel killed."

I twisted away from her. My hands balled into fists. "Stop it."

"Oh no, little Tommy had no trouble doing that."

"I was ten years old."

"Yeah, yeah, you were a kid. But you still had the guts to call the police. You knew they'd send an army after they heard your little story."

"That's not fair."

It *wasn't* fair. I didn't know the police would react the way they did. I didn't want them to shoot up the house, to kill Walter and Mabel. I just wanted them arrested and sent away so they couldn't keep hurting me.

"I needed protection."

Daisy huffed. "You were angry, and it was Walter and Mabel who needed protection."

"Stop it. I was a scared little kid."

"You had enough backbone that day to trick the cops into coming to the house fully armed."

"That's not true," I said. "Stop lying."

"You triggered the shootout by firing the gun through the window. You knew the cops would overreact if someone started shooting from the house."

Daisy lied. That wasn't how it happened. I'd called the police that afternoon after Walter beat me. I said I was in danger, and I was. I mentioned that they had lots of guns in the house and that my folks hated cops, but I didn't shoot any weapon.

No, Daisy had it wrong.

Maybe I had a gun in my hands when the police arrived, but I didn't pull the trigger. Not on purpose. It was an accident, I swear to God.

I sat there, covering my face as I fought the urge to run away. What if Daisy was right and I was more a Lyle than I could admit. Maybe the only difference between Walter and me was I was a coward *and* a killer.

I looked at Daisy's eyes, desperate to see some sign of mercy.

"Don't hate me," I said. "You're all I got."

Her eyelids turned into slits, and her pupils shrunk to hard dots.

So I begged. "Please give me another chance."

It was her lips softening over clenched teeth that signaled she was cooling off.

"Don't leave me, sis. I need you."

Daisy squeezed her fists so hard they shook. She turned away, saying I looked too pitiful to hate.

"Go upstairs and sleep in one of the guest rooms. You're in no condition to drive home."

I did as she directed me and quickly climbed the stairs toward the bedrooms. I knew Daisy would eventually get over her snit; she always had. After all, I wasn't the only Lyle kid who had no one to love them.

Chapter Fifty-Five

S aturday morning, I awoke late. The previous night of terrorizing Gloria Arbuckle, and begging my sister for forgiveness, had worn me out. Daisy had left the house by the time I found my way to the kitchen. A note on the table said she'd be gone for the day.

She drew a heart at the bottom of the message, adding a line about talking to me on Monday.

I guessed I'd returned to Daisy's good graces. That fact didn't make me feel like celebrating, that's for sure.

The rest of my weekend I spent holed up in my house and tried to avoid thinking about the terrible state of my life. When Monday morning arrived, I had stopped wobbling enough to answer the ringing phone. Daisy didn't let me even say hello.

"I need you to get in touch with Eleanor," she said. "She'll hear first about Arbuckle's resignation."

"So, all I have to do is call her, nothing else?"

"You only need to find out if Arbuckle followed through, you hear me?"

"I hear you."

We disconnected the call, and I heaved a big sigh. That wasn't going to be too bad. Wanting to get it done right away, I dialed up Eleanor. Her answering machine instructed me to leave a message. I didn't. Daisy had cautioned me never to leave recorded messages.

My calls to Eleanor continued every hour, and soon the sun settled below the tree line. Mrs. Pressman hadn't once answered. I doubted she'd gone out for the day, what with her limited funds. More likely, she identified my number and refused to pick up.

I left my house and motored to the gas station down the street, the one of a few places that still had a payphone. I placed a call to Eleanor's number, and after the second ring, she picked up.

"Yes."

"Hello, Eleanor."

I heard muttering.

"I don't appreciate you ghosting me," I said. "When you do that, it makes me wonder if you're up to something."

"I've been out."

Keeping in mind Daisy's directions, I jumped to my purpose.

"Listen up, Eleanor. Gloria Arbuckle agreed to resign her position. I'm counting on you to contact that lawyer, you know, the one who read the will, and find out if she'd kept her word."

"Okay."

"I expect an update, starting tomorrow morning by ten," I said. "Even if you have nothing, you call me."

I gave her my cellphone number and hung up. It surprised me that she didn't ask me how my little beach house visit with Gloria went.

* * *

Tuesday morning came around, and I stood in line at the unemployment office. I snatched a copy of the local newspaper from a trash barrel. I might as well be productive while waiting to meet with a job specialist. Even if the edition was a few days old, maybe someone in the area posted a hiring notice.

"What the heck," I said, as I caught the small headline of a below-the-fold article. My voice rumbled over the text as I read, saying some words louder than others.

"Leo Dewey, an apparent failed suicide pulled from the channel near the 5th Street Bridge, died."

I doubled over and slapped my thighs, letting a whoop soar to the ceiling.

The people in the line looked at me with gaping mouths. One guy asked, "Did you win the lottery?"

"Pretty close," I said, "Pretty darn close."

I almost danced out of the building and onto the street. My brain crackled with possibilities. That five grand to pay off Dewey next month now belonged to me. It'd stay in my pocket and not go to some miserable creep.

Wait until I told Daisy.

That's when I came to a halt in the middle of the sidewalk.

Daisy would probably rip off my head. Why hadn't I anticipated Dewey taking a dive off the bridge? If I knew him to be so unstable, I could've held off until he killed himself. I could've saved her the money.

She'd probably explode, thinking whoever pulled Dewey from the water found the packet of cash in his coat pocket. Heck, she might wonder if the bundle had fallen out and sunk to the bottom of the channel. She'd make me go swimming to find it. I knew she would.

Maybe I wouldn't tell Daisy. I could wait. Next month, if she asked about the bribe, I'd come up with some story. She didn't need to know now. Let sleeping dogs lie, as Mandy used to say, or else they'll bite off your hand.

* * *

At noon, I stood outside a deli, scanning the posted menu. With that five grand no longer earmarked for Dewey, I could finally have a big, fat tasty meal. However, I wasn't in the mood. A stinking worry had strangled my appetite.

Eleanor hadn't called. I told her I wanted her to deliver an update by ten. Even if she had no news, I didn't want to be wondering if she had screwed us over.

So I dialed her up.

"Hello."

"Hi, Eleanor, guess who?"

"I don't have any news."

"Did you call the law office?"

"Yes, I spoke with Mr. Thornton. He didn't indicate anything had changed."

"Arbuckle should've handed her resignation in yesterday."

Eleanor's voice became scratchy like maybe her throat had grown smaller. "I think you might've scared her off."

"What are you talking about?"

"My bank source called me. She reported that Arbuckle didn't come in yesterday or this morning."

I stared into space and wondered if I'd frightened the woman enough that she went into hiding. I always warned Daisy that Gloria wouldn't roll over easily. Then I felt my stomach knot. What if she decided to use my confession against us and went to the cops? Maybe they had her in protective custody.

That thought started me shaking. I banged my fist against my head. Man, oh man, did I make a mess. Why can't I get through one day without screwing up?

I reported back to my sister, expecting her to erupt. She surprised me by only humming. That wasn't always healthy, in my experience. She had your classic calm-before-the-storm type of personality.

"Just keep your head down," she said, "and maybe things will break this afternoon."

My definition of keeping my head down meant me taking a few hundred dollars from my Dead Dewey stash and going shopping. I purposely strolled into the shoe store where I'd worked for years and bought a two hundred dollar pair of brogans. Before I cashed out, I made the manager, the dude who'd fired me, run through two dozen pairs of shoes before selecting the very first ones I tried on.

At about two-fifteen, my phone buzzed with a number I recognized.

"What's up, Eleanor?"

"I received a message from Thornton. He wants your sister and me to gather for a special meeting tomorrow at one."

"I'll get her there."

Pressman ended the conversation with a grunt.

My ears throbbed as my heart pounded away like a jackhammer. Had Daisy's scheming finally succeeded? I wanted to be positive, but how many times since my sister killed Eric had her plans blown up?

What if tomorrow's meeting proved to be just another fiasco?

My mind reeled off all the possible scenarios. What if Gloria had recovered from my crazed killer episode and decided to go to the police? Maybe she and Eleanor had teamed up, and that's why the old gal froze me out. What if that meeting was a trap, where Daisy and I walked in, expecting millions in cash, and ended up led out in handcuffs?

My stomachache intensified as I punched in Daisy's phone number.

"Hello."

"Daisy, it's me. Eleanor called. You have a meeting tomorrow with that lawyer dude."

I rubbed my gut as I gave my sister the details. She cooed and said, "We may be getting our big payday, Tommy."

"I gotta tell you, Daisy, I worry it's a trap."

I shared my suspicions about Gloria going to the police and setting us up.

Daisy chuckled. "Didn't you say Arbuckle looked as if she was going to crap her pants when you told her about Eric's cracked skull?"

"I don't think I used those words, but yeah, she was scared."

"You might be more of an enforcer than you think," she said, snickering. "I'd better be careful around you."

Daisy teasing me brought on a wave of nausea. I wanted to tell her to knock it off, that I wasn't a thug who broke bones and killed people. I hung up instead.

Chapter Fifty-Six

Wednesday, one o'clock, and Daisy and I sat at the same conference table where Gloria Arbuckle once introduced herself as Daisy's new overseer. Eleanor Pressman, dressed in deep purple worthy of royalty, sat across from us. We said nothing to each other.

Thornton walked in, scratching his head and nodding at Eleanor and then Daisy. He ignored me.

"We're waiting for Ms. Arbuckle," he said, his voice as weary sounding as his face looked. "She's in the restroom, huh, composing herself."

Daisy pulled out her phone and started texting while Eleanor asked Thornton about his family. I sat and mindlessly rubbed my sweating palms against my thighs. If this meeting didn't start soon, I'd rub a hole through my pants.

The conference room doors pushed open, and Gloria entered the room. She sported sunglasses and makeup that did a poor job of concealing the bruising around her eyes. She sat in a chair at the far end, wincing as if every muscle hurt from the effort.

"I think we can begin," Thornton said, his chin rising and falling as he scanned the room.

"Ms. Arbuckle has requested to be relieved of her fiduciary and administrative duties as outlined in the will of Eric Pressman."

The lawyer looked at Gloria. "Is that correct, Ms. Arbuckle?"

Gloria looked at Daisy and then back at Thornton. "Yes, that's my wish."

"Per the codicils," he said, "the administration of Eric Pressman's estate, including operations of Pressman & Son's Savings & Loan, will revert to Eleanor Pressman, his mother, and widow of the bank's founder, Mortimer Pressman."

"Is that correct, Ms. Arbuckle?" Thornton asked.

Gloria turned her face toward Eleanor, "Yes, that's correct."

Thornton harrumphed about it all being very irregular as he passed around forms for signatures from the three women. I half expected the police to come barging in, but I only heard the noise of paper's shuffling and the scratching of pens on signature lines.

"Okay, ladies," Thornton said. "It seems everything is in order."

Then he looked at Eleanor and Daisy. "I hope that you two can resolve any differences."

I wanted to shout an Amen.

Gloria pushed from the table, her mouth tugging down. I watched her slowly step toward the elevators. The woman looked very unhappy and not because she no longer had a well-paying gig.

Daisy, Eleanor, and I followed Thornton out of the conference room. The lawyer walked off to his office while we stopped in the hall. My sister tapped me on the shoulder. "Why don't you go to the garage and get the car. I want to talk to Eleanor."

I did as she asked. Out of the corner of my eye, I caught my sister and Eleanor whispering to each other. Judging from their facial and hand gestures, it wasn't cheery girl talk.

I retrieved Daisy's SUV. The Junker threw a rod or something and leaked a pool of oil in my driveway, so I again tooled around in Daisy's car. While it felt terrific driving a well-built automobile again, it wasn't Baby. No, I'd never get over that car.

After driving around the block a few times, I saw Daisy standing on the sidewalk. She flagged me down.

"I guess congratulations are in order," I said once she slipped in and buckled her seat belt.

Daisy nodded.

"What did you and Eleanor talk about?" I asked.

"Let's say that we were going over the finer points of our agreement."

"Are you happy?"

"I will be," she said. "Now, let's get something to eat."

Daisy directed me to one of the better seafood restaurants for a celebratory cocktail or two for her and a lobster roll for me. Most of our conversation centered on Daisy's plans for her new life as a bank president following her return from her European vacation. When she took a break to order a third vodka and tonic, I brought up something bothering me.

"I wonder what happened to Arbuckle. She looked like she was in a lot of pain."

Daisy snorted. "I guess you got a little more physical with her than what you told me."

I pounded the table. "I didn't touch her."

Daisy cocked her head to the side and closed one eye as she pointed her finger. "Maybe you're like the Incredible Hulk, Tommy. People shouldn't make you mad."

"Stop teasing me."

My sister snickered and patted my arm.

"Okay, settle down, little brother. Everything's good. The bad times are over, and we Lyle kids have nothing but sunny days ahead."

Her mentioning the future reminded me about my own thoughts on the topic. I wanted to ask her a favor. I didn't want to be a bank vice president or a shoe salesman. I wanted one thing from her, loan forgiveness. I could sell my house and make enough to move to the shore. I'd rent a room near the boardwalk, work the season, and scrape by during the winter.

That's what I wanted from her—a quiet life with plenty of time to make amends for all the bad things I'd done for her.

Chapter Fifty-Seven

O
f all the cop bars in the precinct, I liked Cappie's the best. We old timers loved it, so most of the party crowd tended to be heavier and louder than the average patrolman. The room filled with people slapping me on the back and lying about how much they'd miss me. I loved it and hated it all at once.

"So I remember when you transferred here," Tiny Baker said. "You were a semi-legend, so I was worried you might have an attitude."

"Me, an attitude," I said, faking outrage and getting those around us to laugh.

Baker went on and on until whatever story he tried to tell ran out of steam. Like a lot of bad storytellers, he tended to stretch an anecdote so thin it fell apart. I laughed anyway, just to cover the awkwardness.

"Hey, I didn't tell you," he said, "I got a call yesterday from that pest, Eleanor Pressman."

That announcement sucked away what little joy I'd been feeling.

"What did she want?"

"She claimed she had proof that her son was murdered, and she had evidence of who did it."

I hung my head. "I heard that before."

"She wanted you to come by, and she'd give you everything you'd need to arrest the killers."

I smiled before chuckling. "That woman once told me she knew someone murdered her son, and when I asked her how she knew that, she answered, 'mother's intuition.'"

Baker banged his beer bottle on the bar top as he roared, "I love it."

We raised our bottles, "Here's to mothers and their intuition," I said.

"Hear, hear."

I clasped Baker's shoulder and mentioned I'd better spread my good cheer around the room. This could be the last time I'd see most of the crowd. I slipped between the tables, thanking the guys for coming out, using my half-full bottle of beer to feign off people buying me another one. I didn't want to get blitzed and suffer the next day. I'd planned to visit the office tomorrow, pick up my last check stub, and get out of town early.

Chuckie Brown trapped me in a corner and wrapped his big arms around me so tightly I grunted. We spent a good fifteen minutes starting each sentence with, "you remember that time..." and ending them crippled with laughter.

When the stories started repeating, Chuckie took a big swallow of his drink and asked me my plans.

"I hope Baker lets me off early tomorrow so I can get a start for North Carolina."

Chuckie's eyes rolled toward the ceiling. "Surely, that tight-ass isn't forcing you to work until the last hour."

I shrugged, embarrassed to admit that *my* tight ass would probably want to hang around and take in the last hours of my career.

"So, are you all set to go?" Chuckie asked.

"Yeah, I got my utilities scheduled for shut off. The neighbor kid will take care of my yard. I got my direct deposits, and I can pay any bills online. I'll be unencumbered, so I can do what I want when I want."

I chattered on about spending time on the Outer Banks, probably until the weather got cold. I suggested I'd head south, maybe visit Key West before it became submerged.

Chuckie's eyes glazed over. And even though he wouldn't say it, I could tell he thought aimlessly driving down interstate 95 sounded boring as hell. I didn't have the energy to argue with him. I'd already packed my gear and suitcases and left them sitting in the hallway. If my motivation dwindled any further, I'd never escape New Jersey.

* * *

The morning came, and the hangover wasn't too bad. I stayed within my drinking limit of six beers, and snuck away from the celebration soon after midnight. I got out of bed about eight, my knees screaming for mercy, but I pushed through the pain and climbed into the shower.

After a piece of dry toast and a glass of water to wash down my old man pills, I threw out the few remaining items from the refrigerator and unplugged it. It required four trips from the house to my car to squeeze in everything going with me. The sound of the front door slamming shut seemed louder than I'd ever heard before.

Once I backed out of the drive, I didn't take a look at the house, too afraid I'd see Joanie's ghost in a window wondering why I'd left her behind.

I didn't start feeling semi-normal until I whiffed the musty odor of the precinct building. I immediately headed to Tiny Baker's office. I wasn't surprised. He looked like he'd been there for hours.

"Hey, Boss," I said. "Thanks again for the kind words last night."

Tiny waved his hands. "My pleasure, Detective, I meant every word."

My gaze wandered around his office for a second. I didn't know why I stood there, so I broke the awkward silence. "I'm here to get my check and tidy up before the end of the day. Let me know if you need anything."

A sad little smile crossed Tiny's face. "I know you're on payroll until five, but I'll give you the day off. Get a head start. You know hurricane season started already. You're not going to have too much fishing time if you hang around here."

My mouth dropped open. Seriously, what he said touched me. I knew how much he disliked giving me those hours. I better take him up on it since he'd probably regret it by noon.

"Thanks again, Tiny. I enjoyed working for you."

"I'll miss you, Detective. You were one of my best police. I always appreciated how..."

The phone on Baker's desk rang, and he grabbed the receiver from the cradle.

244

CHAPTER FIFTY-SEVEN

"Baker."

A big grin pushed Tiny's cheeks upward. "Larry," he shouted, rolling away from me, "How are you doing, buddy?"

I figured with the jovial tone of the conversation, whatever heartfelt compliment Tiny planned to lay on me had been overtaken by the call with his old buddy, Larry.

I saluted my boss and turned on my heels.

Meandering through the detective's bullpen, I stopped at my old desk. An envelope containing my last paystub rested on top of a small pile of pink message slips. A quick shuffle of the half-dozen pieces of paper revealed all of them had been left by Eleanor Pressman.

"I sure won't miss that," I said, mumbling under my breath. Not that I couldn't blame her for wanting the police to pursue her case. God knew I suspected as much about her son's death as she did. There were just too many times that Tommy Lyle showed up, and people died. And the inconsistencies in the wife's stories bothered me as well.

But why did Mrs. Pressman hook up with the man she thought killed her son? And, what about her ridiculous plan to get Lyle to confess to the crime? It didn't make sense. None of it did.

Ah, forget it, Nick. That case would be one of those mysteries that'd have me wondering until I died. It's time to move on. Your crime-fighting days are over.

Chapter Fifty-Eight

S itting in Eleanor Pressman's living room brought back the memory of my first experience with her. I'd been on the assignment for maybe six days, doing witness interviews, talking to the responding patrol officers, and reading the initial medical report. I got a call from on high. The old gal had rung up the chief *and* the mayor. She expressed, in no uncertain terms, her unhappiness with my lack of certainty that her son had been murdered.

Like most cops, I found working with the wealthy a pain in the rear end. They had a sense of entitlement that floated off of them like cheap aftershave.

But then the rich Mrs. Pressman became the broke Mrs. Pressman, and neither the chief nor the mayor returned her calls. So why did I happen to be sitting there? I kept asking myself that question. Good God, I should be on I-95 somewhere in Delaware by now.

"Here you go, Detective Bongiovanni."

Mrs. Pressman returned from her kitchen with a glass of water. A silky blue robe with a flowered pattern hung on her frame. In a throaty voice, she continued her salutation.

"I appreciate you finally getting back to me."

My knees cracked as I stood to accept the water from her.

"Please don't get up," she said, handing me the glass and slipping onto the sofa next to me. "I have something important to share with you."

"I'm anxious to hear it."

I figured that since my retirement wasn't official until five o'clock, I still had some authority to do police business. Sure, I doubted Eleanor had anything substantial, but her messages sounded so full of desperation. I knew no one else would listen to her, and if she had something worthwhile, I'd pass it on to Baker.

Hell, I'd slip it to Brutkowski. At least I'd know it wouldn't get dropped.

Eleanor pulled a cassette from her robe pocket. "I told you the last time you were here that I'd get Tommy Lyle to confess to killing my son, and I did."

She held out her hand, the cassette inches from my nose. I took it from her, gave it a look, and stuck it in my jacket pocket.

"Aren't you going to listen to it?"

"Why don't you first tell me what's on it and how you got it?"

Mrs. Pressman's head bobbled back and forth.

"Why does that matter. It's as clear as day. He admits to killing Eric."

I puffed out my cheeks and forced my face into something that I hoped looked empathetic.

"My retirement from police work starts in a few hours. I'll gladly pass on all possible evidence to my superiors after I leave you. But that evidence has to be solid, or else they'll keep ignoring you, you understand?"

Her mouth twisted, seemingly fighting to keep from raging at me. After a second of struggling with her impulses, she gave me the background I wanted.

"We have a family beach house down on the shore. It's a beautiful place."

I focused on her steel-gray eyes, nodding after each sentence.

"Eric rented it out most of the season. He was too busy to spend much time there, and I hated the summer crowds."

I responded with a series of, "Huh-uh."

"To protect the property from ill-behaving renters, Eric installed a recording system throughout the house."

I pressed my lips together. Now that's interesting.

"So last Monday, I was down there to check the property. That's when I discovered the thingamajig indicating that the system was activated this past Friday."

The old thingamajig—yeah, her technology skills sounded only slightly better than mine. I wouldn't know what a thingamajig looked like, let alone how to understand what it did.

"So, the property wasn't rented out?"

"No," she said. "Eric kept August open for himself."

"Could it have been his wife? I assume she had access."

Mrs. Pressman's eyes went dark on me as her anger reared up. "*Please,* let me finish. I *know* who it was."

I usually let people run their mouths. It had always proven to be an effective way to learn things. I wondered what explained me pushing Mrs. Pressman to the finish line? Then it hit me like a backhand from an angry nun—Nick Bongiovanni, crime fighter, detective emeritus, a dedicated officer of the law had reached the end, kaput. His presence in that room had been nothing more than an old detective operating on automatic, sputtering as his time and energy petered out.

What a sad final hooray

"I'm sorry for interrupting you," I said. "Please go on."

The woman continued babbling. "The recording was between two people, a man and a woman. I know both of their voices. The man was Tommy Lyle, and the woman was Gloria Arbuckle. They were discussing a plan to steal my share of Eric's estate."

"That's pretty serious."

"Absolutely, it's serious." She tapped her finger on my coat pocket. "You can listen to the tape yourself. I have a player in the study."

"Did you happen to edit the recording?" I asked.

The woman's chin lifted. "Well, of course, I cleaned it up. There were almost eight hours of worthless chatter from Arbuckle talking bank business before Lyle arrived."

I sat back, lacing my fingers. "It sounds like you put a lot of effort into that project."

"Well, I told you I'd get Lyle to confess. And when you listen, that's *exactly* what you'll hear."

Why Tommy Lyle had spent an evening at the Pressman family beach house with a woman I'd never heard of was beyond me. Eleanor did impress me, however, spending hours listening to recordings, hoping to hear something worthwhile. That woman hated Tommy and Daisy Lyle like no one else on the planet.

"So tell me about the woman on the recording."

Eleanor's face darkened, suggesting that her bitter feelings toward the Arbuckle woman matched what she harbored toward Daisy and Tommy Lyle.

"She's a harpy that my foolish son put in charge of dispersing his estate."

When I asked her to elaborate, she gave me a convoluted lecture on improper fund management, a ruined life, the disgusting Daisy Pressman, and some nonsense about auditing her jewelry.

"So it sounded like that Arbuckle woman caused you a lot of grief."

Eleanor shook her head. "Yes, at one time, but she's no longer a problem."

"What happened?"

"She resigned from her job as trustee. She's not the issue here."

I peppered the woman with a few more questions about Arbuckle. I guessed it was my last gasp as a detective. Eleanor didn't take it well. Her voice jumped from breathlessly frenetic to a high-pitched screech.

"That doesn't concern you, damn it. You only have to focus on the part where Lyle admits he and his sister murdered Eric."

Her rudeness brought home to me how foolish I'd been. I *knew* from the start that this busy-work was nothing more than rich people fighting over money. I'd let my curiosity get the better of me and turned every odd discrepancy into something big and important. Didn't I always warn the young guys not to turn every correlation into causation?

"I'll pass the tape on to my boss," I said. "He'll listen to it."

"I don't trust your boss to listen to anything."

Mrs. Pressman grabbed my sleeve and jerked it back and forth. "No one in that department cares about me."

I sighed. The woman had it correct. She'd earned the label of nuisance, and management would always pass her on to any short-timer with nothing to do.

"I gotta tell you, Mrs. Pressman. The whole secret recording thing is problematic. New Jersey requires at least one party being recorded consent to it. I'm guessing neither Mr. Lyle nor the woman agreed to the recording."

My recitation of the law's finer points failed to impress her. It seemed to have tipped her over the edge. She screamed at me, "You're nothing but a lazy cop who doesn't give a damn. You're disgusting. You all are."

I came into that living room feeling sorry for Eleanor, figuring she lived alone, friendless, and only wanted justice. Now, I wondered if she deserved to be friendless because of her vindictive and manipulative nature. What a royal pain in the ass.

"I'll pass it on," I said, with as much civility as I could muster. "But my days of policing are over. I'm sorry."

"I can't believe it," she said, bouncing on the cushion so hard I thought she'd levitate. "I deliver proof that those Lyle monsters killed my son, and you don't care."

We didn't exchange any other words after that. If Pressman wanted the police to eliminate people causing her grief, they'd have to find someone else to do the job. I had to get on the road. I had fish waiting for me.

* * *

I turned my car out of the condo parking lot and headed west toward the interstate. My gut burned, and my head throbbed. How dare that old bag call me a lazy cop? I'd worked my ass off for thirty-years, never slacking. Even when I walked a beat, I did the job one-hundred percent, damn her.

I *always* cared.

About a mile and a half down the road, I pulled into a pharmacy. I had to get some anti-acids to address the fire in my intestines. After a quick purchase, I sat in my car, chewing a few tablets. As I waited for some relief, I noticed the clouds rolling in, all loaded with rain. That would slow traffic and delay my escape even more. Man, I sucked at making a clean break.

As if to reinforce the argument that I couldn't let go of things, my mind wandered back to Tommy Lyle. I always felt in my bones that he'd been guilty of something. Part of me wanted to arrest him and ride out a hero.

Show Tiny Baker and all those other guys that Nick Bongiovanni was a true detective until the very end. I'd never quit an investigation without a clear-cut resolution. I didn't want my retirement haunted by things I didn't do or clues I'd overlooked.

"Ah nuts," I heard myself mumble. Come on, Nicky; suck it up for another few hours. You're still on the payroll. At least listen to the tape.

A slash of lightning crossed the sky, and thunder ripped the air. The noise snapped me out of my swamp of self-doubt and second-guessing.

"You're retired, you dumbass," I heard myself grumbling. "Where would you even find a tape player?"

As big fat raindrops splattered on the windshield, I started my car and slowly nudged my way into traffic. The further I got from town and toward North Carolina, I figured, the less I'd care about Eleanor Pressman and Tommy Lyle.

The rain came down in sheets as the wind pushed it across the roadway. I soon came to a standstill behind a line of glowing taillights. My mind started pulling up all kinds of questions and answers.

How about that cloth remnant? I never got a solid explanation of what created that weird smudge. Shelia Washington seemed convinced that Pressman suffered head trauma twice.

But, Shelia's opinion, notwithstanding, it had been a small piece of cloth and a big conjecture by the lab. That wasn't enough evidence for an arrest, let alone using it as a foundational piece at a trial.

Why did Eric's wife want to cremate the remains so quickly? Had they really done it to avoid a rift, or had it been a way of preventing further examination of the corpse? What about the funeral parlor assistant telling me there wasn't a cremation? I never got clarity on that confusion.

And had Tommy Lyle's argument with the murdered undertaker *really* been about a missing seat cushion?

I had nothing but circumstantial evidence, no witnesses, no weapon, and no proof.

I pounded on the steering wheel. "Come on, you damn traffic."

Leo Dewey, now he bothered me even more. Why would he have visited

Tommy Lyle? Something must have been going on between those two. Considering Dewey's drinking problems, he'd be fertile ground for all kinds of shenanigans.

Maybe Dewey blackmailed Lyle?

Ah, probably not. Lyle had no money.

Then again, his sister had recently come into some do-re-me, so maybe Leo had something on her, but what?

Now Dewey's dead, and that's another aching molar. Sure, he probably fell over the railing, but why had he been walking across the bridge in the first place? Okay, as a drunk, with something like four times the legal limit in his veins, he'd probably gotten lost. I'd never know.

Then there was the nurse at the hospital, claiming the only semi-coherent word she heard from Dewey had been the name, Pressman. What drove that? Good God, what if I'm sniffing down the wrong path. What if the reference had been *Eleanor* Pressman? Dewey might've been working with her and not Lyle? She had the motive for wanting to pin a murder on the brother and sister.

That's an interesting conjecture. That could explain why Dewey visited Tommy. What if he went over to Lyle's house to alert him to the old gal's plans? Knowing Leo, he probably saw a way to get money from both of them.

A roar of laughter shot from my throat. What the hell am I thinking? One of my sacrosanct rules required you to never fall in love with your first assumption. How ironic, me being unable to attach with my second, third, or fourth assumption.

Thank God I'm getting out. I'm too old to play the game anymore.

The traffic wasn't moving, and the storm looked as if it would keep up for another hour. I took a right down an alley and slowly worked through a couple of parking lots. I knew a few residential side streets that would get me out of the traffic jam. It might be a long way to get through town, but I at least I moved forward. I wished I could say the same thing about my brain and that Pressman fiasco.

Chapter Fifty-Nine

I f I wanted to lie to myself, I'd claim it was pure coincidence. But it wasn't. I knew Daisy Pressman lived not far off the road I'd taken as an alternative way to the interstate. Since I was in the area, I thought, why not stop and take one more shot? What did I have to lose? The rain wasn't letting up, and I'd be stuck in traffic thinking about the damn case anyway.

I'd get in, ask the questions, and watch her squirm. If anything useful popped out of her mouth, I'd make a note and attach it to Eleanor's tape. I'd send the package to Baker once I settled on the Outer Banks. Visiting Daisy Pressman would be the last chance I had to scratch my itch.

Daisy's residence was far off the main drag, requiring navigation of a gravel road through a shabby and unattended landscape. I parked along the side of the house and hoped she wouldn't catch a peek of me before I rang the doorbell. I always found people more loose-lipped if they didn't expect you.

I followed up ringing the doorbell with a vicious pounding on the front door. A female voice sounded from behind it. "Who is it?"

"Good afternoon, Daisy. This is Detective Bongiovanni."

A few seconds of silence passed before she replied. "What do you want?"

"I'd like just a few minutes of your time to answer a question or two."

"What's the question?"

"It's raining pretty hard out here," I said. "I'd appreciate you letting me in so we can get this done quickly."

"Leave us alone."

I recognized Tommy Lyle's voice. Even better that he'd be there because I had questions for him as well.

"We can talk now or when you come all the way down to the station in this rain."

Sure, I lied, but I hoped that the foul weather would be enough incentive to get me inside so I could see their faces.

The front door pulled opened, and a sullen Tommy Lyle greeted me. I thanked him as I stepped inside, shaking off rain droplets from my jacket.

"Make it quick," Tommy said, pointing to the first room off the entrance hall.

The space might've been a living room. The walls had nothing on them, and a sofa and two armchairs made up the only furniture. I dropped into one, and Tommy sat in the other. Daisy stood behind her brother. She didn't appear to be the same grieving widow I met two weeks ago. She stared at me and rubbed her hands as if to warm them.

"I have some good news for you. We're about to put to bed the inquiry into Mr. Pressman's death."

I thought at least a weary smile might crack their faces. Nope, they gave me nothing.

"I have only a few questions needing answers," I said, using my friendly but matter-of-fact voice. "You know, I want to make my report complete, so you're never bothered again."

Neither Lyle nor his sister responded. What a tough crowd. I guess they'd heard my shtick too often to be impressed.

"Can you recall whether you used a bath towel to sop up blood the night of the accident?" I asked.

Tommy waved his noggin back and forth. "I know this game, Detective. If we don't recall exactly what we said before, you'll assume we're lying. If we do, you'll think we've practiced it. So what does it matter?"

"The sooner you give me an answer, the quicker I'll be gone."

Lyle threw his hands in the air. "I don't know. We grabbed whatever we could. Of course, we might've used a bath towel. The washer was in the basement. Dirty laundry probably piled up everywhere."

254

"Daisy, is that your memory?"

The woman used only enough facial muscles to answer, "Yes."

"Did you know Leo Dewey before he arrived at the house that night?"

"Nope."

"Did either of you ever meet with him afterwards?"

Daisy's eyes flickered.

"Yes, I did," Tommy said. "I talked to him at the morgue. I wanted to know when he'd release Eric's body so we could schedule the funeral."

"Daisy, did your husband specify in any legal document that he wanted to be cremated after death?"

The woman bit on her lower lip. She looked at her brother and then back at me.

"No," she said, with enough frost to ice a cake. "But Eric often said he wouldn't waste money on an expensive casket for my burial, so I assumed he wanted the same."

Okay, that got my attention. I'd never heard Daisy disparage her husband before.

"I'm confused, Daisy. You told me you cremated Eric, and others have said you buried him. Can you straighten out my muddle?"

Tommy jumped in. "Old Lady Pressman demanded a big funeral. My sister was in terrible shape at the time and didn't have the strength to fight her. So I arranged the cremation in secret while setting up the big shindig Eleanor wanted."

"So, what is the definitive answer?" I asked. "Was he buried or cremated?"

Daisy stepped forward. "There was supposed to have been a cremation, but the damn undertaker swindled us. We only found out later that Eric was actually buried."

I looked at Tommy.

"Did you ever return to the Funeral Home after the service?"

"You know I did," he said. "You grilled me about it at my house."

"That must've pissed you off," I said, turning my attention toward Daisy. "You go to all that trouble to purchase a cremation service, and Eric got buried anyway."

She shrugged. "What does it matter now?"

"I guess you're right unless Eric's mother wanted to exhume the body."

Daisy jumped toward me and shouted, "I won't allow Eleanor to desecrate my husband's body to feed her irrational hatred of me."

The heat of her vitriol knocked me back. I suspected I saw more of the authentic Daisy than I did in my first interview.

"Did you know that the undertaker, Archie London, was shot dead soon after your funeral service?"

"Of course, we knew that. It was in the news," Daisy said. "I know you think we're illiterate, but we can read."

Okay, I thought, now both of the Lyle kids hated me. I'd better throw out a question they'd never heard before.

"Daisy, did you know last Friday your brother was at the Pressman beach house in Point Pleasant with a woman named Gloria Arbuckle?"

The eyeballs of Daisy and Tommy froze in their sockets, and their mouths hung open.

I guessed Eleanor might have something important after all.

"Care to explain what that was all about?"

Tommy's eyes started to water, and he rubbed the side of his stomach. His sister, on the other hand, set her jaw and folded her arms. I watched as she blinked, sucked in some air, and then gave me an answer.

"Gloria is a friend of my brother's," she said. "Is romance now against the law?"

I smiled. I'd have to meet Gloria to believe that answer. I couldn't envision a skinny little creep like Tommy Lyle getting any woman alone with him, at least not voluntarily.

"I spent some time with your mother-in-law this afternoon, Daisy."

The woman's eyes narrowed. "She's my ex-mother-in-law."

I nodded. "Did you know that your husband had recording devices throughout that beach house?"

My gaze pulled to the right when I heard Tommy softly groaning and folding over at the waist. His body shook like he had some devil beating on his insides.

Daisy sprang over to help him, holding up his head, his complexion now looking like cream cheese. "Are you going to be sick?"

"Huh, uh."

She gave me a heated look like I'd sucker-punched her brother.

"I'll get you some water," she said, patting Tommy on the back. "Don't say anything."

I watched her walk out of the living room toward the kitchen. I decided not to wait for her return. I had Tommy half-way to the mat, and I wanted to pin him for good.

"Look at me, Tommy," I said.

He lifted his face, and I saw his eyes bubbling over. I pulled the tape cassette from my coat pocket.

"See this cassette, Tommy. Eleanor claimed if I played it, I'd hear you telling your so-called girlfriend that you murdered Eric Pressman."

Crimson blotches erupted on his cheeks and neck, and he started hyperventilating. I felt pretty ramped up myself. I couldn't recall the last time I'd felt the intense sensation of getting a criminal to confess. Now I'd deliver the *coup de grace*.

"Did you murder Eric Pressman?"

Lyle's jawline trembled.

"Did you kill Archie London?"

I leaned forward, raising my voice. "Did you throw Leo Dewey off a bridge?"

The shadow of Daisy Pressman caught my eye. I glanced up as she stepped back into the room. Everything about her face looked hard, I mean, her eyes, her mouth, everything.

I should've known what was coming.

Chapter Sixty

It surprised me how quickly Bongiovanni's face drained of color. One second his skin glowed red hot as he yelled at me, and the next moment he'd gone all pale, his pupils big and black.

I looked over my shoulder to see what had grabbed his attention. There stood Daisy, holding a revolver in her hands. Before I could blurt out a single syllable, the air in the room splintered at the sound of a round igniting.

I flipped back to look at the detective and hoped my sister had lousy aim. The man's head bent backward in recoil, and then slowly dropped forward. He looked as much stunned as perplexed. The burgundy stain blossoming across his chest made it clear that the bullet had exploded his heart.

I swiveled back toward my sister. A cloud of blue smoke drifted over her toward the ceiling. The gun pointed downward at the floor as if she knew she didn't need to fire a second time.

I screamed, "What have you done?"

Then I bent over and emptied my stomach across the floor.

"God damn it, Tommy, don't mess up my carpet."

I ignored Daisy and struggled to push myself from the chair. Stumbling toward the bleeding man, I cried out, "Call 911."

"Shut up. I'm calling no one."

My eyes skimmed Bongiovanni's body and the ever-expanding bloodstain. My sister nailed it; no amount of help could save him. I clutched the sides of my head. Oh my God, here I go again, back in Hell standing over another man my sister murdered.

"How could you do that?" I said, "Why did you shoot him?"

"We were trapped. I had no choice."

"But you said we were not hurting people anymore."

"It's your fault I had to shoot him."

"How can you say that?"

My sister started circling, snarling and jabbing her finger at me.

"If you hadn't confessed to killing Eric, there would've been no tape."

"That's not fair," I said, throwing my hands in the air. "I didn't know Eleanor was recording me."

"I told you what to say, you idiot. But no, you had to impress Arbuckle by telling her you killed Eric."

Daisy lied. I wasn't trying to impress Gloria. I did what she sent me there to do, scare her. Gloria laughed at me, so I had to do something to shut her up.

"This one's on you, Tommy."

I dropped my head and covered my face, sniffles sneaking through my fingers.

"Oh, stop your crying," Daisy said. "We have to get this cleaned up."

I looked at Bongiovanni's body, slumped in the chair, blood dripping onto the carpet. A sob clogged my throat. "This is too much. This is way too much."

Daisy grabbed me by the collar of my shirt and jerked so hard my head snapped sideways.

"Stop bawling and do what I tell you."

Pushing me toward the dead detective, she told me to retrieve his car keys. "Then go move his car behind the house and leave. You hear me? Go home and stay there until I call you."

I pointed at the dead man. "But how are you going to clean this up?"

Daisy barked at me. "I've been cleaning up your messes for the past month. I can handle this one."

Maybe Daisy had every right to be angry, but her answer didn't make sense. How could she dispose of a body, dump a car, and clean up a living room covered in blood? And what did she mean by cleaning up *my* messes?

"What messes are you talking about?"

Daisy waved me away like a buzzing fly. "Go on, do what I told you."

"No, I'm not leaving," I said, determined to regain some of my paper-thin dignity, "until you tell me what messes you're talking about."

My sister's pupils shrunk into those black dots again. "Did you wonder why you were never arrested for stealing office equipment from London's funeral home?"

I flinched. "How'd you know about that?"

Daisy folded her arms; her feet planted wide as she readied her dressing down.

"London had a security camera running that night. I saw it all; the sound of gunfire and then you running down the hall, all buggy-eyed, carrying damn office equipment like you'd robbed Fort Knox."

"But how'd you know that?"

"You think I didn't have someone tailing you all this time? They went in after you cracked London's skull and finished him off. Lucky for you, they were professionals and discovered the security camera."

I stood hunched over, wondering what she meant. Who did she have following me around? How did Daisy know people who murdered as a profession? When my guts twisted at the thought, I decided I couldn't handle the answer. I just wanted to get out of there.

I approached Bongiovanni's body, trying not to look into the man's lifeless eyes. I patted his jacket and got lucky. The car keys rested in an outside pocket. The cassette, the one he claimed contained my confession, laid on the floor.

For a moment, I wondered if Bongiovanni had told the truth about the recording. I shuddered to think how close I came to confessing. Of course, what good it would've done him. Daisy had already come back into the room to terminate his investigation once and for all.

* * *

My clock read fifteen minutes past midnight, and I'd been home for hours. I hadn't slept. How could I, with the image in my head of Bongiovanni's chest, boiling with blood. And my body hurt like hell. Kneeling on the floor of my bedroom in prayer, tortured my knees. But such was the price I had to pay to negotiate with Mandy.

"You heard Daisy say that I didn't kill Archie London. I didn't think I did, but now we're sure."

I bowed my head; my tightly interlocked fingers bleached of any color. "I'm not saying I didn't hurt Archie, but knocking him senseless wasn't the same as killing him."

I rolled my shoulders and shifted my weight from one knee to the other.

"And I don't care what my sister said. I didn't hit Gloria. You know that."

My mind pulled up the memory of Gloria at that last meeting. She moved hesitantly, hurting, her brashness gone. Then, like most times in my life, the truth made itself apparent long after the fact.

"Damn you, Daisy." I slammed my hands on the bed and screamed. "I didn't hurt Gloria. Your hired gangsters, your so-called professionals, they smacked around the poor woman."

A burst of heated bile surged up my throat and choked me. How could Daisy, my sister, manipulate me like that? She knew I hated hurting people, yet she let me think I was some brutal thug. How could I be so stupid? Walter had it right all along.

I *was* a moron.

Chapter Sixty-One

I arrived at Daisy's house around lunchtime. It had been four days since I last saw her. She offered me some leftover carry-out Chinese, but I passed. For all I knew, she'd poisoned the orange chicken or something.

"So you wanted to talk about the future, huh," she said.

"Yeah, I do. I have a plan."

She grinned and pointed toward the living room. "Come in here and let's talk."

Oh great, she's taking me into her killing field to talk about my future.

"How do you like the new furniture?" she asked, pointing to the two stuffed chairs, both with price tags hanging from them. I also noticed the carpeting pulled up, and the hardwood floor refinished. The smell of varnish still hung in the air.

Daisy directed me toward one of the new armchairs. "Sit."

I guessed if my sister intended to shoot me, she wouldn't put me in an expensive new chair.

"So, tell me what's on your mind."

"Well, let me get to the point," I said, leaning in toward her, my back arched. "I'm done being your patsy. You manipulated me and risked my life and liberty, all so you could get rich."

I thought my sister would get angry, but she didn't. She grinned as her neck flushed. "I know, and I'm sorry."

I couldn't believe her response.

"I'm your only family," I said, shouting. "And you treated me like a fool, a big nobody."

Daisy frowned, slowly shaking her head. "What can I do to make it up to you?"

Now I got pissed. Daisy gave me a half-ass apology and then tried to buy me off. Since that was kinda the reason I came over, I decided to let her comment pass. I told her exactly how she could make amends. I said I needed a break from her and this town, adding, "As bank president, I want you to forgive the loan on my house."

"Now, why would you want that?"

I stood because my heart pumped blood so fast I thought it might pop my eardrums.

"I want to sell my house, take whatever money I get out of it, and move to the shore."

Daisy walked over and hugged me. "I know I've put you through the wringer," she said, gently rubbing my back. "But I hate the idea of you going off where I can't keep an eye on you."

I supposed I could've interpreted that last sentence as meaning she worried about me and wanted to be sure I'd be safe. Maybe if I had been five years old, that'd make sense. But knowing I had the honor of being the only witness to her hands killing two men, I suspected another reason.

"So you want me around," I said, pushing her away, "because you don't trust your idiot brother?"

Her eyes twinkled.

"No, no, Tommy, I want to create a family for you and me, one that we never had with Walter and Mabel."

I laughed at her. I couldn't help it. Her, Daisy, creating a family, that's silly.

"I'm serious, you, me, and a husband and lots of cousins, aunts, and uncles."

"What are you trying to tell me? You're not making sense."

My sister smiled and then she blushed. It stunned me.

"I'm in love," she said.

"What? How'd you have time to date anyone?"

"Oh, it was love at first sight."

My fingers dug into my scalp. Daisy did not fall in love at first, second, or third sight. I knew my sister, and this development couldn't be good.

"You'll love him, Tommy, he's the best."

"I don't think so. The men in your life always caused me troubles."

Daisy giggled as she grabbed my arms. "No, no, you have to meet him. You'll adore him."

My sister cupped her hand around her mouth and shouted, "Come in here, darling."

A wide-body filled the hallway from the back of the house, dressed in a white terrycloth bathrobe. If my jaw hit the floor, I didn't hear it because my ears had been stunned into deafness.

"Hey, Tommy Boy," the man said. "Good to see you again."

Big Jimmy reached out and pulled Daisy into his grasp and planted a wet kiss on her lips.

Once Jimmy stopped sucking the wind out of my sister, she explained how they met. After I sold the artwork and sporting gear to Weasel Snell, Jimmy decided to introduce himself to the new widow. She claimed he swept her off her feet, and he smiled like she spoke the truth.

I had a hard time maintaining the phony grin on my face as I watched the love birds snuggle. I knew their love-at-first-sight stunk. I figured Jimmy saw an opportunity to get into the banking business, and my sister found a partner who could keep undeserving hands out of her money. In a sick way, Jimmy matched up better for Daisy than Eric ever did.

"Okay," I finally croaked out a response. "I'm happy for both of you."

Jimmy waved me closer and wrapped his arms around my shoulders and squeezed the air from my lungs. Somehow I felt it less a heartfelt embrace, than a demonstration of how easily he could crush me.

Daisy tapped her fingers together, her eyes sparkling. "I must excuse myself and run to the grocery store." She'd promised Jimmy that she'd use his mother's calzone recipe and make him dinner to celebrate their one-month anniversary.

The last celebratory meal I remembered involving Italian cuisine didn't end well. At least with Big Jimmy, I didn't have to worry about Daisy pushing him down the stairs, at least not until after Valentine's Day.

Jimmy and Daisy nuzzled each other before she left. He walked over and sat on the sofa, his mouth pushing his face upward in a crooked smile.

"Come over here and let's chat," he said, patting the space next to him. I swallowed whatever spit I had in my mouth and joined him.

"You know you kept me busy, Tommy. What with the mortician, the drunk off the bridge, and then than mouthy broad who needed a lesson."

"I had those people under control," I said, rubbing my sweating palms on the sofa's arm. "I only needed a little more time."

Jimmy grinned. "Yeah, more time. We all need more time."

He brought up Eleanor Pressman and how he had to pay her a personal visit. He promised her a half share of the estate, and a longer life. He'd also convinced her to destroy any copies of the beach house tape.

"You know," he said, throwing a wink at me, "the one where you confessed to murdering her son."

I heard my mouth sputtering as Jimmy leaned toward me.

"But killing that detective right inside Daisy's living room, now that's not the way we do business, my friend, and it better not happen again."

I tried to straighten out Big Jimmy's thinking by pointing out that most of what I did, I did in the service to my sister.

"It wasn't me shooting that detective. I had nothing to do with that."

Jimmy's eyelids drooped, and his forehead furrowed.

"Are you telling me Daisy shot that guy?" he asked. He started clutching and unclutching his hands.

"I...I...I am."

Jimmy rolled a massive shoulder at me and caused the springs under the cushions to squawk. "What kind of man hides behind a woman, especially his sister?"

I wanted to explain that I hid behind no one. I'd admit my role in Daisy's crimes, but I didn't murder anybody. Jimmy didn't look like he wanted to hear that his sweetheart could be a cold-blooded cop killer. So I sat there, sweating through my shirt, as the behemoth my sister loved ground his molars.

Chapter Sixty-Two

T he sound of the surf blended perfectly with the bite of the whiskey I held in my mouth. Being on the deck of the beach house, watching the grey Atlantic wash the sand, however, did little to ease the grip of depression.

Daisy had been responsible for both the house and my mood.

My sister never kept her promise to cancel my bank debt. I badgered her for a while before she pushed back and claimed New Jersey bank auditors might be suspicious seeing her dropping a family member's mortgage.

Of course, Daisy knew nothing about bank auditors. Her new boyfriend brought in *his people* to operate Pressman & Sons Savings & Loan. They ran a tight ship and operated far more effectively handling delinquencies. I preferred Eric's spiteful cracks about my character over the threat of a broken finger or two.

Not that I let Daisy backtrack without complaining. I told her I hated living in my old house. Whenever I crossed through the kitchen, I remember that I saw her murder Eric. She didn't want me to share my feelings with Jimmy, so she offered me the beach house during the upcoming offseason.

When I asked her how I would I make a living in Point Pleasant without tourists throwing their money around on over-priced food, drink, and trinkets, she answered with ten thousand dollars in cash. And I didn't feel bad taking it from her.

I took another swallow of the scotch.

My newly acquired taste for whiskey I owed to my sister, as well. I think it started at the party where she and Big Jimmy celebrated Daisy's ownership of the bank. Some of Big Jimmy's pals insisted I share a drink with them. They implied that they couldn't trust a man who didn't hold his own when it came to liquor.

Of course, my memory of how alcohol ruined my old man made me resist at first. But two drinks in, and I found myself feeling loose-jointed and relaxed. The third glass turned those goons dressed in thousand dollar suits into jolly good companions who found me hilarious.

By the end of the evening, I ended up hanging over a toilet, much to the enjoyment of Jimmy's associates. But I couldn't forget the warm feelings the booze gave me, if only briefly.

But even that didn't last. The drinking now failed to make me happy, and it only made my remorse and bitterness more potent.

The buzzing sound coming from my pocket disrupted my wallow in self-pity. Who'd be calling me on my new cellphone?

"Dang," I mumbled as I jabbed the screen, desperate to get to the telephone feature. If Daisy hadn't demanded me getting a new device, I'd been happy never touching another piece of electronics, especially something that could record my voice.

"Hello."

"Hi, Tommy, it's me."

Daisy called from Newark airport, all excited about flying off to Europe with her boyfriend. I tried to be enthusiastic, but her trip brought back a bad memory. She'd lied to me about spending her insurance money on a non-refundable European dream vacation. I found out later she poured her extra cash into more clothing and beauty projects. She'd met Big Jimmy and had set her sights on seducing him.

My sister played me as a sucker for a long time.

We chatted about all the beautiful things she and Jimmy planned to take in. Then her voice broke, like maybe she could cry.

"Just remember I love you, Tommy. I only wanted to be happy."

"I only wanted to make you happy, Daisy."

Those words ended our conversation and left me a little confused. My sister seldom acted sentimental, so the emotion in her voice threw me off.

I guessed she must've been overwhelmed with joy at having secured her dreams. She had a man in her life and financial independence, or at least until she spent her way into the poorhouse. My sister also had the status of being a bank president, and most importantly, the people who could ruin it all were either dead or deep in hiding.

I bet if our folks looked down from wherever, they'd be proud of Daisy. Yup, their girl got what she wanted. I imagined my old man boasting, "That Daisy was always the smart one." And then he'd add something like, "That Tommy was a moron."

Man, I hated Walter, dead or alive.

I raised the tumbler to my mouth and swallowed the remaining booze. I regretted thinking about my old man. He only seemed to show up when I felt bad about myself. Why let old memories ruin such a beautiful day. Most of the tourists had left long ago, and the weather had gotten pretty nice. Even the seagulls weren't squawking over some garbage. It was so quiet that I easily heard the sound of car tires rolling across the gravel driveway next to the house.

I wondered who pulled into my drive. I didn't expect my visitor for another half hour. I walked over to the edge of the deck and looked down at a black Mercedes-Benz.

"Good afternoon," I said to the short, muscular dude exiting the vehicle. His had close-cropped hair, and wore green and white exercise sweats. He wasn't the guest I expected.

"Hello," he said, a lopsided grin etching his mug,. "You Tommy Lyle?"

As soon as I saw how he moved and heard how he greeted me, I knew he wasn't a local. Not that a $50,000 sedan wasn't enough evidence.

"I might be. Who wants to know?"

The man raised his hand to shade his eyes. "Would you mind if I came up? It's uncomfortable staring into the sun."

"Stay right there. I'm coming down."

Even with him saying only a few words, I knew he'd be trouble.

I went through the sliding glass door into the Great Room, stepped through the kitchen, and rumbled down the stairs to the ground level. The

268

visitor stood right outside the door, examining the peeling paint on the house's foundation.

"Looks like your place could use a little maintenance," he said.

That comment made me laugh. "So let me guess. You're one of those college kids painting houses for the summer."

The dude chuckled. "No, but I have people who could give you a good price if you're interested."

I grinned but offered up nothing else. *Enough chit-chat, buddy, who are you and what did you want from me?* A handful of seconds passed, and he took the hint and introduced himself.

"I'm Tony."

My head slowly edged up and down in acknowledgment.

"I'd like to talk to you about a job," he said.

How the dude knew I needed employment bothered me more than that he knew I lived at the beach house. I felt sweat dribble down my back.

"A job, huh," I said. "Why do you assume I need a job?"

Before the man could answer, a pick-up truck pulled to a stop along the beach road. Tony's head swiveled on his muscular neck and watched as two older men climbed out of the vehicle. One geezer carried a big thermos and a cooler. The other reached into the truck bed and pull out a rattling collection of fishing rods.

They nodded at us as they walked between the properties toward the ocean.

Tony's eyes followed the fishermen until they disappeared over the dune. He then looked back at me. "To answer your question, we have a mutual acquaintance who told me you were looking for steady work down here at the shore."

My head flopped forward as I forced down a big swallow. It seemed evident to me that the dude belonged to Big Jimmy's crew. I supposed I should've felt grateful that Daisy's main squeeze looked out for me, but I wasn't.

"I appreciate his interest," I said, "but I'm too old to be climbing ladders and painting houses."

The corner of Tony's mouth arched to one side. "Oh, you wouldn't be painting houses. Let's go inside, and I'll tell you about the opportunity."

My stomach twisted enough to cause me to flinch.

"I'd rather talk out here," I said. The conversation reminded me of a similar one I had with Gloria Arbuckle at the very same location. I didn't like thinking that I now stood in Gloria's shoes.

Tony grinned again. His smirking only made me feel even more uneasy.

"Tommy, my friend, our mutual acquaintance would be very upset if you didn't take his job offer."

"So tell me what the job is."

Tony looked behind him, and then before I could scream, his left hand grabbed my throat, and his right held a gun two inches from my nose.

"Get your ass into the house," he said, snarling as he shoved me backward.

I let my legs give out and fell to the ground. Tony swung the gun, and I lurched sideways, feeling my forehead catch fire as the man made his mark. I kicked my feet, sending gravel flying. No way would I walk back into that beach house. If Tony killed me, he would have to do it where a witness might hear me screaming.

Everything started to go black and I felt the fingers of my right hand digging into Tony's face. The last thing I heard before I felt my head crack open was Tony dropping an F-bomb.

Chapter Sixty-Three

The hammering inside my skull slowly pushed me into consciousness. It took a few seconds before I realized I wasn't lying on the ground in front of the beach house. No, I lay in a bed, a hospital bed. I tried to open my eyes wider to get a better look, but they were too swollen.

I felt a big bandage covering my head and saw a splint on my ring finger. A surge of pain shot from my ribs when I filled my lungs too deeply.

I figured Tony arrived to pound my head and kick in my ribs, because Big Jimmy intended to remove the only witness to Daisy's crimes. I hated to think that my sister knew about it, but easily imagined her negotiating with her lover boy not to make me suffer too long. What were her last words she said to me? Yeah, she mentioned how *she only wanted* to be happy.

All the thinking hurt my brain, and a wet yip escaped from my mouth.

A shadow flowed over me as someone stood up from a chair next to the bed. The big man casting the shade looked at me with beady eyes and grumbled, "You look like shit."

Man, I hated Brutkowski.

"You were lucky I got there early," he said. "Your friend was banging away on you."

"How long did you wait before you stopped him?"

Brutkowski, dressed in a grey tracksuit that must've been an XXXXL, chuckled. I suspected he let Tony get a few more licks in before stopping and arresting him, the bastard. But he spoke the truth. Brute showing up early probably saved my life.

271

"So why did you want to meet with me?" he asked.

I turned away. I couldn't look at the big lug and his stupid, smirking cop face. I probably reached out to him because I didn't know anyone else in the police. I also suspected he'd believe me.

"I got some information for you," I said, before flinching when my ribs lit up.

Giving up Daisy would be hard for me. Sure, she lied and manipulated me into doing bad stuff, but I always forgave her because she was my sister. Pushing Eric to his death had been somewhat justifiable since the dude treated her so cruelly. Finding out she asked Big Jimmy's thugs to work over Gloria was pretty evil. But they didn't kill her. I had to give them credit for that mercy.

I had more trouble dismissing the deaths of Archie and Leo. As cheaters and thieves, they deserved no mercy, but breaking a leg would've been enough retribution. I wondered if Daisy ever considered that option.

Bongiovanni, now that messed me up. She shot him in cold blood, unprovoked, while he sat in her living room. And to come to learn, she pinned it on me.

Sister, or not, Daisy had to pay.

Brutkowski's meat hook of a hand shook my shoulder. "I've been here all morning, Lyle, let's do some talking."

And so I did.

He seemed unsurprised when I said that Eric Pressman's first fall was probably accidental, and his second wasn't.

His head wobbled back and forth, hearing that we'd bribed Leo Dewey to alter his findings. When he asked if I'd thrown the Medical Examiner off the bridge, I felt okay saying, "No, I had nothing to do with that."

"What about Archie London?" he asked.

"I hit him over the head and stole his office equipment, but someone else murdered him."

Brutkowski grunted.

I described how Eleanor and Daisy worked as a team to get Gloria Arbuckle out of her job. His fat face squished. "Who's Gloria Arbuckle?"

"It all had to do with money. She's not important."

My head started throbbing. I figured my next secret might upset the big cop. You know the Blue Wall and all that.

I winched, taking in a big breath.

"And I suppose you'd like to know what happened to Detective Bongio-vanni."

Brutkowski's eyebrows pulled together.

"What do you mean?"

That wasn't the response I expected. I scanned Brutkowski's eyes and tried to read his mind. He seemed confused.

Daisy knew Big Jimmy's men had disposed of the body and the car professionally, as she liked to say. But she wondered why there had been no local news about a police detective going missing. The only scuttlebutt her new beau picked up from his sources in the police department had the detective retired and fishing in North Carolina.

I might've stopped talking if I hadn't seen Mandy standing off in the corner. Rational people would claim it nothing but a manifestation of my guilt. They could be right. I knew that Mandy wouldn't help me gain God's forgiveness if I didn't come clean.

I began my confession with, "Bongiovanni stopped by my sister's house a month ago," and ended it with, "I don't know where they buried him."

Brutkowski shocked me when he started sobbing.

Acknowledgements

The Dames of Detection for their support as publishers of my short stories, and now my novel.

About the Author

William Ade was born and raised in a small town in Indiana during the fifties and sixties. He earned college degrees in early childhood education and special education, working in both fields until 1980. That August, he and his wife of one year moved to the Washington DC area. They had freshly minted graduate degrees, a VW Super Beetle, and no jobs.

Ade's career shifted from education to telecommunications, and he was eventually employed by MCI and then Verizon up until his retirement in 2014. During that same period of time, he and his wife, Cynthia raised two wonderful children into adulthood.

At his retirement, Ade announced to his wife, that he wanted to try his hand at writing. She said that if he was going to do that, he had to pursue it vigorously.

Ade's work has appeared in the *Mysteries Unimagined,* the *Rind Literary Magazine, The Broken Plate, Black Fox Literary, Mindscapes Unimagined*, and the 2018 and 2019 *Best New England Crime Stories.* He writes both literary, humor, and crime stories.

His collection of short stories, *No Time for His Nonsense,* was released in early 2020. His first novel, *Art of Absolution,* came out in July, 2020.

Visit William's website at billade.com
Connect with William on Goodreads

CPSIA information can be obtained
at www.ICGtesting.com
Printed in the USA
BVHW030950140521
607265BV00007B/217